MW01000593

Bear Lust

Bear Lust

HOT, HAIRY, HEAVY FICTION

EDITED BY RON SURESHA

alyson books
los angeles

Manufactured in the United States of America.

This trade paperback original is published by Alyson Publications, P.O. Box 4371, Los Angeles, California 90078-4371. Distribution in the United Kingdom by Turnaround Publisher Services Ltd., Unit 3, Olympia Trading Estate, Coburg Road, Wood Green, London N22 6TZ England.

First edition: November 2004

ISBN 1-55583-818-9

Credits
Cover photography by Chris Komater.
Author photo by Edward Scott Valentine.
Cover design by Matt Sams.

Contents

Dedicated to the memory of Hal Hillman,
1961–2004,
who reveled in his deeply masculine erotic essence and
in the mirth of the bear community

Introduction

Bear Lust is another irresistibly scrumptious plateful of first-rate, hot, hairy, heavy bear fiction, a return trip to the all-you-can-eat buffet served up by this fine publisher in *Bearotica*. The dish now in your trembling paws, however, is seasoned with a completely new range of tastes to tempt your palate and whet your appetite.

This anthology whips up another heapin' helping of strong, captivating stories—unique depictions of bears and similarly masculine folks across time and place. *Bear Lust* attracted submissions from Canada, Europe, South America, and every region of the United States; from men and women—queer, straight, and bi; from bears and bear lovers alike. The mouthwatering spread in these pages features select cuts of fiction from bear-smut veterans as well as tasty treats from lesser-known contributors. Every portion served is fresh meat on the hoof, excepting "Papabear Beau," which was published several years ago in *Daddy* magazine but deserves far wider exposure.

This current homo-macho banquet features plenty of sizzling, spicy, unexpected M2M action with a beefy table full of unique and memorable characters. These savory (and some unsavory) critters include horny Gold Rush cowboys, a Norse god and his ultrahairy smith, frustrated and exploding ex-husbands, forestry students playing with handcuffs, a solitary barber praising the gorgeousness of hair, curious cops undercover at a bear contest, hirsute Roman foot soldiers, a summertime six-way gang bang, an intrepid cub reporter, and a mysterious muscle-bear fantasy in an abandoned storefront—the latter in iambic heptameter, no less. Believe me, there's not a sloppy tale among the group, though there are plenty of sloppy fucks.

Since *Bearotica* was published, we have witnessed mega-icon and sex god Homer Simpson briefly outed as a bear. Even more amazing, we have entered a post-sodomy phase revealing a complete transformation of the GLBT civil landscape. Bear men (and grizzlies, cubs, wolves, otters, and the whole forest of other man-loving critters) and bear communities have earned a place at the table, a recognizable and respectable part of that population. And that's reason enough to celebrate the manly love of woof-licious comrades.

Trail Ride
DALE CHASE

"You got digs nearabouts?" the miner asked. Like most in the saloon, he looked tired and grizzled, as played out as the gold fields.

"Just passing through."

"California, I'll bet."

I grinned. It came up in every conversation, the big gold strike, now a thing of the past but still drawing hopefuls. I wasn't looking for gold, though, just good honest work and maybe someone to share it with.

"Whorehouse up at the other end of town," the miner said.

I nodded, but just then a cowboy sauntered in, pulled off his hat, and slapped it against his thigh to shake off the dust. He was good-sized, a big bear of a man, and he caught me in a way others hadn't. I watched as he made his way to the bar.

He said nothing, didn't acknowledge me in any way other than elbowing in beside me and ordering a whiskey. As he leaned on the bar his shoulder bumped mine, and I knew it was intentional, for this was how things were done. He was looking either to fight me or fuck me. I had to be careful in how I responded, as I didn't want to end up in a scrap out back—although the last time that happened, the fellow I fought threw a few punches, wrestled

1

me to the ground, then pulled out his dick and fucked me.

The cowboy downed his drink, called for another, and bumped me again—but this time his shoulder stayed put. Now I knew. He was one of my kind, was probably hard down below and looking to get into me. And I couldn't think of anything I wanted more after the long ride down from Montana. So far Nevada was emptiness and heat, and arriving here in Ely hadn't been much better. The town had grown up around copper mines but remained hardscrabble, raw. I pushed against the cowboy and he drew a long breath, finished his second drink, and walked out. I followed.

He led me down a side street where buildings crowded in on one another and a sliver of moon kept us deep in shadow. There, what we did was mostly by feel. I undid my pants, pulled down my long johns, and heard him do the same. And then he got behind me, spread my butt cheeks, and pushed a long wet prick into me. I heard the saloon's laughter and music in the background as the big piece of meat pumped in and out of me, and I grabbed my own cock and began to pull because I was gonna shoot me a dickful.

The cowboy rode me hard and fast, grunting the whole time, and when he started letting go of his stuff he growled and groaned. I worked myself faster and felt it start inside my balls, everything drawn up and him still working my backside. The feel of him up there and the knowledge that he was squirting in me made me let go as well. I cried out as I sprayed the ground.

When he finished with me, he pulled out and closed up his pants but didn't leave. I buttoned up and turned to him. "I'm on my way to San Francisco," he said. "If you're going to California, how about ridin' along?"

"Fine with me. I'm John Doss," I said.

"Call me Crow," he replied. "First name's Ephraim, but I don't like it much. My horse is down at the livery, gettin' fed. I'll round him up, meet you back here. We can camp outside of town."

I knew what that meant. I'd had enough cowhands and range riders to know what went on beside a campfire out in nowheres.

Throw down your blanket, get naked, and get at it. My dick stirred at the thought of seeing Crow like that.

We rode in silence for some time, then Crow said, "Here's good," and we dismounted, staked the horses, unsaddled them, and made camp. The fire was small, but it was enough. I watched Crow strip away jacket and shirt to reveal a broad, thickly furred chest. When he lowered his pants and underwear, I got a look at what had been inside me, a big, long cock about halfway along. It grew out of a black bush that ran all up his stomach and made him appear more beast than man. When he was fully naked, he took hold of his prick and began to stroke. "Get 'em off," he said when I just stared. I laughed sheepishly and quickly stripped.

Crow eyed me up and down. I was smaller than him, slighter, smoother, younger. He seemed to like this. He pushed me to my knees and guided his cock into my mouth. "Suck on it," he said.

He let me work him awhile, but after I'd sucked and pulled and tasted his dribble he withdrew and said, "I need me a long, slow fuck, so you get down there on your hands and knees, play pony."

I did as asked and he pushed his big prong up me, but this time he went slowly. I moaned as I felt him snake into my gut and got louder as he eased back all the way, then popped out of me. He did this several times, leaving my hole gaping between strokes, going back in so slowly I wanted to scream. I wiggled and squirmed and he murmured low, "You like getting fucked, dontcha," and I moaned "yes" as he popped out of me again. When he hesitated and I began to whimper, he ran his finger around my rim, teased me. "Fuckhole," he said. "Goddamn fuckhole." And he put his cock back in.

He rode me for what seemed hours, and when I complained that my legs hurt, he laid me over a saddle and fucked me that way. I came twice while he used me, and as we were miles from anyone, I made it known. Crow responded to my cries by shoving his meat into me all the harder, which made the climax even more intense.

The horses, tethered nearby, began to snort and stamp. Crow remarked, as he kept going in and out of me, "They want to fuck too. Their horse cocks are hard, big things all swollen up. Can't play with themselves like a man, poor beasts."

My bottom felt raw when Crow let himself come. "I'm gonna do it in you," he said as he picked up speed and began to pound me. "I got me a load to put up your hole," and he cut off talking while he did just that. He took time to empty, shoving in and out and growling and moaning until he slowed, then stopped. When he pulled out of me and sat back, I felt his hands on my bottom, then his fingers playing around my hole. And then his breath. He had his face down there, and I let out a cry because nobody had ever done that. I felt his tongue on me, licking of all things, then going inside.

"Sweet Jesus!" I cried but he kept on, tongue like a little prick fucking me, then finally just feeling around in there, like he was trying to get at what he'd squirted in me. His mouth was plastered against my bottom and he was like a starving animal until he gave me a final lick and retreated.

I rolled off the saddle onto the blanket. The fire was nearly out. Crow got up, went to gather bits of wood and scrub. He traipsed off stark naked while I lay with his juice running out of my backside, thinking about his tongue.

As he worked the fire back up, I looked at him in his squat, everything about him big, especially that prong hanging between his legs and the fat balls beneath. "We'll rest awhile," he said, and he stretched out beside me.

"Why California?" he asked. "You after the gold?"

"No," I told him, "just opportunity, and I've never seen a big city like San Francisco. Been working my way across the country, on cattle ranches mostly. How about you?"

"Same. I hooked up with a wagon train awhile but had to leave when I was caught fucking the wagonmaster. People threw up a stink about it, got religion and all, eternal damnation. You ever run into that?"

I laughed. "Hell, yes, but the other times make up for it. I've had some good stuff, bunkhouses mostly, no religion in there, just cowhands working their pricks in the dark. Then one finds out you'll take it in the ass and he crawls into your bunk, gives it to you and doesn't care who hears, and next thing you know they're all coming after you."

"You like that?"

"Yeah, but it doesn't take long for them to start fighting each other, and then the foreman, if he's not one of the ones doing me, asks me to leave and the guys have to go back to their hands. And the last time it was just the foreman. He had his own cabin and he had me come up there and suck his prick. The others knew what was going on, wanted me to do them too, but the foreman wouldn't have it. I had to get out of there. Dangerous."

Crow's hand went down for his cock as he spoke. "I'd have stayed with the wagonmaster, and I think about him sometimes, how he'll get to where he's going and those people will scatter and he'll be on his own, all because he gave in to their fire and brimstone. He was a good man. We started in down by a river, in a patch where you couldn't see. I stumbled on him bathing, clothes in a pile on the shore, except he wasn't washing, he was playing with himself, knee-deep, cock hard, hand working. He saw me approach, looked at me square-on but didn't stop, and I saw his spunk squirt and decided then and there I had to have me some. So while he was still there in the water holding himself, I stripped, waded in. And I bent him over and fucked him. And he carried on something as I did it, even came again. Afterward, we got up on the shore and sucked prick until we heard others coming along. So we dressed and acted like we hadn't even seen each other.

"From then on, I did him regular. There was several single men on the train, some with their parents, ripe as hell, but I kept my distance even when I'd find one in the bushes, pants at his ankles, pulling on his cock. Some of them I think was doing each other, but I kept to Graydon. That was his name, the wagonmaster.

"He had his own wagon, said it was his last trip across, planned to get him a place in California, settle down. When I wasn't on my horse, I rode up beside him and we'd sit there, dicks hard, aching to do something. That last night, I crawled into his wagon. I hadn't done that before, always slept outside, but I woke up in the middle of the night with a hard cock and went to him. Everyone was asleep, or so I thought. I kept quiet, crawled in, put my dick into his mouth, and he sucked like he was starving, but he wanted me to fuck him, stuck his bottom up at me, begged me to put it in him. I knew better. Something told me not to, but how do you resist an ass bared to you when your dick is hard? So I got into him, started going at it, and of course the wagon is rocking and pretty soon someone is behind us with a candle.

"I finished, I'll have you know. All the yelling and commotion, I knew it was over, that I'd be turned out, so I was gonna have me this one last fuck and I started going at it all the more, sweat flying, and Graydon is pulling on his prick and then we're coming and God knows how many are watching—and how many of their dicks are hard because of it. When I pulled out of him I turned to them, cock still wet. Didn't try to cover myself. A woman was there, and two men. She didn't say nothing, just stared at my prick while one of the men was spouting his religion and the other tried to pull the woman away. I was asked to leave that night.

"They let Graydon stay on because they needed him, but I'll bet his trip was hell to pay the whole rest of the way. I haven't fucked anybody since him. You're the first."

He reached over, began to rub my cock, then got down to my balls, rolled them in his palm. I spread my legs, raised them to give him access, and he turned toward me. "I'm gonna have to do you again before we sleep," he said. He worked a finger back to my hole and pushed in. His cock was hard again and I reached for it, ran my palm up and down its length. "Roll over," he said.

I would have liked him to go at me from the front, but most men didn't do it that way. One of the bunkhouse crowd had, though, took me on my back with my legs spread, held high. I'd loved that because I could watch his face all screwed up when he let go. But I also loved it from behind, like the animals. If Crow fucked a horse or bear it would be the same, get around behind and stick it in. Now, as his big piece of meat snaked up into my bowels, I groaned with pleasure. And as he began to ride me, I wondered if maybe I might take Graydon's place.

When Crow finished with me this time, he just rolled off and fell asleep. I stayed awake as the fire died, raised up on one elbow to look at him. I'd never seen a man with such a pelt and sure to God never had such a cock in me. His size and his animal look made me feel protected, safe. He could challenge anybody or anything and emerge the victor; he could fuck who he damn well wanted. I squeezed my butt muscle thinking about how he'd been up there, how he'd be up there again, and part of me wanted to get over there and suck on him, crawl around in that fur until his prick was up and I could climb onto it, get it up inside me, and ride him until he gave me more of his spunk. As it was I left him at rest, prick soft but still a thing to behold.

Next morning I awoke to Crow's cock pushing into me. He lay behind me, leg thrown across to get at my bottom. It was like he hadn't slept and was simply continuing what he'd begun the night before.

The day was young but heating up fast. Due to be a scorcher even though it was spring, a time when the desert is most hospitable. I knew Crow wanted to fuck early, then get on with the journey. His thrust was urgent, strokes quick. He reached around and grabbed me. I was hard and wet, and it didn't take much work with that thing pumping my backside for me to let go. Pretty soon he was grunting and I started spewing juice and knew he was too, up inside me, which I liked more than anything. I wanted to ride along later on with his stuff running out my hole.

"We'd best get a move on," he said while his cock was still in me.

"Yeah, I guess so. Getting hot."

I clenched down on him and he chuckled. "Maybe later on we'll find us some shade and I'll fuck you."

But there was no shade to be found and no water. Our canteens were empty when we rode into Carson City at dusk. "Let's get us a room, have a bath," Crow said. "I'll pay."

As much as I wanted to get naked with him, I wanted more to wash away the dirt and sweat. A tub and hot water were brought up to the room and we stripped and washed, then lay down on the bed together all clean.

"I haven't been in a bed in a long time," Crow said. "Can't recall exactly when it was." He ran his hand over the straw mattress. "Fine, just fine," he added. "Now why don't you get down there between my legs and suck my dick."

He was soft and I thrilled to bringing him along, running my hands though his pelt as I sucked his fat knob. He let me play awhile, feeding on him while my hands explored his chest, found his tit nubs in the fur. Finally he grabbed my head and thrust into my throat. I then began to seriously work him and he growled, "Hell, yes."

I'd had many a cock in my mouth, especially in the bunkhouses and, of course, that last foreman, but none were the size of Crow's. Most were a decent mouthful, nothing more. Crow's meat filled me, and I gobbled and fed until he began to moan, then bucked up and let go. His cream spurted into my throat, great salty squirts, and I swallowed it all. When I pulled back and sat up, he was still hard.

"Crawl up here and give me yours," he said, and I went up onto his chest, rubbing my butt over that fur until I leaned forward and put my prick into his mouth. As he began to work me, he reached back and bunched the pillow so he was more upright, and then he lay sucking on me for a while. I looked down at him, face tanned, lined yet still handsome, thick black hair peppered with gray, and I looked at his lips around my cock and how his mouth worked as he sucked. It was too much, and I let go my load, squirted into him, which made him suck all the more.

I tried not to cry out, as we wouldn't want others to know what we were getting up to, so I held my jaw shut, keeping in check the pleasure scream that churned up all the way from my crotch.

When I was empty, I pulled out of Crow's mouth and he stuck his tongue out, licked the tip of my rod, played around a little. "I need to fuck you," he said. "Slide back and sit on my thing."

I eased back, rose up to straddle his lower part, and eased my bottom onto him, felt that snake go up me. He took hold of my hips and made me bounce on him, and I got the idea, took over, went at it. Like fucking myself, riding cock. I pushed down onto him over and over, which drove him up into my gut, then I raised up to almost let him out before dropping back down. Crow lay with his hands behind his head, watching me do it, but my legs finally grew tired and I grew still.

"OK, get off," he said. Then, "Off the bed, around to the foot."

He put me standing at the bedpost, holding it with both hands, bent forward. And he got behind me and shoved back up my hole and resumed the fuck.

"I like it standing," he said. "Bed's good for some, but this is how we're meant to do it, being animals and all. Bull, bear, man, all the same, hard pricks in need of a fuckhole."

I had to admit I liked it this way. The rough feel had always appealed to me, even in the bunkhouses, but this was better because I was feeling for Crow, the way he'd lost Graydon and not had anybody since. Something had begun between us—fucking, yes, that was part, but there was more now, something that might grow when we reached our destination. We would continue on to California, visit San Francisco, then maybe get us a spread, some cattle. For now I savored the feel of him in me, fucking like the animal he was.

Balsam Poplar Buds

JEFF MANN

"The scientific name is *Populus balsamifera*. The buds are resinous, thus the reference to balsam. Pay attention to the buds and the bark, not the leaves. The leaves, remember, will be scattered on the ground or under the snow by the time your final exam rolls around."

It's hard to take notes in dendrology class today. First of all, it's raining. The sort of steady October drizzle that conjures up wraiths of mist in the hollers, strips the maples of their fiery leaves, soaks into your shoulders, and makes you wish you had a flask of bourbon hidden in your backpack. At this altitude—the top of Chestnut Ridge, smack-dab in the middle of Cooper's Rock State Forest—the rain's unseasonably cold, and I'm beginning to shiver.

I'm standing here with a bunch of other forestry majors, and we're all madly scribbling away on clipboards stuck inside clear plastic bags to keep the water off our notes. Dr. Norris looks like a hobbit and has got to be 30 years older than any of us, but all us young bucks pant to keep up with him when we take these woodland field trips. All afternoon he's been climbing nimbly up rocks, pointing out red maple, chestnut oak, sourwood, and now one solitary balsam poplar.

10

But the rain isn't the only reason note-taking is hard today. Dr. Norris is telling us that the balsam poplar usually doesn't appear this far south, that its native area is Canada, but I'm only half-hearing him now because I'm looking at Travis.

Travis and I have several forestry classes together: ornithology, aquatic seed plants, and dendrology. My grade in every one of those classes might be better if he weren't around, because my concentration goes all to hell every time I look at him. If my grade point average slides another few points, I'll lose my scholarship, and then I'll be fair and squarely fucked. I'll have to return to my pissant hometown and bag groceries at Kroger.

If only Travis would wear a grocery bag over his head, I'm thinking as I study him, trying to make light of this painful obsession. But that wouldn't end the problem, of course. Even with his handsome face hidden, there'd still be the width of his shoulders, the hair on his forearms, the denim curves of his ass to make me ache. I've seen his chest bare once, and I'd give just about anything to see it again. Still, seeing him shirtless that one lucky day at the lake sure hasn't helped this paralysis I feel when he's around.

Morgantown is a pretty cool university community, and it's a world I like a hell of a lot more than Hinton, my far-too-heterosexual hometown. There's a gay student group that meets on the West Virginia University campus once a week, plus a gay bar down the street that's busy every weekend, a friendly hole-in-the-wall where I've scored a few times. Hinton, on the other hand, three and a half hours south, is an old railroad town fallen on hard times, full of fundamentalist preachers and empty storefronts. If I flunk the next dendrology test and a few more quizzes in ornithology, I may end up having to go back there, and it'll all be Travis's fault.

"Be sure to examine the buds," Dr. Norris reminds us. "Their resin is one way to distinguish the tree from its relatives."

Dutifully, we surround the tree and take turns sniffing. When I take a pointy amber bud between my fingers and rub, it feels like it's been dipped in molasses. When I hold my sticky fingers beneath my nose, they smell like musk. They smell like luck, like

I've just been rubbing a man's cock or fingering his ass or sweaty armpit.

The rain's turned into a real downpour now, and besides, class is almost over, so we're all heading back to the bus. I study Travis as he strides silently a few feet in front of me. I admire his purposeful gait—he's so fucking butch—and every few seconds I lift my fingers to my face and breathe in that balsam scent.

Every time I'm around him, I'm constantly trying to memorize details, as if my memory could possess him even if my body can't. Mental photos I'll pore over later, in bed alone, stroking my own chest and crotch, wishing he was there beneath the tattered family quilts with me.

Travis looks to be my age—early 20s. He's a little shorter than I am, I'd say around 5-foot-10, and he looks a little like me: dark-haired, beefy, and bearded. We both look like young lumberjacks, mountain men, the kind of guys I grew up around down in Summers County, the kind of men I've been having rough and vigorous fantasies about since high school. According to my psychology textbook, these desires make me not only a narcissist but a fetishist and sadomasochist as well: I'm attracted to men who resemble me, and I like to tie them up or have them tie me up. Sometimes I worry about that, wonder if I'm sick in the head. It's an anxiety that makes me slow to act, makes me afraid my longings will never be welcomed or understood by anybody.

Right now Travis is wearing a black toboggan cap and a baggy army-green jacket darkening with the steady rain, but I've studied him enough to know that beneath those bulky layers, the guy's got just the kind of build I like, the kind of build I myself have developed using a rusty yard-sale weight set three times a week. He's got big shoulders and arms, prominent pecs, a moderate beer belly, and a round ass. His face is handsome and aloof, with heavy-lidded eyes, long eyelashes, and a neatly trimmed brown goatee. His auburn hair is thick and wavy. He sports long sideburns and, most days, enough cheek stubble to make a good start on a full beard. Usually he's got on the kind of outfit that most us forestry majors wear: jeans or denim overalls; lumberjack boots or cowboy boots; a scruffy T-shirt, thermal undershirt, or flannel shirt.

And, most maddeningly, the detail I dream about most, dark wisps of chest hair are constantly curling over his shirt collars. I want to follow that dark smoke down under his clothes and bury my beard in that soft moss, in the smell of resin.

Another flight of fancy, the sort that often interferes with my note-taking, the sort hot guys always inspire in me. Rain's dripping off my baseball cap, and my feet are freezing, despite thick socks and heavy boots. Winter's on its way, and this time of year my lonely fantasies all revolve around heat. God, it'd be fine to have Travis in my arms, naked and warm all night long, in my little bachelor's bed. The heater's humming; the rain's tapping impatient fingernails against the windows as I press my chest against his back. His breath is deep with sleep, but beneath my fingers his nipples are hardening into little nubs, like balsam poplar buds.

By the time we reach the bus, I'm walking a little awkwardly, stroking my hard-on through my pants pocket. My lesbian buddy Dora sits beside me, and all the way back to Morgantown I'm gazing with thinly veiled longing at the back of Travis's head, three seats ahead of me. I alternate this reverential stare with pained expressions of lust whispered into Dora's sympathetic ear.

"Goddamn, look at those shoulders! Dora, you know what to get me for Christmas," I groan. After many years of high-school isolation in a small redneck town, I'm really pleased to have a queer compatriot in forestry, someone safe to whom I can vent my growls of lust.

"Honey," she mock-drawls, "Ah can feel you *wantin'* him!" Then, seriously, "Christ, Allen, have you even *spoken* to the guy?"

Got to admit I haven't, though once, during an ornithology field trip, he did speak a few words to me. He's too fucking hot, and I know my shy self well enough to realize that I'd be a stammering idiot if I tried to strike up a conversation. Plus he's so quiet he seems unapproachable. Sits in the back of the room in every class, never says a word, stroking his brown goatee and looking stern.

No, I've never had the guts to speak to him. But every now and then, either in classes or in the corridors of Percival Hall, our eyes meet and hold for a few seconds, before my cowardly gaze veers off. Every now and then, ever since that day I saw him stripped to the waist, ever since that day he caught me staring at the dark hair on his chest.

It was the second week of fall semester, and our aquatic seed plants class had bused out to Cheat Lake to glop around in the mud and listen to Dr. Keener lecture about the wide variety of Appalachian waterweeds. First of September, and the weather was still hot, an uncomfortable fact that metamorphosed into one hell of a blessing. Within 15 minutes of getting there, several guys had stripped to the waist.

I tried not to stare. Being openly gay in that crew of macho straight guys would have been pretty risky. But years of drooling over men have helped me develop amazing powers of peripheral vision. Anybody watching me would think I was completely absorbed by Dr. Keener's discussion of arrowhead flowers, but what I was really doing was watching Travis out of the corner of my eyes and hoping he'd take his cue from our classmates and pull off his shirt.

And eventually, so he did. First he rubbed impatiently at the dark sweat stain spreading over the front of his gray T-shirt. Then, abruptly, he tugged the shirt over his head and off, then tucked it carefully into a back pocket of his faded jeans.

The blood pounded in my temples; my cock stiffened against my pants; any moisture in my mouth dried up like a garden in dog days drought. I peeled off my own T-shirt. I mopped my brow with it. I wiped my own hairy, sweat-moist chest and tried to look normal. I looked away, looked at goldenrod blooming on the edge of the lake. Then, drawn irresistibly, I looked back. The clumps of hair I'd seen curling over his shirt collars were only the highest needles of an evergreen tree—hemlock? spruce? fir? larch?—that spread its branches over his torso. The fur was curly and dark brown. Like circling eddies in a river's waters, its swirls matted his big chunky pecs and covered a little curve of beer belly before disappearing into the top of his jeans. As when I'd tried to distinguish details of an unfamiliar landscape as they disappeared in the dusk, I could just barely make out his nipples and, in the deep cleft between them, a small silver cross. When he reached one arm up to cock his baseball cap against the sun, I could see his biceps swell and bushy hair fan out in his armpit.

Suddenly I could see myself with my face in those pits, lapping away like some honey-hungry bear who's raided a beehive. First one pit and then the other. Then a determined tongue-search for those nipples.

It was then that Travis caught me staring. I was so lust-drunk I'd forgotten myself, forgotten how dangerous it might be to let my desire be glimpsed by a guy who was surely straight, a guy who would very likely find that desire disgusting. His eyes met mine, dark, distant, and solemn. I gave him a curt nod and shifted my gaze away as calmly as I could. I swallowed hard, wiped my brow again, cast about desperately for something else to focus on. Dr. Keener was talking about pickerelweed now. Behind him, a straight couple floated silently by in a rowboat.

I was pretty tense the next time I ran into Travis, only a couple of days later, one foggy morning during ornithology lab at the arboretum. I was afraid he'd figured out what my steady gaze at Cheat Lake meant. I was afraid he'd shun me, and I was determined to ignore him.

Fat chance of that. Fighting the urge to look at Travis, I felt like some asteroid losing its battle with gravity, bursting into flames as it enters the atmosphere, leaving a smoking crater as it slams into the side of the planet.

Led by Dr. Williams, about 20 of us were tramping around a cattail-lined pond when a great blue heron, frightened by our noise, took to wing. "There! Look!" the teacher shouted. The huge bird, long-necked, long-legged, rose into mist, flapped silently through the silver maples, and soared out over the Monongahela River.

A long, awed silence, as all of us stood stock-still watching the bird disappear into the misty distance. "Pretty damn amazing, huh?" a deep voice drawled at my elbow, a voice I didn't recognize.

To my consternation and amazement, Travis stood right by my side, in denim overalls and a camouflage T-shirt, unsmiling. I'd never been this close to him before. Those eyes into which I stared were brown. Those lips were beautifully shaped, framed by his dark goatee. Suddenly I was terrified.

Just before I'd mustered the courage to choke out something stupid like, "Yeah, big bird, all right," the professor shouted, "Follow me, folks!" and suddenly I was looking not at Travis's handsome face but at his broad back. A few seconds' hesitation, and I'd missed my chance. Dr. Williams led us over railroad tracks and toward the sound of a drumming flicker. I followed Travis up the slope, watching his ass every step of the way and cursing myself for being a tongue-tied coward.

My daddy's a farmer. He brought me up to love the outdoors, and I guess that's why I've ended up in forestry. I spent my teens by his side, gardening, baling hay, and chopping wood. One day I'd like to be a ranger or a forest-fire fighter, and sometimes I think I like trees better than people. But Daddy's a great reader as well—got an English degree on the G.I. bill before heading home to keep up the family farm—so he also raised me to love books. This semester, my only break from forestry courses is a British lit class.

It's an October afternoon, a week after the rainy day at Cooper's Rock when I snuffled the balsam poplar buds. A week after I lay in bed in my lonely apartment, smelled the sticky balsam on my fingers, and jerked off, pretending that fading scent was Travis's pits or crotch. Today Indian summer has opened the floor-to-ceiling windows of E. Moore Hall, and the filmy curtains waft and sway, fingered by a warm breeze.

I'm as restless as those curtains, hunched over a textbook in the lounge, trying to concentrate on some poems by W.B. Yeats. Problem is, Yeats writes a lot about desire, so between stanzas my mind wanders. It's as if someone keeps slipping a photo of Travis on top of my textbook, a picture inserting itself between me and the page. Travis at Cheat Lake, chest and belly hair glistening with sweat. Travis in ornithology lecture last week, meeting my eyes occasionally, chewing on the head of his pen. Travis tied to my bed, thrashing about beneath my caresses, his unwilling struggles slowly grading into thrusting eagerness as I take his big dick down my throat.

"Aargh!" I grunt. Dora's at my elbow reading for mammalogy, and she only has to check out the wild look on my face to know what the problem is. She rolls her eyes. "Grow some balls, Allen! Introduce yourself! You see him three days a week!"

"Yeah, yeah," I sigh. The next poem's "Never Give All the Heart." Yeah, right. I shake my head, shuffle the pages, and stare out the window at falling sycamore leaves. I'm just about to start reading again when I look down the room and see Travis walking toward us.

Shit. I've never seen him in E. Moore Hall before. I can't get over how meaty his chest is. His skin's all warm and musky and furry beneath that black T-shirt and army pants, his body's only yards from me, and there's nothing I can do about it. He might as

17

well be on another continent. It feels like my fingers, my cock, my tongue are all in prison, in solitary confinement.

Our eyes meet as he approaches, and this time I hold his gaze rather than shyly dropping my glance. There's just the slightest evidence of a smile as he nods, says "Howdy," then passes us, his chunky ass heading on down the hall, out the front door, and into the bright afternoon of chrysanthemum bloom and leaf-burn.

"Wow!" whispers Dora, nudging my thigh beneath the desk. "He spoke!"

As the shock inspired by his sudden appearance ebbs, a detail comes floating up out of my confusion. The T-shirt he wore said PRAIRIE STREET GYM. When I drop my eyes to the textbook again, a line from Yeats's biography leaps up at me: "I shall be a sinful man to the end, and think upon my death bed of all the nights I wasted in my youth."

Prairie Street Gym is nothing special, a musty rattrap basement in the warehouse district. And I'm so poor this semester—been ordering tonic water at the gay bar, since I can't afford gin—I can barely scrape up the membership fee. But I've wasted enough nights. Yep, I'm only 21, but sometimes, lying alone in bed at night, watching the Pleiades wheel over Morgantown, I can feel time flying. I don't want a bunch of regrets to poison my last years. If there's one thing reading literature does, it's remind you of mortality. Carpe diem poems just convince me of how hot Travis would look belly-down on my bed while I tie his hands behind his back, then work my tongue up his no-doubt-hairy ass.

Only my second visit to this gym and major luck comes my way, as if fate's impressed with my long-delayed attempt to take action and decides to be generous for once. I'm right in the middle of my second set of preacher curls when Travis shoulders through the front door and heads for the locker room.

"Jesus," I grunt, gathering my courage, determined to speak to him. When he comes out of the locker room five minutes later, dressed in baggy gym trunks and a tight white T-shirt, I resume my set, hoping to impress him with my biceps. He sees me almost immediately and gives me the half-smile and nod I've seen before. Instead of coming over, though—shit, he's as standoffish as I am— he stretches for a while before settling into some bench presses, weights a good 50 pounds more than I lift, I notice with envy.

I start another set of curls, watching the muscles of his chest bulge and relax, bulge and relax, but then I see my chance and decide it's time for sit-ups. There's an incline board only a few yards before him, and every time I lower myself into the first half of a sit-up, I can peek up his shorts and get a dim glimpse of inner thigh and shadowy jockstrap. Given the chance, I think wickedly, hoisting myself up and down on the bench with the rhythm of an oil rig, I'd chew that aromatic jock until it dripped, then peel it off him and stuff it in his mouth.

My belly's going to ache tomorrow, I realize, as Travis finally rests the barbell on its stand and rises from the bench, giving me an excuse to stop too. We're standing about three yards apart, both panting and stretching, meeting each other's eyes occasionally, saying nothing, when I see my opportunity. One T-shirt slogan got me this close; another T-shirt slogan will get me closer.

"Hey, you play guitar?" I say, trying to keep the nervous quiver out of my voice. Stretched across that great set of pecs is a Martin guitar logo.

Travis looks startled, as if a corpse suddenly spoke or a stone began to dance. He grins. Not that distant half-smile, but a real grin framed by his brown goatee. He grins real big and then he slowly nods.

"Yep, I got me a fancy Martin. It was my uncle's. He died in a mine explosion a few years back, left it to me."

From the sound of it, he's from my neck of the woods, and I've got to ask what we mountain folk almost always ask when we meet someone new: "Where you from?"

19

"Down Beckley way. Stanaford. Y'ever hear of it?"

Now I'm grinning, delighted to find that we have something in common. "Well, hell, sure! I'm from Hinton, just down the mountain." I step forward and extend my hand. "I'm Allen Ferrell. Don't we have some classes together?"

"Travis Hood," he says, grabbing my hand hard. "Pleased to meet ya. Yep, I've seen you in ornithology, right? That morning with the heron?"

He's a coy one. Surely he remembers not only speaking to me as that great bird swooped off through mist but also how my hungry eyes ran over his bare chest that day at Cheat Lake. "Oh, yeah, the heron!" I say, trying my best to be casual. As if I need a reminder of the first time I heard his voice.

My next words, fraught with consequence and with possibility, are more casual still. "Hey, I play guitar too," I say suddenly, crossing my hands behind my head and stretching first my right triceps and then my left. "Got me a Yamaha at home. You wanna work up a few tunes together sometime?" Being gay makes some of us terrific actors. An eavesdropper might assume from the flat tone of my voice that I could care less what Travis's response will be.

He looks at the floor for the space of four seconds, and my heart starts sinking fast, my throat getting dry and tight. He strokes the silver cross around his neck, then lifts his eyes to mine. "Sure," he says. "What kinda music you like to play?"

Nothing like bourbon to get in a guy's pants, I always say. I've had to borrow the money from Dora, my funds are so low, but she's a sweetheart. "Cook me up some of those enchiladas sometime, or a pan of that yummy eggplant parmesan," she'd said, handing me the twenty, "and then we'll be even." It's Evan Williams, cheap but tasty, and Travis and I are drinking it straight.

For the past two years I've been renting this cozy two-room

apartment on Lorenz Avenue, high above Sunnyside, Morgantown's student ghetto. I love the view from here, love to watch
summer storms roll in over the town, though it gets pretty windy
on this hilltop in winter, and sometimes snow blows in around the
loose panes of the windows, like it is tonight. I've got a few candles
going, and Travis and I both sit cross-legged on my bed taking
turns on our guitars. I'd never realized before how convenient it
can be not to have a living room.

I drop a few strings into G-tuning to show off my rendition
of Joni Mitchell's "The Circle Game," and Travis sings along,
improvising a harmony. He's a baritone too, and we sound pretty
good together. Our voices braid around one another like honey-
suckle vines.

"Hey, that sounds damn fine!" Travis enthuses, slapping my
back, then reaching for the bottle of bourbon on the bedside table.
Shy or proud or frightened or ashamed of our own desires, we've
both carefully kept our distance up until now. Tonight, though, a
snow-blustery Saturday night in late October, after some delivery
pizza and a few jiggers of booze, we're talking like we've been buddies for years.

Travis is smart and funny, much to my surprise and relief. Not
like some of the guys I've fucked, who've turned out to be hot in
bed but dumb as rutabagas once the sex stops. We've talked about
Raleigh County—his father's life in the mines, his mother's obses-
sive Bible-quoting. We've talked about Summers County—my
father's vegetable gardens, my mother's prize-winning carrot
cakes. We've complained about how pissed we get when Yankees
hear our West Virginia accents, roll their eyes, and then make jokes
about *Deliverance.*

Of course, my big problem with *Deliverance* has always been
that Ned Beatty got raped by the hillbillies, not sexy, furry Burt
Reynolds. As it is, I'm sure hoping that either Travis or I will, to
use the film's notorious phrase, be "squealing like a pig" by
evening's end. God knows, now that I've gotten Travis drunk
and on my bed, it'd be a crying shame if those coils of rope and

that tube of lube beneath my bed weren't put to use.

It's Travis's turn, and he's singing Stevie Nicks's "Landslide." I watch his fingers move through the chords, following that bass run from C down to A minor seven, then back up. As he sings, I'm hearing even more reasons to take a chance and make a move. Suddenly I'm wondering how he'd look with a goatee full of silver.

We take a break, fingers a little sore, watching the earlier uncertainty of flurries thickening into determined snow outside, whitening the roofs of the houses down the hill. "Hell, it's only October!" Travis growls, taking a swig from the bottle and letting his guitar slide to the carpet. "Cain't believe how hard it's snowing. I don't wanna drive home in this! My pickup ain't—isn't—worth a damn in snow."

Now *there's* a entrance begging to be taken. I grab the bottle from his hand and take a big mouthful, hoping my old friend Evan Williams will wash away the fright. "Well, look, man, y'can just stay over. You don't wanna drive drunk on a Saturday night with cops lyin' in wait all over Sunnyside."

"You sure?" Travis looks dubious, eyeing my bed's narrow width.

"Hey, you've found you some Southern hospitality here! I'll sleep on the floor, if you'd like." I'm trying to appear gallant, but of course I'm hoping like crazy that he'll opt for other arrangements.

"Nah, this is your place. Why don't I…"

I guess it *is* Evan Williams, or Yeats, or Stevie, or Joni, or just the thought that Travis could leave, right now or tomorrow morning, and I'll have to live the rest of my life knowing I could have touched him if I hadn't been so much of a coward. Whatever the reason, I almost feel like a soldier tearing into battle when I choke out, "Well, I wouldn't mind sharin'. If you don't."

"Uh, no," he says quietly. He takes another gulp of bourbon, and his hand seems unsteady. "That'd be all right, I guess." He tugs at the silver cross around his neck. He clears his throat and turns his head toward the window, either to watch the snow or to avoid looking at me.

Damnation. Now what? Have I read him wrong? "OK, well,

lemme play you one more song," I stammer. "Let's see, let's tune this top string back up to E…"

Suddenly what felt like fate is degenerating into pathetic illusion. I'm feeling a little nauseated. How could I have ever believed he'd want me? Wait'll Travis tells all the guys in Percival Hall about the big queer. I'll be a laughingstock.

Nervous and scared, I tighten the tuning peg too fast, and then—*zing!*—the string snaps.

"Ow!" Travis grunts. I look up, and he's got his big, hairy hand over his right cheek.

"Oh, hell!" Instinctively I bend over and pull his hand away. There's a tiny line of blood seeping up amid the stubble, right under his cheekbone.

"Jesus, I could have put out your eye!" I gasp. "I'm so sorry."

Travis's hand tightens around mine. Only inches apart, our eyes lock. Silence gathers around us for several seconds like that snowstorm outside. He gulps once; I gulp once.

Then I kiss his cheek, right on the cut. I kiss it because, I realize with a dizzy shock, I love him. Because he's beautiful and butch, smart and funny. Because he's the kind of guy I've been wanting ever since I figured out I wanted guys.

I kiss his tiny wound again, and he doesn't pull back. He just breathes heavily. Then I lick the blood off his cheek, run my fingers through his hair, and kiss him on the mouth. Our beards push together. His mustache mixes with mine. His tongue slips between my lips, and his arms wrap around my shoulders.

My guitar's jammed against my ribs, the last wall between us, and I tug it out of my lap and drop it onto the floor, where it bumps Travis's guitar and both instruments resound with the impact. "Oops!" I whisper apologetically, but Travis whispers back "C'mere," and we're kissing some more, mouth mashed against bourbon-scented mouth.

It isn't long before I've gotten my fingers beneath his thermal undershirt and am feeling the fur I've been dreaming about for months. Now I'm tugging the shirt over his head and pushing my face into his thick chest hair. Soft curls atop hard curves: It's like the moss-covered sandstone boulders I used to play on up at Hilldale, on my grandparents' farm. And yep, the scent and then the feel of balsam poplar buds, his nipples getting stiff as I lap away at them like a painter cat at a pool of rainwater.

"Wait a moment," Travis says, and he fumbles with the clasp of his necklace for a few seconds before dropping the cross on the bedside table. I shuck off my sweatshirt, and his mouth is on my tits now, rough and eager. His hands press the hard lump in the front of my jeans, tugging at the zipper, pulling my dick out.

For a few minutes I'm sitting on the edge of the bed and Travis is on his knees on the floor, rubbing his goatee up and down my cock. Then, with his foot, Travis pushes the guitars back against the wall, and he pulls me down to the carpet. We're lying side by side, hairy bellies rubbing together and kissing hard, when Travis suddenly stops.

"Whoa, Allen. Hold on!" he whispers, staring at something over my shoulder. What the hell? When I roll over, I realize he's noticed the rope and the tube of KY beneath my bed.

Lube is par for the course. Rope is not, at least not in most queer boys' bedrooms. "Uh," I manage sheepishly, "yeah. My kink stash." I'm a little flustered. It's one thing to be gay, it's another to be a leather-sex enthusiast.

When I look into Travis's eyes, however, they're gleaming, and it's not with amusement or scorn or fear, the usual responses I get from vanilla boys. "Oh, jeez!" he says. "You into that bondage stuff?"

"Uh" appears to be my word of choice tonight. Inarticulate, I grunt and nod.

"Oh, man," Travis gasps, rolling on top of me. "Look, I, uh, me too! Or," he continues, kissing my bearded chin, "I've always wanted to try it."

With that, he pushes up off me. He stretches one arm beneath the bed, pulls out the coils of rope, and drops them onto my chest. Now, to my ecstatic disbelief, Travis props himself on his knees and puts his hands behind his back. He stares at me for a second, then lowers his gaze to the floor. I can barely hear him whisper, "God, Allen. Do it."

I'm guessing it's a religious thing for both of us. All those pictures of a long-haired, bearded Christ secured to the cross, his holy muscles swelling with the strain. Plus, when you're brought up in the Bible Belt and led to believe that your kind of lust is sinful, it's a moral release to be tied down. Any control you have you've given up, and with the control the responsibility, as if free will were a falsehood and fatalism could free you of fault. You can take it up the ass or down the throat and tell yourself you're helpless, it's not your doing, it's not your choice.

That's what's going through Travis's mind, I suspect, because sometimes it's what I think when I'm lucky enough to find myself in his position. But, hell, the really, really beautiful ones bring out the top in me like gangbusters, and it doesn't take much in the way of candlelit rope-work before I've gotten Travis's wrists knotted behind his back and started slamming my dick against the back of his throat.

He's choking by the time I slip my hands beneath his elbows and lift him to his feet. I lead him to the end of the bed, peel his jeans down to his socks, then bend him over till his chest is against the mattress and his ass is in the air. The wind's rattling those loose windowpanes as I cup my palms over the fur-dark cheeks of his ass and pry them apart. Maybe he's never been rimmed before, because the yelp he makes sounds like surprise, but his ass is as musky as poplar resin too, and pretty soon I've got my face buried as deep as I can, flicking my tongue around and then into his hole like a bee working over the nectar-brimming bell of a sourwood flower.

I'm really going to town when I hear him grunt "Allen? Allen?" I pull my face from his ass. "Yeah?" I say, my hands holding his hips. I look at his bound hands and the pool of hair in the small of his back, thanking God or whatever angel allowed this. Allen Ferrell is one man determined *not* to waste the nights of his youth.

Travis tests the rope around his wrists—no way he's getting loose, 'cause I know how to tie a knot—then says, "You gonna fuck me?" I can't tell whether he's hopeful or fearful, but I'm guessing it's both.

"Yep. If you'll let me."

"*Let* you? Hey, man, I'm helpless. I guess you're gonna do what you want."

"Yeah. Well, then, I'm gonna fuck you." I slap his ass and grin.

Wind grinds away at the eaves outside. "Allen?" Big ole guy that he is, Travis sounds like a little boy. Tentative. Ashamed.

"Yep?"

"I, uh, make a lot of noise when I come, so you should…" He trails off, then presses his face against the quilt.

He can't ask for it, but I know what he wants. It's what I want too. It's the last kinky detail that would make this evening complete.

Without a word, I reach into my gym bag, which rests on the desk only a foot from my elbow. When I start working the balled-up jockstrap into his mouth, Travis goes "Uufff!" like the breath just got knocked out of him. I stuff the jock in, really pack his cheeks tight. Don't want to wake the upstairs neighbors.

"That what you wanted?"

He nods. "Mmm-hmm." He nods again.

I haven't washed that jock for two weeks, and I'm betting it smells and tastes pretty strong. But based on the way Travis is groaning—"Uhhhh! Mmm-hmm. Uhhhh!"—and humping the baseboard of the bed, my guess is he's enjoying that musky mouthful as much as I would if I were in his position.

When I start greasing up his asshole, though, Travis starts shaking violently, like one of those quaking aspen leaves we studied a few weeks ago in dendrology. "Relax!" I urge, unrolling a rubber onto my very thankful prick. Then it occurs to me. "Hey, you ever been fucked?"

He lies there silently for a few seconds, clenching his bound fists, candlelight flickering over his broad ass. Then he shakes his head and starts shivering even harder.

I remember the first time I got it up the ass. Big football jock who just pushed it in. I almost passed out. Ended up sore for a week.

I look down at Travis again, and the gratitude almost chokes me. God, he's beautiful. Gently I stroke his buttocks with the back of my hand before squirting more lube on my fingers. "Travis, I'm real proud to be your first. No way I'm gonna hurt you. We'll take our time."

Travis reaches for his clothes as soon as I untie him. I've fucked him for a long time. Slowly and carefully, over the end of the bed. Then tenderly, deeply, with his legs over my shoulders. Finally, fast and hard, on his belly. I've filled up my condom and he's shot all over the towel spread out beneath him. But now he jerks the jock from his mouth and starts fumbling for his underwear.

"Whoa, Travis! Where you goin'?"

He won't meet my eyes. "I need to…"

Then I grab his arm, and he looks at me. Dark eyes, moist and frightened. Despairing. Full of shame.

"Allen, this is wrong. How can you even speak to me now that I've let you—"

Travis shakes his head and reaches for the cross resting on the bedside table.

All that fucking fundamentalist shit. "Oh, no!" I snarl. "You're not gonna let the Baptists ruin the best night of my life. You're stayin'!"

With that, I wrap my arms around him and hold him hard. For about 10 seconds he struggles against me, cursing quietly and shaking his head.

Then, abruptly, Travis goes limp, gives in. His head rests on my shoulder with a sigh, and he starts shaking again. I pull him into bed with me, heap the quilts over us, and curl against his warm back.

"Isn't this a sin?" Travis whispers.

I kiss the muscles of his bare shoulders. I press my face into his hair, run one finger over his wounded cheek, pat his furry belly, and hold him closer, breathing in his balsam scent.

"Never give all the heart," Yeats said. As if that's the sort of thing you choose.

The Third House on Russell Road

THOM WOLF

Finding where Eddie lived was not as difficult as I expected. The suburb just outside Durham was a small-enough place. I asked around, casually, at the pub, the supermarket, the park. Not wanting to seem desperate, I dropped his name into conversations, wondering if anyone knew him. I even asked my one-night stands. In a community like ours, where everyone has had everyone, the odds that the guy whose dick I was sucking had at one time sucked Eddie were stacked in my favor. At 3 A.M. one Saturday night in a pitch-black corner of the gardens, my diligence paid off.

"Eddie? Is he that big, fat fucker?"

I saw the man's face for a moment, illuminated by a flame as he stuffed a cigarette between his lips. He was short and podgy, with pockmarked skin. From the brief feel I'd had around his torso, he was in no great shape himself. He tucked his cock back in his jeans, exhaling smoke over me as I straightened up, my legs aching from being down there so long. The secondhand smoke went some way to ease the acrid taste of his spunk. "He lives on Russell Road, doesn't he?"

"I don't know. Does he?"

"I'm sure he does," the man said, walking away, "if I'm thinking of the right bloke."

It was the wrong direction, but I passed down Russell Road on my way home. There was nothing much to see: a narrow road lined with terraced houses—old houses, modest, each front door opening straight onto the main footpath, cars parked either side of the road. He could have been in any one of them. There was no way of knowing. At this time of night there was no evidence of life other than a scattering of lights shining from a few upstairs windows. Most of the houses were in darkness, their curtains closed. I smiled as I turned the corner at the end of the road, heading for my own home. I knew where he lived. I was getting closer.

I passed down Russell Road whenever I had the opportunity: taking a detour back from the pub, changing my jogging route. Sometimes I would walk out that way with no other reason than a hope of seeing him. I varied the time, going by early morning, before work, at lunch, early evening, late at night. I grew bolder, chancing a look through the windows of the houses I passed. I saw neat little sitting rooms with modern furniture and walls painted in primary colors. Eddie wouldn't live in a house like that. In the photograph, he was lying on an unmade bed, his hands behind his head, his hard cock reaching for the furry swell of his gut. It didn't reveal much of the room itself: a glimpse of wall, cornflower-blue, behind the brass bed rail in the upper left corner of the frame. Blue, a man's color. I couldn't imagine Eddie living in any of the bright living rooms I could see into. I continued my search.

Two weeks later he was there. Number 18 Russell Road, third house from the end of the terrace. The living room lights were on and the curtains had been removed from the window. In November the nights cut in early so that at 6:30 it was black and cold. Through the bare window I could see right into the heart of his home. The furniture was covered in old dust sheets splattered with paint. Eddie was straddling two stepladders, his strong legs forming a wide bridge as he put paint on the walls; it looked like he was painting it the exact same shade as before, a light barley color.

I'd only seen one photograph, the picture of him on the bed, but I recognized him. He was dressed in an old pair of overalls— stained with the evidence of previous painting jobs—with a ragged gray T-shirt underneath. He had his back to the window. His hair was the same as in the photo, slate-gray and seasoned with white, the short fuzz on the back of his head indicating a recent cut. He turned his head, adding paint to the roller, and I caught a glimpse of the dark, peppered whiskers that covered his upper lip and chin. He was broad from top to bottom: thick shoulders, barrel trunk, big arse. His body was like a small house, solid and well-constructed.

Daring to creep closer to the window for a better view, I watched him work his way along the wall. I'd seen enough of his picture; I wanted to see the real man in motion. The muscles of his forearms bunched and flexed beneath their fur as he rolled the paint across the wall. He stretched, reaching the widest area possible before moving the ladders. With one foot on the rung, the other leg straight, it was a great position for me to admire his mighty fine arse, so big and meaty. I could stuff my face in the crack of those juicy mounds and not come out for hours, just biding my time down there, slurping and sniffing and basking in his fullness.

He stepped back to inspect the finished wall, wiping his hands on the seat of his dungarees, smearing more paint. I withdrew a few feet to just beyond the range of the window, hoping I would go unnoticed in the dark. Now was not the time for him to see me. Eddie smiled to himself. His eyes wrinkled, and I saw the deep laugh lines cut all the way from the corners of his eyes to his mouth, just like in the picture. He gathered up his equipment and left the room. The kitchens of these houses were in the back, but there was no point following him round—the yard walls were so high that there was nothing to see but the upstairs windows. I looked up and down the road, checking the windows across the street. Now that I was so close to Eddie, the last thing I needed was to get busted by some nosy neighborhood watchperson.

Half an hour later, I saw the living room light go out. The front door opened, and Eddie left the house. He had changed into jeans, a tucked-in checked shirt, and a black jacket. He didn't see me as I hovered behind his neighbor's transit van. He walked to the end of the road and turned left. I followed, keeping a safe distance. He walked quickly and purposefully, his hands tucked in his pockets and his breath ascending in the cold night air.

I followed him to a pub called the Kingfisher. I'd heard of the place but had never been inside. It was quiet, done out quite traditionally with wood-paneled walls and low beamed ceilings. The walls were decorated with old farming equipment: a polished tractor panel, a pitchfork, shovels, buckets, and other restored equipment that I didn't know the names or uses of.

Eddie headed for the bar. I stood behind him as the barman pulled two pints for another waiting customer. I watched Eddie's face in the mirror behind the bar. His mouth was set in a straight line, his eyes narrowed. My own face was reflected just over his shoulder. For a moment he looked at me, but he showed no signs of recognition.

You won't recognize me, Eddie—not from the photograph I sent you. It was an old picture, I've changed a lot since then, from the thin chicken who shaved his chest and worried about the calories and fat in everything he ate. I've changed for the better, like you wanted me to. I'm a man now, just like you wanted.

"Is it too late for food?" Eddie asked the barman, when it was his turn.

"No, we're serving till 10," the man explained, handing over a menu.

"I know what I want," Eddie said. "Half roast chicken with chips, peas, and gravy. And a pint of bitter, please."

The barman tapped his order into the computer and pulled Eddie his drink. "Take a seat. I'll bring your food over when it's ready."

Eddie picked up his pint, took a sip, and headed for the non-smoking dining room.

"I'll have a pint of bitter," I told the barman, glancing at the menu. "And the roast chicken too. I want the same as he had."

"Take a seat. Won't be long."

I headed for the dining room, which was fairly quiet. A family of five were finishing their ice cream, and a middle-aged couple sat in silence, not even looking at each other while they ate their dinner. There was an even greater array of restored farming equipment hanging on the walls in here; I saw a tin bath and an old-fashioned sewing machine. Eddie sat at a table in the corner, his back to the entrance. I headed for the table beside him, deliberately angling my seat so he could see me. He had already drunk a third of his bitter. He wiped his 'stache on the back of his hand after each mouthful.

Finally, he looked my way. I raised my eyebrows and smiled. Eddie nodded.

"Is the food good?" I asked.

"Not bad. Nothing fancy, but the portions are a good size and it's cheap."

"Do you mind if I join you?" I asked. "I hate eating alone."

His kitchen would have been small and homely, if it had not been stuffed with furniture from the living room: a coffee table, bookcases, lamp stands. The pictures he had taken off the walls were stacked in the corner, between the fridge and the washing machine. From what I could see, the photographs were all of the same two people, a boy and girl, ranging from childhood to adult. The grown boy was a junior version of Eddie.

We sat at his table, drinking beer, listening to David Bowie on a portable CD player. The paint fumes were making me dizzy. Eddie rested his elbows on the table, arms folded, listening with interest to my fake history—macho stuff, like my girlfriend kicking me out after checking my Internet history file.

Like so many people, his photograph did not do justice to the real man. His small eyes sparkled while I talked, the exact same color as his hair. His teeth were large and square and slightly gapped in front. I could see down the open neck of his shirt, where black and gray hair curled across his chest. In his profile he said that he was 52. Most men, it's fair to say, lie about their age. I always do. The kind of men I'm interested in rarely want to know a guy under 35. Eddie didn't. I guessed his age to be near 55. Didn't matter. I wanted him even more.

"What's the story with your girlfriend?" he asked.

I shrugged and tried to sound genuine. I didn't want to tell such an elaborate lie that it would trip me up later. "We were young when we started going out. I didn't know any better. Soon we had a kid, and we've been together ever since."

"And you've been playing away from home?"

I gave a mournful nod. "It's the only way I can be happy." I reached for his hand across the table. There was paint under his fingernails. "Let me suck you."

Eddie stood up, shoving back his chair. He rived open the fly of his jeans and hitched up his shirt, revealing the hairy abdomen I had worshiped in digital JPEG form. He dug a hand into his jeans and tugged out a fat tube of soft flesh. No underwear—I hadn't expected that. I scrambled round the table, on my knees by the time I reached him. His soft cock had started to fill. I was delighted to see the foreskin, which covered his hard cock in the photo, hung over the edge of his flaccid dick by a good inch. I flicked the fleshy tip with my tongue, feeling the foreskin shorten and retract as the organ it protected grew hard. I took him in my mouth, just the head, and sucked, tasting piss and sweat and the distinct flavor of precome. I held him between my lips while my eyes traveled upward, over his belly, searching his face. The steely eyes twinkled. "Go on, son," he said.

The scent of his groin was more intoxicating than the paint fumes. I'd waited months to get his cock in my mouth and now that I had him I was high. I widened my jaw and swallowed, taking the blunt end down my throat, hoping he was impressed. His dick throbbed, nudging my tonsils. I dug my fingers into the fabric of his jeans, feeling the hair and muscle beneath, experiencing him with all my senses. Eddie grabbed a handful of hair and drew me off his cock. The hard, wet organ popped out of my mouth, drooling precome and saliva. His foreskin retracted behind the head, the knob glistened, and I couldn't resist kissing the tiny pink lips.

"Over the table," he said.

I stood, hoping he would kiss me. Eddie grabbed me by the shoulders and spun me around. I put both hands on the table to support myself. His hands went around my waist, grasping at the fastenings. The weight of his belly pressing against my back made me desperate; I wanted this man like never before. He hauled my pants halfway down my thighs, exposing my arse.

"Nice," he said, slapping my butt.

I grunted. "Thank you."

Rough fingers grasped my arse, kneading the ripe flesh, crushing my cheeks together, riving them apart. My arse was worthy of his attention. I'd been working hard, transforming it into the sort of big, meaty rump Eddie would adore. I'd stopped shaving too, and had cultivated a nice blond bush inside my crack. My arse was so fine these days, I'd fuck it myself if I could. Eddie snuffled in the funky crevice, shoving his nose deep into the bush, sniffing. His beard scraped against my skin. He poked at my hole, wiping his tongue around the area in decreasing circles. I fell forward on my elbows and shivered as his tongue, warm like wet velvet, slivered inside my arse.

"The back pocket of my jeans," I told him. "Lube."

Eddie retrieved the sachet. "I'll get a johnnie," he said.

"No," I hissed. "Fuck me bare."

He tore the sachet, lubing me with his fingers, shoving deep into my arse. I listened to the sounds of my hole, squelching and sucking, as Eddie fucked one, two, three fingers into my arsehole. He stepped back, fisting a palmful over his cock. His belly pressed against my back, feeling wonderfully full at the base of my spine. His left hand went around my waist, the right guided his dick into my crack. His cock head felt juicy and warm as it pressed against my ring. I rolled my hips back, telling him how ready I was. Eddie rested his chin on my shoulder and entered with a groan. Finally, his big bear club lay fully in my arse, exactly where I wanted it. Months of patient planning had paid off. This big fat bastard who didn't fuck chickens was fucking me now. He loved me—all 23 years of me.

He wrapped a thick elbow around my neck and brushed his beard against my neck, grunting with every thrust. When my hole was loose enough, he could pull his cock all the way out of me and shove it back in without guidance. Each time his cock slipped free, I felt like I was missing something, but the brief frustration was worth it when he pushed inside again. His thrusts became less controlled, his dick started stabbing at my hole in an erratic rhythm. He tightened his hold on my neck and dumped his load deep inside my guts. When he withdrew for the last time, I felt a wonderful wetness trickle down my thighs.

It took until the end of the week to see his bedroom. I'd hoped I would see him sooner, but Eddie claimed his time was tight; he was working overtime and had his home improvements to complete. The living room was still not finished when I returned to Russell Road, properly invited this time. The room was covered in dust sheets, the kitchen still cluttered with furniture.

"What's left to do?" I asked, surveying the room from the foot of the stairs, determined to get into his bed that night.

"A few finishing touches," he said, scratching his beard, "varnish the wood, hang a new light fitting."

"Sounds cozy," I said, grabbing his crotch, kissing him, tasting beer on his breath.

The bedroom was large and simply decorated with a large pine wardrobe and bedside dresser. The walls were blue, just like in the picture. A large Monet print, framed above the bed, seemed out of keeping with Eddie's tastes. *Water Lilies*—not what I expected. I wondered if it had been a present, maybe from one of the kids. He hadn't mentioned his family. On my last visit, I'd managed to steal a small picture of the brother and sister. I'd scanned the image into my computer and had the original in my bag, ready to return when the opportunity arose.

The bed was made up with dark blue covers, different from the photograph, but the large brass head rail was familiar. Eddie lay on top, facedown, naked, one leg raised and bent, his arse ready for my lips. Dark fur covered the back of his legs, growing lighter across his pale buttocks. His back and shoulders were surprisingly smooth. He had a fading tan line, which left his buttocks several shades whiter than the rest of his body. There was a tattoo on his right cheek, a red rose, its colors weakened with age. Entwined around the stem of the rose were the names Eddie and Beverly. Eddie and his ex-wife? Or the names of his kids? I would have to find out. In time he could have the tattoo recolored or removed. Either way, Beverly had to go.

I lay down between his heavy thighs and pressed my face against his arse, taking it in via sight, scent, and touch. His crack was oak-brown and fragrant. I spread his cheeks, needing both hands to part the hefty mounds, revealing a dark, nutty hole. I buried my face in the crack, eating his arsehole like it was my first meal in days. Eddie's moans were muffled in the pillows, but the way he squirmed his hips let me know I was doing it right. His arse was strong and savory. I was not disappointed. I teased the lush brown pucker, circling with just the tip of my tongue until he was writhing in ecstasy.

"Son, that's just beautiful," he growled.

I like a man who shows appreciation, especially when I eat him out. My last bear, Dave, would lie there in silence while my mouth slaved away at his hole—the ungrateful bastard. Big mistake. But Eddie wasn't like Dave, I could tell that straight away. I knew from his photograph that we would be perfect together. I was right.

I wandered, widening my range, dipping down to his balls and following the seam back to his hole. Eddie's ring was juicy and wet; I could enter it easily, if I wanted to. But I didn't. Fucking Eddie was not part of my plan. I chose him for his brawn, his masculinity. I wanted a dominant daddy bear, not some slack-arsed pussy.

Eddie tied my wrists to the brass headrail, fastening the rope tight. There was no give in any of his knots.

"Legs," he commanded.

Rolling through my back, I got my feet up on the rail, either side of my wrists. He secured me at the ankles. My hamstrings ached from the position. My cock was hard, drizzling precome into the blond mat surrounding my navel. My arse was off the bed, raised for my daddy bear.

"Son," he said, giving my cock a firm tug, "I've got just what you want."

"I want you," I gasped.

His face creased into a smile, his gray eyes twinkled. "You're going to get me."

Eddie took a swig from the beer on his night table and spat it out over my cock and balls. Cool, foamy liquid dribbled down my body, trickling under my balls, into my arse crack. Eddie took another mouthful and spat it out, a direct hit on my arsehole. I groaned, pouting and winking my arse lips at him. He massaged the opening, stroking, swirling, poking, slipping a blunt finger inside. I squirmed as much as my bounds would allow. I wondered if Eddie could read my mind; he seemed privy to every desire I had.

I'm so glad I was right about you, Eddie.

From his bedside dresser came a value-size tub of lube. Eddie took his time, scooping out a thick white wad, slowly working it into his palm, getting his whole hand coated. He started on my hole, inserting two, three, four fingers into my opening, slipping back and forth with a smooth wrist action. In went his thumb, fingers to the knuckle. "Enough?" he asked.

"No," I gasped. "More."

His paw was huge. My arsehole resisted. Through gritted teeth I bore down on his hand, sweating as Eddie pushed. I felt the width of his knuckle. It seemed impossible—he was beyond me. I strained at the bindings. Then my arsehole gave, engulfing his entire hand. Eddie closed his hand into a fist and began to thrust, slowly turning, fucking my gut. I wanted to devour him, absorb him, suck his massive bulk from head to toe into my body, via that tiny opening. I began to rock, rolling through my hips. My head was in another place. When I came it was a tidal wave, washing over my guts and chest, saturating the hair I grew especially for this moment.

Eddie slept soundly. I lay awake for a while, listening to his breath as it rumbled in his chest. He had asked me to spend the night. Tomorrow, he said, we could do something together—anything I wanted. The thought made me smile. I had what I wanted for now.

I eased quietly out of bed. Eddie slept innocently. That was good. It gave me a chance to explore the house undisturbed. Eddie might think I was nosing, invading his privacy, like Dave used to. Which was ridiculous. I only wanted to explore the house, get a feel for the place, suss out what I liked and what I didn't. Like the pictures of his family. They'd have to go for a start. I didn't want them staring disapproval from the wall after I moved in. I wasn't keen on much of the color scheme either, but those things would easily be changed.

The house on Russell Road and the bear who lived there did not disappoint me. They had potential.

Forged by Stålbjörn
FURR

"Lord Hephaestus?"

At the sound of the unfamiliar voice, Hephaestus looked up from his work and replied, "Yes…who are you?"

"I am Thor, one of the Aesir from the land of the Norse. I've come quite some way to see if you are able to help me. I have been searching for a smith capable of a very special job, and from what I'm told it seems you may be my only choice."

Hephaestus looked over his visitor with interest. Thor was tall and broad-shouldered, but the first thing that caught the eye was his thick flaming-red beard, worn quite long. His hair was perhaps a shade or two darker, held back from his face by a golden headband. He wore knee-high boots trimmed with fur, an embroidered tunic with a hammer of unusual design hanging from the belt, and a heavy bear-fur cloak. "Welcome, Lord Thor. If you give me a moment to finish this, we can discuss your problem—but you might want to take off your cloak. Even as used to the heat as I am, I don't wear much here in the forge," said Hephaestus as he gestured at the breechcloth and sandals he wore.

"Thank you," said Thor, draping his cloak over a stool and moving closer to the door, where it was a bit cooler. Hephaestus finished setting a ruby into the pendant he'd been working on; absorbed in his work, he failed to notice Thor's gaze looking him up and down appreciatively. Hephaestus was also broad-shouldered, with the powerfully muscled arms and chest that blacksmiths naturally develop. Strong legs and thighs balanced his powerful torso, and nearly all of his olive skin was covered with curly black body hair that had the same texture as the thick beard covering most of his face. As Hephaestus had turned away, Thor caught sight of a deep red glow in the dark eyes under bushy black brows, but in the forge it could have been a trick of the light.

Setting the pendant aside, Hephaestus turned to his guest. "So, what brings you to me?"

"Mjolnir, my hammer. It's a rather long story, but suffice it to say that Loki the Trickster interfered with the forging, leaving it with an awkwardly short handle. The difficulty is that it's enchanted, and any normal smith would ruin it trying to alter it."

"Ah, I see…but what about the person who forged it for you originally?"

Thor sighed. "Eitri the dwarf is difficult to deal with at the best of times. He demanded a ludicrous quantity of gold to even try, while at the same time saying it couldn't be done. It was at that point I decided I needed to seek a smith both more powerful and more talented than him." Hinting, Thor grinned. "Not to mention one easier to deal with. You've already been far more courteous than Eitri."

At this, Hephaestus noticed the sweat cascading down Thor's handsome face and soaking the armpits of his tunic. "Let us discuss this further in my chambers, where we'll be more comfortable." As he passed close by Thor, the scent of the sweaty Norse god made Hephaestus's cock lengthen and his balls twitch. Leading Thor through the corridor, he didn't see Thor's similar reaction to his own scent, and to the sight of his furry, broad back tapering down to a hairy, muscular butt, only the crack of which was covered by the skimpy breechcloth.

When they reached Hephaestus's chambers, he gestured Thor

to a longue, telling him, "Make yourself comfortable. I'll get us something cool to drink." On his return with four large tankards—two of cold water, two of cool wine—Hephaestus found Thor sprawled casually, having divested himself entirely of his tunic and boots, leaving him wearing little more than a skimpy, sweat-soaked breechcloth. His powerfully built body was carpeted in lush red fur—much as Hephaestus's body was in black, except that Thor's was only somewhat wavy, while Hephaestus's dense pelt looked shorter because of the curly ringlets his hairs formed. Thor had his hands behind his head, allowing the male musk from his sweat-soaked armpits to fill the room.

Despite his full hands, Hephaestus managed to rearrange his suddenly much larger dick inside his breechcloth more comfortably. "If he's offended by my appreciation of him, he can keep looking for a smith," he muttered just before smiling broadly and coming to Thor's notice. "I'm glad to see your idea of comfort is similar to my own. Here's cold spring water for thirst and wine for enjoyment." Hephaestus set down Thor's tankards on a side table beside the longue. "Perhaps I should have a look at Mjolnir while you refresh yourself."

Thor handed Mjolnir over as he reached for the tankard of water and said, "Certainly. And thanks. I knew your lands were much warmer than ours—especially now in winter—but I had no idea of the heat of your forge. I admit to some surprise that anyone could stand it for long. Certainly, the forges my mortals use—or even Eitri's—do not get so hot!"

Hephaestus raised an eyebrow, saying, "I suspect none of them are heated by the very blood of the Earth, as mine here at Aetna is." Noticing the intricately designed metal bracers on Thor's forearms, he asked, "And did Eitri make those fine bracers as well?"

"Yes," Thor said, "and in fact they are necessary for me to wield Mjolnir." He stripped them off and passed them over. "You may need to examine them as well to fully understand Mjolnir's nature."

Thor guzzled down his water and then began more slowly on

the wine, while Hephaestus examined the hammer and bracers, feeling out the patterns of their enchantments. Finally, Hephaestus set them aside, saying, "I will have to make a more careful study to be certain, but I believe I can do what you wish. I will warn you— there is a chance that any work on Mjolnir will ruin it, but I feel that chance is small. The decision will have to be yours."

"How long will this deeper study of yours take?" asked Thor.

"A day or so. The enchantments are indeed complex. If you wish to remain here with me while the work is done, you are welcome."

Thor looked at Hephaestus with his piercing, sky-blue eyes. "You're not at all what I was led to expect."

"What?!" said Hephaestus, a bit startled by the change of subject.

"You were described to me as a master metal smith and jeweler, of course, but to be blunt I was told you were ugly and crippled. Certainly, I noticed that you limp a bit, but I have to wonder at the blindness of someone who would describe you so."

"I do have a bad leg. I used to be able to walk only with a stout staff, but I exercised—both my body and my patience—and reduced the problem to a limp. As to ugliness, well, what consti- tutes beauty is a very subjective thing. What you were told doubt- less comes from what the other Olympians think of me. It's a somewhat complicated situation."

"I would be interested to hear of it, if you choose to tell me."

"I won't bore you with the long history of all this, but it comes in part from the fact I don't fit the Olympian male ideal. For one thing, I'm far too hairy—like a black goat, as Aphrodite once said. My beard is thick and unruly, instead of lying neatly like that of Heracles, or appearing patriarchal and imposing like Zeus's. Furthermore, I am looked upon with derision because I am alone among the Greek pantheon in that I routinely do heavy work at my forge and anvil. Zeus would not do without the thunderbolts I forge for him, Aphrodite and Hera their jew- elry, nor Eros his arrows of love…but that only intensifies their distaste for me." Hephaestus flexed one massive, hairy arm, adding, "It doesn't help that my craft has given me a build like a mortal laborer rather than the athletic leanness of Apollo."

Thor rose from his lounge and approached Hephaestus, who also rose as Thor drew near. "Lord Hephaestus," Thor boomed, "I do not share the misguided opinions of your fellow Olympians. In my lands I am patron of craftsmen, and I have respect for those who pour their sweat into stone, wood, and metal to create tools and items of beauty." Thor clapped one beefy hand onto Hephaestus's shoulder and continued, "And you are a fine figure of a man— which anyone who prefers men to beardless youths can see!"

The red glow in Hephaestus's eyes grew and brightened. "Indeed!" he exclaimed—and the glow brightened further to the rich orange-red of a bed of hot embers as his arm lashed out, grabbing Thor by the back of his neck. Caught off guard, Thor found Hephaestus's lips pressed to his; a charge, like a trail of hot sparks, flashed through his body. Thor's hand slid up to grasp Hephaestus by the back of the neck as Thor's tongue plunged into his mouth. Hephaestus countered with his own and, as their tongues wrestled back and forth, their free hands removed what little the two still wore, leaving their stiff, drooling cocks bare to grind against each other's hairy belly as they continued their embrace.

The kiss finally broke, but Hephaestus quickly moved on, licking and nibbling first at one of Thor's meaty nipples, then tonguing his way through the sweaty red forest on Thor's chest to the other. Back and forth, until he stopped in the middle, licking down the slightly denser center trail, past Thor's navel, his silky beard caressing Thor's rigid tool all the way down. He breathed deeply of the potent musk of Thor's crotch as he nuzzled the red-furred balls, and then slowly he licked his way up the twitching, drooling shaft. He had just begun to work his tongue into Thor's foreskin when Thor grabbed him by the chin, tilting his head up. Thor's eyes had turned a dark slate-gray, the color of storm clouds, and they sparkled with what seemed to be miniature flashes of lightning.

Thor fought to get his words out, whether because he was breathing so hard or because of a rising tide of animal lust that was overwhelming rationality, Hephaestus couldn't quite tell. "I am...going to...fuck you...*so*...*hard*!" Hephaestus winked up at Thor, and promptly swallowed his shaft all the way down, trailing his mustache along the top and grinding his furry chin into Thor's balls when he hit bottom. Thor let out a thunderous bellow that shook the mountain and frightened some of the residents—except for the smiths, who just smiled at their apprentices and remarked that Lord Hephaestus must have a special guest.

Hephaestus pulled back, again stroking the top of Thor's shaft with his mustache and stopping just with the head still in his mouth. As he worked his tongue into Thor's foreskin, his mouth filled with thick, sweet-salty precome. Hephaestus swallowed some but allowed most of it to simply run out of his mouth, soaking his beard and dripping down into his sweat-drenched pelt. Hephaestus released Thor's cock, skinned back the long foreskin, and rubbed the ripe head across his precome-slathered beard, the smell of Thor's musky manhood causing his own dick to drool freely.

Hephaestus suddenly found himself pulled to his feet, Thor's hands still in his armpits. There were few even among the gods physically powerful enough to manhandle him so! Thor growled, "Your bed, or I take you here!"

"The bed, then," said Hephaestus, grabbing Thor by the cock and leading him down a hallway, noticing that Thor wiped his sweaty hands on his beard. Hephaestus grinned and shoved him up against the wall, pushed an arm up out of the way and began rubbing his beard through Thor's ripe, sweat-soaked armpit fur. Thor growled deep in his throat, gathered some of the thick slime pouring from his cock, and began working two fingers into Hephaestus's fur-shrouded arsehole.

Finally raising his beard from Thor's armpit, Hephaestus asked, "How do you want me?"

"All fours!" Thor grunted.

Hephaestus dashed to the bed, quickly bracing himself so he wouldn't find himself beaten senseless from having his head dashed against the headboard by Thor's thrusts. To Hephaestus's surprise, the first sensation was of Thor's beard brushing across his hairy rump, followed by his tongue plunging deep into the hole. "Oh, yes, Thor—yes!" Hephaestus exclaimed. Thor spread the furry cleft wide and ate like a starving man at a banquet, tongue-fucking Hephaestus's arse as deep as he could manage, prompting Hephaestus to grunt loudly in pleasure and push back against Thor's face. "Yes! I love your tongue up my arse and your beard on my balls! Fuck me hard, Thor!"

Thor did just that—plowing the full length of his long, thick shaft into Hephaestus all the way to his crotch fur with one steady thrust. He paused for a moment, then started fucking, gradually picking up the pace until only Hephaestus's strong arms were keeping his head from slamming into the headboard with each thrust. The bed was creaking and groaning loudly—if one could have heard it over the grunting, moaning, and swearing of its occupants. Both sweated heavily: Thor's was copious enough that every time he slammed into Hephaestus, he shook loose a shower of droplets, which pattered onto Hephaestus's back in a sort of counterpoint to Thor's thrusts. There, they combined with Hephaestus's sweat and trickled down Hephaestus's hairy buttocks, producing a wet smacking sound every time Thor's loins slammed against them.

Abruptly, Thor collapsed onto Hephaestus's back, slamming his cock in as deep as it could go, bit into the muscle at the base of the Greek's neck, and grunted loudly. Thor came so forcefully and copiously that with each shot some of the hot jism splattered out of Hephaestus into Thor's hairy crotch.

As Thor's orgasm began to fade, Hephaestus rolled him over onto his back, then remounted Thor's still-rigid cock—Thor gasping as his sensitive cock was once again in the Olympian's tight, slick hole. Hephaestus rode Thor's cock while pounding his own tool with two hands—just one of his big hands was not quite able to touch fingers around his thick shaft. Hephaestus stared into Thor's eyes, and Thor saw that the glow in Hephaestus's eyes had become a brilliant yellow-white. Hephaestus slammed his furry arse down on Thor's cock, and sped up his hands on his own. Never breaking his stare into Thor's eyes, he growled louder and louder, until finally he broke into a bestial bellow as his cock spewed great splats of come, covering Thor's face and torso with gobs of the thick, jelly-like jism.

As Hephaestus's orgasm began to fade, Thor grabbed his buttocks and leaned forward, catching the tip of Hephaestus's cock in his mouth and taking the last shots of his load, his tongue exploring the folds of the foreskin as he did so. Ever so slowly, Hephaestus slid down, eventually forcing Thor to release his cock. He plunged his tongue into Thor's mouth to taste his own juices there, and the pair once again began kissing passionately, smearing Hephaestus's load between them. Thor's cock finally softened and slid out of Hephaestus's rump and their kissing gradually slowed, eventually leaving the two of them sleeping soundly in each other's arms.

Thor woke first. Soon realizing that he and Hephaestus were virtually glued together—mustache, beard, and chest hair—by Hephaestus's now-dried ejaculation, Thor chuckled deeply, awakening Hephaestus, who likewise began to laugh as he realized their situation. Fortunately, there was a flagon of water and a rag handy, and with care the two managed to separate without ripping out many hairs. "We'll have to be careful about that next time," said Thor.

"Yes, indee—" began Hephaestus, only to be cut off by a kiss. "But later—I need to get to work on that hammer of yours." Catching the mischievous look on Thor's face, he amended, "The one you wear on your belt, not the one between your legs!" After noting that Thor's appetite at the table was the equal—at least—of his appetite in bed, Hephaestus sent him out hunting so he could focus on the work at hand without being distracted by either Thor's lust or his own.

On Thor's return in the afternoon, Hephaestus had good news for him. "It seems it's going to be much less difficult to alter Mjolnir than I thought," Hephaestus said.

Thor looked puzzled and asked, "Why is that? You said earlier you'd need a day or so just to work out the enchantments, and I was only gone a few hours."

"Well, they did *look* complicated at first but, after thinking about it for a while, I saw the basic logic and everything suddenly made sense. It also helps that the part I thought would be the biggest obstacle—the enchantment that makes Mjolnir unbreakable—has turned out to be a huge help!"

"You're going to have to explain that to me," said Thor.

"Well, it's really not an enchantment of unbreakability to begin with. They used one that causes Mjolnir to instantly repair itself. It's so fast you'd never see it happen, but for our purposes the difference is enormous. All I have to do is craft a handle extension that, under the right circumstances, Mjolnir will accept as part of itself, and it will be as if it were originally forged that way."

Thor thought about this for a while and then said, "I think I see what you mean. How do we proceed from here?"

"I plan to make up some mock handles that we can temporarily fix to Mjolnir with wax, so we can find the right length and weight for proper balance. Then, I'll craft the actual handle extension, and we'll fuse it to Mjolnir."

"We will?"

"Yes. Mjolnir has…bonded to you. For this to work, you need to be involved."

"Involved how?"

"The final quenching will have to be done with your own body fluids." At Thor's shocked look, Hephaestus hurried to add, "It need not be blood, though that would work. You might simply piss all over it and that would work as well."

At that, the shock left Thor's face, and a few sparkles appeared in his eyes as he said, "I have some ideas on that point, but when shall we test the mock handles for balance?"

"Tomorrow morning. I've already made a few, but I want a bit broader range to be sure we get it exactly right."

"So we'd do the actual alteration later tomorrow?" Thor asked. Hephaestus nodded.

"In that case," Thor went on, "what do you think of me quenching Mjolnir in the come I'll shoot with you fucking my furry Norse arse?"

Hephaestus's cock became erect so quickly that it loudly slapped against his belly, already trailing threads of precome. Thor looked surprised for a moment and then roared with laughter, finally finding the breath to say, "I'll take that to mean you like the idea!"

"*Very* much so! I certainly enjoy getting fucked myself, but I have been hoping to get a chance to fuck you since our first kiss!"

Thor looked slightly abashed as he said, "I hope you'll...take it slowly, at least at first. I've never let anyone fuck me before."

"Let me guess—the status thing, right? It's fine for, say, the captain of one of your Viking longboats to fuck anyone on his crew, but no one fucks the captain. So, who would one of the Aesir allow to fuck him?"

"That's part of it. I've also never found any of the other gods particularly attractive that way. You're a peer—you drive me crazy with lust, so why not do it while I have the chance?"

"I can see your point, but here's something to consider," replied Hephaestus. "I have no problem with the idea of getting fucked by a mortal; in fact, I visit some of the finest metal smiths in the Olympian domain on a fairly regular basis. While the Greeks generally have a similar idea about what goes on between two males, there's also the simple fact that I'm a *god,* and my followers are quite happy to do whatever will make me happy. I suspect that if you showed up on a Viking longboat, screwed half the crew, and let the captain fuck you, they'd probably see it as a blessing of enormous magnitude."

Thor burst out laughing, then said, "You know, you're probably right! I just never thought of it that way. I'll have to give that idea a try."

"Besides, once you let the captain fuck you, just roll *him* over and fuck him until he begs for mercy!"

The flickers of light in Thor's eyes grew a bit more intense as he said, "I like the way you think, my friend!"

"Right now, I think I should get back to making those mock handles. If you can stand the forge for a while, you can give me some idea as to your preferences on the handle extension and how you want it decorated."

"Lead on, Lord Hephaestus!"

The two spent the rest of the afternoon in the forge discussing hammer handles and weapons design in general. While Thor was sweating freely, he simply made up for it by drinking vast quantities of cold spring water and the occasional tankard of wine. Finally, Hephaestus declared himself finished with work for the day and ready for dinner.

Over their meal, the two continued discussing various issues regarding the next day's work. "The only bad thing," Hephaestus said, "is that we're not going to be able to reenact last night tonight. After all, we need to conserve our strength—and your come—for tomorrow!"

"Are you saying I wore you out so much last night you're afraid you wouldn't be able to perform as required tomorrow if we enjoy each other tonight?"

"No, I'm just wondering how often you can spew enough jism to cover your hammer!"

"As often as I want to—but now that I think about it, it seems right to hold back a bit the night before the first time a hairy, sweaty beast mounts me and rides my arse until I blow a load the size of Odin's ego!" Hephaestus simply grinned back at him, a deep orange glow lighting his eyes.

The next morning they awoke, breakfasted, and bathed together in one of the warm springs near Hephaestus's forge. Outside it was a glorious, clear sunny day, and they set to the task of testing to see exactly how long and heavy the extension for Mjolnir should be. One of Hephaestus's samples was nearly right, and with a little more weight added to the butt, Thor proclaimed it perfect. Hephaestus bade Thor to go relax while he forged the actual piece to be joined with his hammer. "We'll do the joining later this afternoon before dinner," Hephaestus told him.

Thor—never much one for "relaxing"—had fallen asleep on a lounge when Hephaestus finished his work and came in to fetch him. Hephaestus grinned and took a moment to admire the furry Norse sprawled carelessly across the lounge before awakening him with a kiss. "Mjolnir's ready to be joined. Are you ready to get fucked?" Hephaestus asked playfully.

"Let's get to it!" said Thor, leaping to his feet and heading off to the forge. There he was surprised and delighted by the extent of Hephaestus's preparations. Mjolnir was laid on a low table topped with polished obsidian. In front of the table was an odd contraption with a large padded bar a bit lower than chest height.

"What's this thing?" Thor asked.

"To be blunt about it, it's a fuck brace. You put your knees there and there, and lean forward, resting your chest against the padded bar."

"I don't understand why we need it."

"Because we need your come to shoot all over Mjolnir, I can't fuck you on your back. If we tried doing it standing up, we'd be constantly fighting for balance, and I want you to be able to relax. This way, you won't have to worry about falling over or being out of position when you're ready to shoot."

During the explanation, Thor had been kneeling by the table, examining Mjolnir and the new handle. "It looks finished already!" he exclaimed. "The workmanship matches so closely, I can't tell where the new handle begins!"

Hephaestus came over and pointed out the hairline seam, saying, "It is work I'm proud of. It's quite a compliment that even you couldn't see the joining until I pointed it out. And speaking of joining…" Hephaestus pulled off his breechcloth with one hand and with the other brought the Norse god's bearded face into his crotch.

Thor immediately began lapping at Hephaestus's hairy, sweaty balls and rubbing his beard into the surrounding sweaty black tangle. Hephaestus groaned in pleasure and began drizzling precome freely as Thor worked his tongue along the underside of his shaft, letting his mustache scrub the top side as he worked his way out toward the head. Reaching it, he slowly swirled his tongue into Hephaestus's foreskin, working it back and gradually swallowing the thick shaft until his nose was buried in musky crotch fur. He then worked his way slowly back, getting a large smear of dick lube across his mustache and one side of his beard as Hephaestus' cock popped out of his mouth. "I think that's enough of that," said Hephaestus. "Get on the brace."

Hephaestus showed Thor how to position himself, and as he did so, Thor saw how Mjolnir was perfectly positioned. Thor found he was surprisingly comfortable; while there was a stout bar for him to hold on to, his hands were free and his view of Mjolnir was clear for when he'd need to aim. As he settled himself, he felt Hephaestus's beard at the back of his neck. "Just relax and enjoy yourself." Hephaestus's beard trailed down his back, brushed across his furry rump, then burrowed inward. Thor gasped as he felt Hephaestus's tongue begin lapping around his hole, then grunted as it worked its way into him. The energetic rimming made Thor's already stiff cock drool freely, and he began pushing back against Hephaestus's face.

At that sign, Hephaestus backed off and started working his cock head up and down Thor's sweaty, saliva-slicked cleft, adding his own thick cock-juice to the mix. Every time the head slid past Thor's arsehole, Thor would twitch or gasp just a bit; as that reaction faded, Hephaestus started pressing in just a bit as the head passed. After several passes and gradually increasing pressure, Thor groaned and Hephaestus's cock began sinking in. Patiently, slowly, Hephaestus kept up a gentle pressure and in that way slid his entire thick length into Thor's no longer innocent fuckhole. As the last of Hephaestus's cock vanished into Thor and his chest fur ground against Thor's back, Thor let out a little moan. "Are you all right?" asked Hephaestus.

"Just wishing I'd thought to get Mjolnir worked on a long, long time ago."

Hephaestus ground his crotch against Thor, saying, "Better now than never!"

Hephaestus moved inside Thor, shallow and slow at first, but with increasing depth and power until Hephaestus was long-dicking Thor fast and hard. The fuck brace groaned under the strain, and Thor was thankful for the heavy padding on the chest bar as he was rhythmically slam-fucked against it. He could see the sparkling in his own eyes reflected in the midnight obsidian of the table, and he could feel Hephaestus's heat against his back, along with the sweat showering down. "Oh, yes, it feels so good…oh, yes, oh, yes, oh, *yes*! Oh, *yes*!" Thor's chanting of approval guided Hephaestus's rhythm, keeping Thor moving closer and closer to release.

"Oh, yes, oh, *fuck*, oh, *yes*—I'm close, Stålbjorn! Fuck me harder, make me come!" Hephaestus grabbed Thor's shoulders and began pounding with all his considerable might. Thor grabbed his slimy tool with his hands and stroked once, twice, three times, then let out a bellow that shook the forge as ropes of thick cream jetted from his cock and drenched Mjolnir, covering the tabletop. As Thor's arsehole tightened around Hephaestus's cock, he let go and began pumping his own load deep into Thor's gut. At the sensation of being filled with Hephaestus's hot juices, Thor bellowed again and his orgasm renewed itself, another series of massive shots of Norse jism splattering all over the now-glowing Mjolnir. Hephaestus collapsed on top of Thor, grinding their sweaty pelts together and plowing his cock deep into Thor one last time. "I don't know whether to consider myself foolish or fortunate," Thor panted, "in not discovering this pleasure earlier, or in waiting for one so proficient!"

Hephaestus laughed heartily. "What a sweet-talker, and *after* he's come, at that!" Hephaestus slowly dismounted, then helped Thor up from the fuck brace.

The obsidian tabletop was covered with puddles of Thor's

come, outlining Mjolnir. The come that had landed on or near the hammer had vanished. Thor picked up his hammer and carefully checked for the seam, which had disappeared. The balance was perfect, and just holding it he knew that his hammer was stronger than ever. Thor grabbed Hephaestus in a bear hug, exclaiming, "Thank you, my friend!" Hephaestus slipped his tongue into Thor's mouth, and the two kissed long and passionately.

Finally, the kiss broke and Hephaestus asked, "By the way— what was that you called me just before you came? Stålbjorn, I think it was?"

Thor actually blushed a bit, then he grinned and said, "It means 'steel bear,' in honor of your craft, the quality of your tools"— Thor grabbed Hephaestus's cock—"and the strength with which you use them!"

Hephaestus laughed and led Thor off to the dinner table— knowing that if he was hungry, the walking Norse appetite known as Thor would be ravenous after the kind of exercise they'd had.

Dinner proceeded quietly. Thor was obviously troubled about something and, as the meal drew to a close, he finally spoke. "I really, honestly, don't want to offend you, but I need to get back home. As much as I'd like to spend another night with you, my duty to the mortals who look to me for protection is weighing heavily on me. I hope you'll understand…"

"I had hoped you could stay the night, but I won't be offended if you leave after dinner. I understand your obligation, and I respect it. I hope you'll remember that you're always welcome here."

Thor's face relaxed into a smile, with that familiar sparkle of tiny lightning in his eyes. "Thank you, Lord Hephaestus. You likewise are always welcome to visit me. I would love to show you our part of the world—in particular, a quiet, private little meadow I know of."

The glow in Hephaestus's eyes brightened noticeably at that as he and Thor both rose from the table. "I look forward to it, Lord Thor." Hephaestus handed Thor his clothes as he began to dress. "I hear the summer days in your lands are very long, just the thing for us to enjoy such…natural beauty."

Thor looked up from lacing his boot, and the two burst into laughter simultaneously. "Farewell, my friend," said Hephaestus.

Thor grabbed Hephaestus in a powerful hug and growled, "Not farewell—see you soon."

Thor released Hephaestus, turned, and quickly took his leave. Hephaestus watched after him for some time, then headed for his workshop. He had an idea for a statue and had in mind just the right copper alloy to match the shade of Thor's beard.

Feeding the Bear
TULSA BROWN

"Hey, Joey! Come on out front."

My father's voice sailed over the clamor of the full restaurant and through the narrow window of the kitchen galley. I was sure it was a hallucination—he'd never interrupt me during breakfast. I had eight eggs, two scrambles, and a country-style omelet all frying on the big grill, a full pen of home-fries sputtering in the hot grease, not to mention a hockey puck sizzling on the gas stovetop. Who the hell could eat a burger at 7 A.M.? I wondered.

"*Joe!*" The thunder in his voice snapped me awake, an obedient flinch that ran through me even though I was nearly 20. A second later, my sister Rosa appeared in the galley doorway.

"He means it, Joe," she shrugged. "You'd better get out there."

"Shit." I grabbed a fresh apron off the hook and tossed it at her, to protect her waitress uniform. "I've got four number 2's, a flip with extra spuds…"

I rattled off the orders on my way out, wiping at my face with a towel. I'd been hustling for an hour in the kitchen's inferno, and I was dripping sweat and grease. Nobody knew the mayhem of the breakfast rush better than my dad, Frank Caparelli. What the hell was so important?

He was standing beside a full double in section three—two tables pushed together to seat 10. Our restaurant, Frank's Grill, was more than a simple diner. There were 20 tables in the long, L-shaped front room, with a narrow galley kitchen, an office, and a staff room in the back. There was nothing trendy about the red vinyl seats and striped tablecloths, but on a morning like this the place bustled and shone.

Dad beamed as I came up, and he thrust an arm around my shoulders. At 50, he was short, dark, and powerful in a wiry way, an Italian Popeye who wore his cook's cap and whites as proudly as any serviceman's uniform.

"Here he is, the smart one in the family. I'm lucky to have him for the summer. Home two days from university and he's already putting the old man to shame. Joey's so good on the grill, you'll never know if it was me or him who filled your plate."

The gush of parental pride was embarrassing enough, but for the first time I noticed his audience: some of the burliest, hard-bitten workmen I'd ever seen. It was a solid wall of big bodies in blue and green, faces bright with sunburn or already burnished by work and wind. They clutched coffee cups with rough, scarred hands, their hairy forearms crowding the table like a log jam.

At 5-foot-10, I was two inches taller than my dad, the same wiry muscles spread over a bigger frame, hardened by a winter of the run-and-tackle lunacy of rugby. Yet in that instant, I felt like a kid. Even sitting down, these guys dwarfed me.

But each of them must have had a father too. With knowing grins, they gave me good-natured nods. I smiled back, trying to inch away. The scrape of a chair made me look to the far end of the table.

I don't know if the world moved when the big man stood up, but my end of it certainly tilted. He was a golden mountain towering over me by four or five inches, his enormous round shoulders briefly blocking the morning light through the window. His nut-brown hair was streaked blond by long hours in the sun—even the bristles on his forearms glinted gold. His broad torso didn't taper into his belt; he was a solid trunk, with huge thighs that strained at the denim-blue work pants. I was mesmerized by his silver belt buckle, the abrupt, short curve of his belly above, and the bulge of his fly underneath.

I saw this all in one moment. He reached forward and gripped my hand in a strong, meaty clasp, his brown eyes glimmering with good humor.

"If you're feeding me, boy, you've got a *big* job ahead of you."

The table burst into laughter. I grinned stupidly, nailed in place by one fact: He was still looking at me.

"Joe, you're burning," my dad said.

No shit.

"Joey." He nudged me and I smelled it too: faint, acrid disaster wafting from the kitchen. I bolted without a goodbye, more laughter ringing after me. I chased Rosa out of the kitchen, dumped four orders in the trash, and started again, my body moving with the measured panic of a high-speed robot. But I was still too dazzled to be angry, the image of that golden giant throbbing in me like a pulse.

My father, I realized, had been priming me for months before I arrived home, telling me about the condo complex going up a few miles west and the boon it would mean for Frank's Grill. Business in our family's restaurant had always been brisk, so I hadn't understood his excitement, or his pride.

"These guys," my father had said, "don't go out to *dine*. They sit down to eat, and that's why they come here. I know how to fill a plate. They're big men, lifting with their backs all day. They'll work harder before they go to bed tonight than you and me will all week." He stumbled a bit, embarrassed. "I'm not saying computers aren't, you know, work, but…"

Yeah, Dad. Sure, Dad.

Yet as I scraped the burnt and broken eggs off the grill that morning, I had a dawning of what he meant. Hunkered around the table in a solid wall of animal brawn, those men radiated the labor that had shaped their bodies, the weight they'd lifted and pounded and wrestled with, and not in any gym. It was a vivid reminder that machines don't build things—men do. And those men like to be fed.

I'd been taught my craft by Francesco Guido Caparelli, the high priest of short order.

"The kitchen," Dad had said, "is no place for a woman. OK, at home you gotta let 'em. But here, when you're cooking *professional*, you need strength and balls." He whacked off the head of a whitefish with a single chop of the cleaver.

I'd been cooking since I was 14, and in truth, I've always loved the fast pace and kick-ass action. I could hold eight orders in my head at one time, crack two eggs in each hand, and not break a yolk. It took rhythm and endurance and sometimes acrobatic skill—in the middle of a big rush, I was Jackie Chan.

Yet nothing I did in a day, whether here or boring myself silly in computer sciences, compared with the raw power I'd felt beaming from those bodies, especially the golden grizzly. I still buzzed from the intensity of his brown eyes, the wordless animal glint that had lingered on me. I didn't even mind that he'd called me "boy."

"Hey, Frank, tell the kid. He does good grub!"

The distant words turned my head. The men from section three had finished and were leaving. I craned and twisted, trying to see them through the galley window, but the angle was wrong. Without thinking, I got up on the counter and peered out. The giant was the end man, not lagging behind but herding the others with an easy, rolling gait. At the door he turned and glanced back—and grinned at me.

Shit!

My face flamed to be caught gawking, but I didn't have time to agonize. The sound of approaching footsteps got me off the counter in a hurry.

Dad was glowing and pleased, happy with the morning bustle still in progress. He put on a clean apron and set about briskly clearing workspace. My heart thudded with one question. I took the basket of home fries out of the grease and shook it deftly, trying to sound nonchalant.

"So that's the crew you were telling me about?" I said.

"A few of them."

"Who's…the one who shook my hand?"

"Cole Buckland. He's the papa bear."

The words burned through me in a laser ray of porn. I almost dropped the spuds. But I was pretty sure my father didn't know the gay connotation it had.

"Oh, what's that?"

Dad was leafing through the orders. "That's what they call the guy who coordinates the trades on a site, who schedules the work so the men don't get in one another's way. If there's a dispute, it goes to the foreman. If he can't resolve it, they take it to Cole." He looked up and grinned. "That's the bear part. I've heard he's slow to boil, but then—look out! That's a whole lotta man to piss off."

It was hard to concentrate the rest of the morning. There was way too much potential in every plate of eggs and sausage. When our lunch help showed up at 10:30 to prep, I stole away for a break.

In the Caparelli establishment, cleanliness came ahead of godliness; we even had a shower stall in our little staff room. I gratefully stripped off my grease-stained uniform and set the water.

A year earlier, I had told my family I wanted to do something—anything—that didn't involve a restaurant, and I registered at the first university that would take me. Actually, my only goal had been to get a hundred miles from home and lay every guy who looked at me right. In a week, I was bored with my courses in computer-assisted design; in two, I loathed them. But I never mentioned that when I phoned home. I didn't have the guts.

The nights had made up for it. My dark Italian looks paid a lot of tabs in the gay club near campus. Most of the men were too small and smooth for my liking, but what the hell: all the parts worked. Every now and then, after a game of rugby, someone from the other team looked across the grass at me, smoky eyes revved by more than the run, and that made for a good night. Bigger was better.

But Cole Buckland was his own category. Even now I was still riding the hot rush he'd laid on me, thrilling to the memory as I soaped my body, the familiar flat planes swirling with dark hair. I'd been with guys bigger than me, but never a man who was…overwhelming. A papa bear.

Forget it, Joe. The best ones are always straight.

Yet I knew that gaze, hungry and territorial. Straight guys didn't look at you like that.

And if you're wrong, "that's a whole lotta man to piss off."

Tell it to my hard-on.

I stopped talking to myself—there was nothing else to say. I was stiff and needy with an electric charge of lust that burned out the other circuits. I stroked myself and saw him again, imagined him unbuttoning his denim shirt, revealing the broad pecs and furry pattern of golden brown hair, the deep hole of his navel, and the solid, fleshy belly resting on top of his belt. I saw one big-knuckled paw yank the clasp open and the other unzip the straining bulge.

You've got a big job ahead of you, boy…

I came so hard it wrenched me, one hand on my twitching cock, the other on the tiled wall, my balls pulled up tight as wallops of pleasure shook my body, come leaping into the warm spray. I shot again and again, tremors pumping up the joy from some well deep inside me.

I leaned against the shower wall, trembling. This wasn't about the parts that worked, a fun run and quick lay on a Friday night. I felt electrocuted, as if I'd touched some deep trip wire of want, a mainline of need that I couldn't exactly name and didn't how to get. But damn it, I had to try.

The crew came in for breakfast every day. I almost gave myself whiplash straining to catch sight of Cole Buckland's large, golden presence through the narrow window of my galley. I made sure to heap the spuds higher on his plate, fill and dress his breakfast burgers into towering works of art. It gave me a little rush of pride to do it and a bigger one to see the plate come back empty. I was giving this man something he wanted, at least.

But I wanted more. Dad let me off every afternoon from 2 until 4, and he usually gave me the car. I always wound up in the mall parking lot across from the condo construction site. In 80-degree heat, my dad's old Pontiac was an oven, the dense air laced with the spicy, lingering scent of his cigarillos. Perspiration trickled down my temples and streamed under my T-shirt as I scoured the site through binoculars.

The men were sweating too, shirtless backs gleaming as they worked, hairy legs bare below ragged denim shorts. I knew some of them caught hell for it, but it was too hot for protective clothing. Way too hot. My imagination simmered at the sight of the knotty, gnarled electricians tugging cable, the huge, hairy bulls hauling sheetrock on their broad shoulders. With a glimpse of Cole Buckland, the steam blew my lid right off.

I'd zoom in until he was close enough to bite. I loved the wild brush on his forearms, the wet rings that darkened his work shirts, even the outline of his wallet in the back pocket of his jeans, jutting out with the press of his solid ass. Most of all, I was entranced by the way he moved. He walked differently than the others, more of the big man set back on his heels, an unhurried, swaying strut that must have vibrated the floorboards. Even with the site's noise the men heard him coming, and they always perked up with new energy. It wasn't fear, I thought, just…respect. They knew who the papa bear was. And if they didn't, they found out.

I never saw the fight start. My sights that afternoon were trained on Cole's rugged face, his thick fingers thoughtfully stroking his lush beard while he studied a schedule. Suddenly he looked up, eyes flashing. He threw down the clipboard, whipped off his hard hat, and leapt into a run.

Against the outside wall of the condo row, a small crowd had gathered. Through the onlookers, I could see two men grappling—the turbulent shuffle as they shoved and tugged at each other, each trying to land the first blow. Cole Buckland charged into the group like a bull. The muscles on his massive back twitched as he reached in and tore the scrappers apart, a single, mighty wrench that sent them staggering in opposite directions. One man stumbled to the dirt, but the other caught himself in a few steps, then turned in a hot rage and lunged at Cole's back.

My stomach flipped; I almost called out. But the papa bear spun swiftly around and caught his attacker with both hands, then plowed him back into the wall. A second later he yanked him off and slammed again, a gust of animal force tempered by chilling expertise. The pinned man's furious face was a blank slate now, his feet barely touching the ground.

I was swimming in my own sweat, the images of power and aggression rolling through me in a low thunder, erupting in a smack of sex, coupled with alarm. I was bewildered and very, very hard.

Cole Buckland finally released the workman, who tottered a few steps, stiff with shame and resentment. The crowd fell back, their usual respect tinged with new caution, even fear. They were dogs smelling the mark of a dominant male, sprayed on flesh instead of a tree. I thought Cole would simply chase them back to work, but in less than a minute he walked up to his attacker and threw an arm around his shoulders, a rugged, masculine hug of goodwill, or forgiveness. Even at a distance, I saw the tension leave the smaller man's body, a physical sigh that rippled out through the rest of the group. Cole calmed them all with that single touch, and the men drifted back to their jobs, talking and even laughing.

I was gripped by awe. I rubbed my bulging crotch, writhing

on a hook of lust and envy. How would I ever get under that man's arm?

I drove back to the restaurant, daunted. It was quiet in the kitchen, clean counters gleaming, the lull before the dinner rush. Dad had spread a dozen piles of the week's orders in front of him, studying them like tarot cards.

He saw me looking. "You know what a successful restaurant is, Joe? Fifty percent listening. You watch what a guy orders, then ask him how his mom used to make it. Anybody can fill a man's stomach, but you feed him here." He tapped my chest, my heart. "Give him home food and you've *got* him."

He seemed to catch himself then, and turned aside, gathering up the orders. "I know I should be explaining this to Rosa. I guess I'm just glad to have you home."

The words were in my mouth. I wanted to tell him, but how could I? He'd already paid my tuition for the coming year.

I turned my attention to the good advice he'd given me: how to bait a line. I'd been studying Cole's plates like the rumpled sheets of a bed, and I knew what he liked. Burgers for breakfast—the man was definitely a carnivore. And I had a secret weapon in that department.

"Ma," I said when I arrived home that night, "can I have your recipe for meat loaf?"

The next morning was carefully planned. Just when the order for section three was ready, I sent Rosa on an errand into the storeroom and carried out the plates myself, five on a tray and three scalding my bare arm. Dad was leaning on their table, blocking my way while he told one of his favorite stories.

"So the guy says to me, 'I'd like to get that waitress in the sack.' And I picked up my cleaver and said, 'Oh, yeah, which one—my daughter or my wife?' "

They howled with laughter and thumped the table, long seconds before they noticed me standing there with my arms breaking. My father shot me a sharp look as I set out the plates, but I said, "Dad, the laundry never delivered the tablecloths. They said we should just flip the dirty ones over."

Smoke almost came out of his ears. He charged away, invoking saints the Vatican never heard of. I trembled with nervousness and arousal as I sidled up to Cole Buckland's solid, square-shouldered form and slipped the heavily-laden plate in front of him. He noticed the two-inch thick wedge of meat loaf that crowded the eggs and looked up at me, mustache twisted by a wry smile.

"What's this?"

"A test-drive," I said. "We're thinking about adding it to the dinner menu, but we wanted an expert opinion first." I was certain he could hear my heart. "If it's any good, stop by after work and pick up the rest to take home. We close at 8."

He raised an eyebrow—a direct hit. In fact, his bare gaze could have melted the uniform off my body. I sauntered back to the kitchen, but my hopes were doing handsprings. I was Jackie Chan *and* Bruce Lee behind the grill that morning, flying on the hottest rush, walking on fucking air.

At 11:20 A.M. I heard a pounding on the service door in back of the kitchen. When I heaved it open, I was surprised to see one of the workmen from the site. He handed me a sealed envelope, smudged by the dark grit of his hand.

"Cole wanted me to run this over," he said, grinning. "Maybe it's his lunch order."

I closed the door and leaned against it in the dim hallway.

Hi Joe,

That's the best meat loaf I've ever had in my life, and you are one hot kid. Real hot. But I'm probably a rougher ride than you're used to, and your dad owns a lot of knives. Call me up in a few years.

Cole.

Whenever you cruise, there's the chance you'll lose: I knew that. Sex is a game you never win all the time. But Cole's note nailed me, the words ripping into my skin like a spray of buckshot. Over the day, the wound festered in the kitchen's greasy heat, and by the middle of the supper rush I was slamming pots and kicking the oven door shut. Bruce Lee had become Bruce Willis. Dad shot me dark looks down the steel counter, but he couldn't afford to stop when we were so busy, even to give me shit. As soon as most of the tables were at the coffee and pie stage, his firm hand closed around my wrist.

"Why don't you knock off early. Take that mood for a walk."

It wasn't a request, and anyway he was right. There was somewhere I had to go. I changed into jeans and a T-shirt and fired my whites at the laundry hamper on the way out. I dug my hands into my pockets and started to walk.

By the time I reached the work site, the daylight was yellow and slanted, and long shadows stretched toward dusk. The row of side-by-side condos looked like the half-eaten carcass of a dinosaur, a silhouette of stark bones against the failing day. Summer here was short; the men worked twelve-hour days to make the most of it. It was almost seven o'clock as the last of the crew walked to their cars, tired and dirty, shoulders bowed.

I was betting that Cole would be the last to leave. When I crept close enough to see him, my nerves pulled taut, the electric kick-start of lust and anger, and a bit of fear. I had walked a long way to tell him one word. But I was going to say it, even if he put me into the wall.

He was in the unit on the end, down on one knee as he rifled through a big metal tool case. Plaster dust lined the creases of his denim work shirt, and his sun-lightened hair was matted and dark, still ringed by the mark from his hard hat, which was on the ground. I stole up through the bearing posts, my heart running.

"You chickenshit," I blurted.

He didn't answer, just closed the tool box with a solid clang and flipped the latch shut.

"I didn't give a rat's ass about 'no,' but you should have had the balls to say it to my face."

He got to his feet and I felt a clutch of alarm. Even paces away he towered over me.

"Like the balls it takes to sit in a car with a pair of binoculars?" Cole said.

The news was a blow, a slam of shame that squeezed my breath out. He knew I was spying on them, that I came day after day to drool like a hungry stray. But how the hell had he seen me? The mall parking lot was across a four-lane highway and always full.

Cole reached into his breast pocket and tossed something to me. I flinched to catch it, a small, dense metal cylinder that I first thought was a piece of pipe. I quickly discovered the sections telescoped out—a spyglass.

"Do you know what they pay me for, Joe? To see everything, hear everything that goes on at this site, or around it. If the same car shows up day after day, I've got to know if it's some nut who wants to sabotage the job…"

Or some horny kid squeezing his dick. Well, that kid now felt like the stupidest shit in the world. I closed the spyglass and tossed it back, my skin turning to ash in waves of fire. I wished there was a hole I could fall into, but Cole was still looking at me.

"If you want something, be man enough to ask for it. Don't skulk around. Why didn't you just show up after work, like this?"

Because you're 10 feet tall, I thought, *and the rest of these guys are 8.*

"I don't have steel-toed boots," I said.

He knew what I meant, anyway, and his gaze softened. "No, but you're one hell of a fry guy, and that's something. When you feed this crew, they're set for five hard hours. Every man's a better human being after a good meal, especially me." He grinned and patted the solid, comfortable curve on top of his belt. "There's already five pounds here that belong to you. It'll be 10 by August."

The words slung around my shoulders like an arm, pulled me close even though I hadn't moved. I grinned back at him, my hopes rising.

A blue hush was lowering onto the site, deepening the shadows around us. I remembered all the times I'd stared at this place, the fantasies I'd played out in my mind with this papa bear in the tantalizing caves of the half-finished rooms. Now I was really here, inhaling the earthy scent of raw wood and plaster dust, and Cole Buckland was looking me over like dinner. I felt a serious surge against my zipper.

But nothing would happen until I made it happen. He was waiting, head cocked, hands on his hips.

I took a breath. "I think I'm ready for any ride you want," I said, backing up into one of the rooms.

He found me, seized me in a rugged embrace, and wrestled me back against a wall. One of his legs spread my two apart and I thrust my bulging crotch against his thigh, riding it like a horse. I pushed my face blindly against his thick neck, enjoying the sharp, acrid smell of a day's labor on him—sweat and dust and the animal musk of effort. When I opened my mouth on his skin, the sea-salt bitterness flooded me.

I fumbled with his shirt buttons, wanting to rub my face in the bushy forest of his chest, but he took firm hold of my jaw. He tilted my face up with deliberate control, pinned the back of my head to the wall, and forced my mouth open with his. The papa bear called the shots on this site. That potent message and the hot shock of his tongue tore through my body and ignited in my balls. I moaned deep in my throat, a vibration of need and surrender, his cock a cudgel against my hip.

At last Cole pushed himself away and took a few steps back. Shadow colored the golden mountain in shades of gray, the stark tones of the hottest wet dream. But his eyes held me in my place against the wall. With a faint smirk and easy patience, he unbuttoned his shirt and shrugged it off. I caught my breath at the broad power of his massive shoulders and chest, the thrilling contrast of flesh and hair, a forest that flattened on its way down into his belt. I rubbed my hard-on through my jeans, waiting for the word.

His thick legs were spread in a conqueror's stance. Biceps bulged as he tugged open his buckle, the deft movement sending a tremor through the curve of his belly—with a rush of pleasure I remembered some of it belonged to me. When he unzipped and released his cock, I groaned in a helpless wave of want. The big head gleamed, a taut bell mounted on a shaft that looked as thick as my wrist. Cole stroked himself languidly, grinning with wickedness.

"See something you want, boy?"

"Please," I whispered.

In an instant I was on the plywood, kneeling between his big, dusty work boots, devouring him. He held my cheek with one hand while he thrust and drove into my eager mouth, stretching me wide, his deep, growling satisfaction stoking me. I hung onto his big thigh to steady myself and tugged on my own throbbing cock with my other hand, electric pleasure burning in a circle from my mouth to my balls and back again, humming with a single, searing thought: I was feeding the bear and he was feeding me.

I shot between his legs, far out onto the raw wood floor, christened this place of men with my come.

Spasms of bliss were still twitching through me when Cole closed his fist in my hair. He tugged me off with a smooth, powerful pull that left me panting, my mouth open and wet, gazing up in surprise.

"Tell me what you really want, Joe."

He could see through me to that mainline of hunger, pulsing at my core. Maybe he saw it all along. My heart pounded in my ears.

Ask for it.

"I want to be your boy," I said.

The sound came up from his balls, a deep rumble of triumph and lust. He reached under my armpits and hauled me swiftly to my feet, the same gust of strength that had pinned a workman to the wall. With an iron grip on the back of my waistband, he marched me over to a darkened corner of the room. I pitched forward onto a stack of five full bags of dry concrete with a little gasp. Damn, that was solid.

Cole was unconcerned, his breath rising behind me like a storm. He yanked my jeans to my ankles and then left me, bent over and bound, my ass naked to the air. I clutched the bags beneath me, hanging on in excitement and terror. Had I really asked for this?

I heard the rattle of his tool case and then the sharp, distinctive crackle of a condom wrapper. When I felt the slippery nudge of his thick finger greasing me with lubricant, I arched my back and pushed up against it.

"Yeah, you show Papa Bear what you need, little Joe."

The name was a rough caress that made me moan. Cole swung deftly behind me, an instinctive, animal movement of possession. His naked thighs blazed against my backside, the slick head of his enormous cock forced into me like a fist. I cried out into the curl of my own arm, but then I was there—pinned under the big body I'd hungered for. I felt completely opened by the long, slow burn, his unyielding pole of force and fire. My tight ass ring throbbed; my balls contracted. But I wanted this, the steady, overwhelming power of him driving into me.

Cole lifted my hips as if I were a rag doll, positioned me for a deeper strike. The slam forced the air out of my lungs and sent a steel-wool grind of pleasure tingling from my ass to my balls, and even up my spine. The sound came from the dark center of my neediest fantasies.

Oh, yeah. Ride me hard.

Cole hammered me again and again, the slap of flesh and our urgent breath echoing through the unfinished rooms. The whole building seemed to vibrate with our fucking. When he shot at last, his low bull's roar of release nearly tore me open with pride. I was exactly where I wanted to be. He pulled out and my muscle that had been so ravaged at first now glowed with pulsing heat. The big man had branded me.

We sat on the floor afterward, almost dressed, watching the twilight deepen through the hole in the roof. Cole leaned against the wall and I lounged between his legs, his broad, hairy chest the most comfortable bunk in the world. I had to keep swallowing back the wonder that I was really here, the amazement at what you could have if you had the courage to ask for it.

Cole kissed the top of my head, then lingered, inhaling my hair. "You smell like a burger."

I laughed. "I'm a cook. We're not even going to talk about what *you* smell like."

"So when do I get the rest of my meat loaf?"

The thick, possessive tone of his voice made my heart leap, but there was something else I had to do first.

"Tomorrow," I said softly. "Tonight I've got to talk to a little Italian guy—about a job in the fall."

Cub Makes Headlines!

JAY NEAL

Mike paused in his typing and looked up. The editor of *The Weekly Gazette* was standing by his desk, chewing an unlit cigar and scowling at him. When he had Mike's attention, he pounded his fist on the young man's desk in a hard-boiled editorial way.

"Kid," the editor said, "I've got an assignment for you."

"Yes, sir?" Mike wondered what was coming.

"Bears," the editor said, as though he'd said all he needed to say.

"Bears, sir?"

"I keep hearing things about these bears," he said as though he had said more than he felt he needed to say.

"What are bears, sir?"

"How the fuck do I know! That's your assignment: Find out! You're the reporter. Report! We need the story on bears! Who are they! What are they! Where are they! Why are they!"

"You forgot 'when,' sir."

"Fuck when, when is now! Find out! Are they some sort of secret organization? Get the secret! They may have something to do with bikers. Are they the new crime gang in town? Are they dangerous? Should our readers hide their food and lock their doors at night? Get the story!"

"Yes, sir. But why me, sir?"

"Because Chuck's doing something important. Besides, you're the cub reporter!" The editor barked a laugh at his witticism and rolled the cigar to the other side of his mouth. "Not to mention that you look the closest we've got to a biker. Now get going! And don't show your sorry ass around here until you've got the story!"

The editor swung around and stomped back to his office, where, no doubt, he'd continue cracking walnuts with his teeth. Mike sat, looking a little shell-shocked, pondering how to begin his assignment.

This felt like it was going to be his toughest assignment yet (CUB FACED WITH HAIRY SITUATION), but he knew deep down that he could make it as an investigative journalist (CUB REPORTER EXPOSES BEARS). It was a challenge, but he felt up to the task, certain that he would prevail (CUB TOPS BEARS). Sure, there might be personal dangers involved (CUB SHOOTS AS BEARS MAUL), but he'd do it. He'd get the story!

If only he knew where to start, how to find them (CUB HUNTS BEARS). If they were bikers, maybe a gas station would be a good place to start. If they were a criminal gang, a police station might be more likely. But if they were something like a sports team, then maybe they'd hang out at bars after games, socializing (BEARS HANG AT BARS, CUB DISCOVERS). That's it! He'd ask Flash, the social-events reporter, for a lead.

Mike pushed back from his desk and hiked across the newsroom to the farthest desk in the style section. There Flash sat in his corner, nearly hidden behind a desk piled with invitations, announcements, programs, thank-you notes, and other social ephemera. Pencil in mouth, Flash concentrated on his typing, two fingers at a time.

Mike pushed a pile of papers aside, sat on the corner of the desk, and spoke briskly. "OK, Flash, give me the dish. I need information, and I need it fast." He slapped his thigh once to punctuate his rhythm. "I've got an assignment from the chief and no time to waste."

Flash watched this performance without blinking an eye. When Mike had finished, Flash removed the pencil from his mouth, tapped his pursed lips a few times with the end of his pencil, then tipped the pencil toward Mike.

"Hon, you want my advice on your newspaper career? Lose the Kate Hepburn and try Spencer Tracy instead; you're never going to be Woman of the Year."

Mike slumped a bit. "Darn. I thought I'd finally gotten the accent right."

"Oh, sweetie, it's not the accent, it's your feet. They're way too big—"

"They are not big!"

"To look good in low heels. Besides, the full beard gives you away. Hepburn was much more a Vandyke type, in my opinion."

"Well," Mike grumbled, "who was asking anyway?"

"Hon, you're the one who rushed over here with your flannel on fire. So tell me what's got your boxers in a bunch."

Mike leaned over the desk and lowered his voice to a conspiratorial whisper. "Bears."

Flash leaned toward Mike, his eyes wide with feigned surprise, and whispered back: "Bears?"

"You know," Mike said, waving an arm vaguely in circles, "bears!"

"I know what you mean, hon, I just don't understand why you're asking me."

"Because you know about these things."

"And you don't?" Flash asked.

"No. Why should I?"

"Well, just look at you."

"Me?"

"Yes. You."

Mike stood up, held his arms wide open, and looked himself over.

"Why me?" he asked, perplexed.

"Oh, merciful Judy, because you're such a bear yourself."

"Me?"

"You!"

Mike stood, waiting for Flash to say something he could comprehend.

"You know. The beard. The body hair. The belly. The winsome smile and cuddly, huggable demeanor that makes someone just want to scratch you under the chin and call you snookums."

Mike raised his bushy eyebrows and shrugged his cuddly, huggable shoulders.

Flash reached behind him and pulled forth a trashy tabloid. "Honey, we need to get you enrolled in Bear 101 right away." He opened the paper from the back and began looking through the classified ads. Mike came around the desk to watch.

"How about a 'Bear Beer Blast'?"

It sounded a little dangerous to Mike. "I don't know. A blast? Besides, it's next week, and I need the story now."

"OK," Flash continued reading, "how about a nice, snuggly 'Big Bear Hug'?"

"Maybe, but it sounds like a euphemism for something. Besides, it costs 20 bucks and I don't think the boss would go for it."

"Aha!" Flash announced. "Here it is: 'Bear Games Night.'"

"Hmm," Mike said, "I guess it sounds safe enough."

"Depends," Flash said, arching an eyebrow, "on who's the game."

"At least it's free, but what is it? It sounds a little nefarious."

"Honey, I'm sure it'll just be a bunch of fat slobs playing poker, drinking beer, and belching while they scratch their balls. Exactly the thing to indoctrinate you."

Mike was wary. It still sounded questionable, but then, he *was* the cub reporter, and a journalist goes where the story takes him. He felt his resolve stiffen.

"But Flash, this is investigative journalism, undercover stuff, ferreting out the facts. I'll need a good cover story, some sort of disguise that can get me in there without suspicion so I can get the whole story."

"I've got it!" Flash actually snapped his finger'
lowered his voice to create the proper underc...
don't you go as a bear?"

Mike thought Flash might be pulling his leg and decided that
silence would serve him best. So, he winked in a knowing, undercover fashion, took the paper that Flash held out to him, and headed back to his desk.

Flash called across the newsroom: "And your cover story is sex!"

Mike's face turned red. He headed faster back to his desk. When
he got there, he settled in and studied the announcement in the
paper. "Bear Games Night" sounded like…sounded like…what?
He couldn't seem to picture a bunch of gangsters playing
Scrabble, even if they did look a lot like him. He still didn't understand what Flash had meant when he said that, but he was determined to get the story, and he was convinced that the story started
with bear games.

The newspaper announcement had a phone number for the
organizer, someone named Doug. A bear named Doug sounded
pretty normal. Mike picked up the phone and started dialing, but
he put it down before it could ring. Whatever was he going to say
to a bear named Doug? He pulled his well-thumbed copy of
Interview Tips for Cub Reporters from his desk drawer and looked
through it for helpful suggestions. None seemed particularly
applicable.

Mike set his resolve, picked up his phone again, dialed, and was
soon talking to the bear named Doug, who seemed remarkably
easy to talk to. Mike asked whether he might join the bears for
Games Night ("Of course! Visitors are always welcome!") and got
directions. He tried to glean a little information for his story without being too overt, but he didn't get much. Doug at least had a
nice voice, big and round and warm and friendly. Was that what a
biker or a gangster sounded like on the phone?

It was getting late in the day and Doug's place would take some
time to get to, since Mike couldn't yet afford a car. That left him
just enough time to get himself home, take a shower, put on his

good flannel shirt, nuke a few frozen burritos for dinner, and make his way by bus and foot to his evening's destination. He grabbed his cub reporter's pocket notebook and headed out.

Shortly before 8 o'clock Mike was standing on the sidewalk in front of Doug's suburban bungalow. Earlier, as he walked down Doug's street, he thought he spotted a couple of big guys with beards going in the front door. They could have been gangsters; it was hard to tell in the near dark. There had been no further activity. The porch light was on and the coast was clear. He was ready to go in.

The doorbell was answered by the very imposing host, a big guy, taller and bigger around than Mike, with short onyx-black hair and beard. He wore jeans and a flannel shirt, but in a different plaid from Mike's. He must have been the kingpin of the operation but, to be honest, he didn't look all that dangerous to Mike.

"Hi, I'm Doug. You must be Mike." He shook Mike's hand and led him in through the door. "Come on in and say hi to the guys. Make yourself at home."

Inside, Mike was surprised to find the room filled largely with amply sized men with beards—*friendly*-looking men with beards, when it came down to it—variously arrayed around card tables, rolling dice, moving game pieces around game boards, dealing cards, and throwing poker chips into piles. He felt considerably relieved to discover that most of the guys there actually did look quite a bit like him.

"Guys, say hi to Mike." A dozen or more hands waved in the air; some of the guys looked up from their games to give Mike a quick visual evaluation. Mike waved to the room at large and indulged in his own bit of visual evaluating, surveying the variety of beards and body shapes. He'd never before been around so many men who were so gentle, so massive, and so hot-looking.

Doug was steering Mike across the room, pointing out the games in progress. "That's Ricky, Dave, Jake, and Pete at the mahjongg table; their play gets pretty competitive, so be careful. Likewise for Booboo and Stan with their dominoes. Joe over here would love your company, but you should know that he has a strong cribbage fetish and only gets off while pegging out."

Indeed, Joe was grinning widely and gesturing feverishly, but Mike just smiled back and continued his tour with Doug.

"Over here at the big table is the Monopoly board, and I see the guys saved a place for you. What do you say?"

"Sounds fine, if I can remember the rules."

"Don't worry," Doug said, "they make it up as they go along anyway. Reading from left to right: Nick, Rod, Sam, and Barry."

Mike shook hands left to right: extra stout with long blond hair and beard (Nick); tall and muscled with a shaved head and a brown mouth-beard (Rod); pocket-size with wavy brown hair and an incandescent smile framed by a full beard (Sam); and husky with short red hair and beard (Barry). Mike was thinking that it might be difficult to concentrate on the game—not to mention getting the bear story—with opponents as attractive as these guys. They sat down to play.

Mike ended up with the racing-car token. He would have preferred the schnauzer, but apparently Sam always got the schnauzer. Besides, he was here to get the story, not to *be* the story. The car certainly didn't help his luck any, since he rolled last. The real estate market was hot, but he managed to buy only Baltic Avenue and the Water Works since he was always last to get to the good ones. No monopolies for him tonight.

The game rolled on and the trading stayed friendly. The other guys built houses and hotels, but Mike only paid rent; their piles of money increased, but his decreased alarmingly. It seemed he'd better get started on his investigation before it was too late. Several approaches came to mind, but he decided to go with something subtle.

"So," Mike asked, nonchalantly rolling the dice, "what do you think really makes a bear?" He moved his racing car to Park Place, trying not to notice the looks of incredulity from the other players. Barry owned Park Place and Boardwalk; Mike handed over all but 20 of his remaining Monopoly money.

"OK," Barry said, "I'll bite. For me it's the beard. There's nothing quite so individual or beautiful or sexy as a beard. Whether it's short and stubbly or long and fluffy, full or cut in a Vandyke, it completes a man's face and turns his mouth into an object of such sensuality that it is impossible not to kiss him."

Barry abruptly stood and stepped toward Mike, grabbed Mike's beard to pull his face up, and leaned over to give Mike a long, wet kiss that lasted until it was Barry's turn again. He let go of Mike and took his turn with the dice. Mike looked unusually thoughtful.

"I'm not sure I agree, Barry," Rod said as Mike took his next turn. Mike was happy with the roll since it meant passing Go, until he found that he had landed on Oriental Avenue, where Rod had a monopoly. Not only was Rod well-developed, so was Oriental Avenue.

"Uh-oh," Rod said, "looks like someone's going to lose the shirt off his back."

"I don't have enough money for the rent," Mike said. "What do I do?"

"Doug did explain, didn't he," Rod was saying, "that we play Strip Monopoly?" As Mike pondered the implications, Rod walked over behind Mike and started unbuttoning Mike's shirt.

"For me, it's a furry body," Rod explained. He pulled Mike's shirt off and started rubbing his hands across Mike's chest. "When I rub my hands across a bear's body fur it makes my fingers tingle and sends sparks through my whole body that seem to electrify my dick."

He kissed Mike on the back, just between the shoulder blades. "If I were to give you a tongue bath," Rod said as he sat down, "I'd get so fully charged that I'd probably go off without ever touching myself. So it's definitely body hair for me."

Mike made a mental note about body hair as play continued around the board. His next roll, a double, brought him to Pennsylvania Railroad. Nick owned all the railroads.

"Let me guess," Mike said to Nick. "My jeans?"

Nick nodded. Mike stood and shucked off his jeans, leaving

him in his plaid flannel boxers. Nick reached over and began rubbing his hand in large circles on Mike's belly.

"For me," Nick said, rubbing, "it's definitely a bear's furry belly. Nice and full and just soft enough not to hurt my ear when I lie down on it to give him a nice, long, unhurried blow job. With a good belly, I can suck a bear's dick for hours and never get a sore neck. It's *got* to be the belly!"

Mike was ready to agree; his dick was starting to agree too. Nick's rubbing his belly had made his dick hard, and he was afraid it would poke out the fly in his boxer shorts. He sat down quickly and picked up the dice to distract himself, since he had to roll again. His next roll brought him to Chance.

"Aha!" he exclaimed, a bit relieved. "Chance!" Then he read the card while the others looked on expectantly. "Uh-oh: 'Go to jail. Go directly to jail.'"

"All right!" Sam yelled, jumping up from his chair. "Strip search!" He pulled Mike's chair out of the way and yanked Mike's shorts down to his ankles. "Definitely," Sam said as he stroked Mike's furry ass, "it's a furry ass and asshole. Mighty good eatin'!" He spread Mike's cheeks and shoved his face in between, energetically licking Mike's asshole with his tongue.

Sam may have mumbled further explanations, but Mike was too distracted by the exquisite tingling feeling of Sam's rimming tongue to notice. Leaning on the game table with Sam's talented tongue probing his asshole, he didn't notice that the others had cleared away the Monopoly board.

Neither did he quite notice how he ended up on his back on the table. Soon enough, though, he did notice many additional sensations. No doubt his legs were draped over Sam's shoulders, since it was still Sam's tongue licking from his asshole to his balls and sucking there awhile before heading back down to visit his asshole again.

From the length of beard draped across his belly, he deduced that it was Nick's head resting there, hence Nick's mouth that was warm and moist and sucking on his dick. Surely Nick *could* go on like this for hours, but Mike didn't think he'd last nearly that long.

Given his proclivities, it must be Rod who was leaving wet tracks in Mike's chest fur with his tongue, not to mention the unexpectedly exciting twinges that came when Rod tweaked one nipple between thumb and finger, or nipped at the other with his teeth. Each tweak went directly to Mike's dick, which jumped inside Nick's mouth; each nip caused Mike's asshole to clamp down around Sam's tongue. The stimulation was becoming overwhelming.

From glimpses of red hair and red beard, direct visual evidence told Mike that it was Barry's mouth clamped on his own, their tongues pressing moist and firm against each other's. Fortunately, Barry's arms held him solidly against the table, otherwise his thrashing about from all this pleasurable torture could have hurt someone.

The tension of the evening, the excitement of his undercover investigative reporting, the thrill of getting the real story about bears at last—all of it was gathering now in Mike's groin, building up explosively. Barry's kissing, Rod's tongue bath and nipple play, Sam's tongue tango on his asshole, Nick's mouth riding his dick— they were all driving Mike at breakneck speed toward his climax. His back arched against Barry's hold, his muscles tensed and his nipples stiffened in Rod's mouth, and his asshole held on to Sam's tongue for dear life as his moment arrived and he shot load after load after load into Nick's hungry mouth.

Time passed. Normal sensation returned at last. Mike could finally breathe again. He opened his eyes to see his smiling game partners standing around him, drips of come in Nick's long beard. He heard cheers and applause in the room around him. He felt like he'd finally gotten somewhere at last. He had arrived.

Mike had his story now, and it was big. Really big. No longer a cub reporter he. In his afterglow, he drifted afloat and imagined his new office, a new desk, a new nameplate on it that read MIKE BARR: BEAR REPORTER. He had the story, but he couldn't imagine what the headline would say.

Licking Volodya

DANIEL M. JAFFE

The moment I entered the bookstore, I noticed him behind the counter—dirty-blond hair, bushy beard with a few small patches of gray, stocky build. His long-sleeve white shirt, buttoned at the collar, hugged pecs so thick and massive I wanted to march right over to the counter, reach across, and grab them, feeling those hard nipples press against my palms. But being 19 and still a virgin, I wasn't about to make a pass at a stranger. And in Moscow, of all places.

I'd come from New Jersey to spend the summer studying Russian literature at Moscow State University and to get a feel for the culture. Of course, I'd fantasized about meeting men here, far away from home, somewhere nobody knew me, where I could feel more at ease finally coming out. I'd imagined walking through the Kremlin's Armory Chamber museum, ogling gem-encrusted Fabergé eggs, when some bearded soldier would come up to me, lead me at rifle-point to a guardroom, barking, "You want eggs? I'll give you eggs." He'd drop his trousers to reveal huge hairy balls that he'd force me to nuzzle and lick. Or some bare-chested, furry sunbather in Gorky Park would wink and jerk his thumb over at a cluster of bushes; I'd follow to find him on his knees with his mouth open and tongue ready to lap.

Or some husky guy would grope me in the red-marble darkness of Lenin's Tomb, or on a shadowy hidden staircase in St. Basil's Cathedral, or behind the pillars of some 18th-century Arbat neighborhood mansion. Or on a trolley or in a taxi or on goddamn Red Square with tourists milling around—fuck! I fantasized about sex everywhere…I just didn't have a clue how to find it. Russian hospitality was legendary, but what was I supposed to do—walk up to a fuzzy stranger in the Metro and ask, "Hey, comrade, I'm a horny American; wanna take me home and have some international relations?"

I wasn't likely to experience any wild encounters at the hotel where we students were staying, the Ostankino, nicknamed the Ostinkino because of the perpetual stench emanating from the communal restrooms. My roommate, a guy from Oregon, was as skinny and hairless as I was, not at all my type. Besides, all he kept saying every time I suggested we study together was, "Fuck Dostoevsky—I want some Russky pussky."

One day, after participating in a seminar on Russian satire, I went into a bookstore on Tverskaya Boulevard for a copy of Russia's first gay-themed novel, written nearly a hundred years ago. And off went my "bear-dar" like a Geiger counter in a Ural Mountains uranium mine.

The bearded salesman behind the bookstore counter was helping a couple of schoolgirls wearing pink ribbons in their blond pigtails. I stepped in line behind them. That's an advantage of traditional Russian bookstores—all the bookcases are behind the counter, so customers absolutely have to ask the salesman for help. Some say the system was designed to minimize theft and maximize employment, but I think it was designed to help shy cubs like me cruise without being obvious.

The hunk's smile, unusual among dour-faced Russian salespeople, accentuated his bright blue eyes as he spoke to the schoolgirls in a gentle voice, "How may I help you future poet laureates?" The girls giggled, then answered him, and as he turned and reached for a volume of Leskov's stories, I watched two melon-sized ass muscles flex through his thin gray trousers. I could run around the counter right now, I thought, and crouch low so that no customers would see me, then I could yank down his trousers, grab his cheeks, and bite them, lick them, press my face against them, feel him tremble and squirm. Then I'd spin him around, discover how hard he'd become, lunge forward and—

"Are you OK?"

"What?"

"Are you OK?"

Good God, he was speaking to me. While daydreaming, I hadn't noticed that he'd already wrapped the book for the girls and had sent them to the cashier. He was now talking to me.

"Uh, yes, sorry. I'm fine."

He smiled, and I noticed a crooked eyetooth among all the other straight ones. Was this the same smile he'd flashed the girls, a plastic salesman mask slapped on a hundred times a day? Or was this grin just a bit broader, his upper lip higher now over the eyetooth, revealing a hint of personal interest in me?

"Kuzmin," I sputtered the author's name.

"Ah, one of our finest poets." Those prudish Soviet censors had done their best to hide the fact that Kuzmin had written a gay coming-out novel in the early 20th century, but now, in post-Soviet times, more and more Russians were learning both about his prose and his gayness.

Would the hunky salesman know all this? "Actually," I said, "I'm looking for Kuzmin's novel, *Wings*."

"Ah," he said, nodding his head and broadening his grin. "A wonderful novel. A wonderful novel, indeed. Very much ahead of its time."

"That's what I hear."

"You know what it's about?" he asked, leaning a bit closer over the counter.

Our gaze held, and I felt certain that we understood each other. "Yes," I said, "Yes, I know it. I've read it in English, but I'd love to read it in Russian."

"Ah, English. That's your accent. From London?"

"No, a small town near Philadelphia."

"America," he said in that way Russians do, always with a mix of fanciful longing and wariness. "Tourist?"

"Not exactly. A student." I launched into an explanation of my summer-study program, prattling on about our various seminars and readings—anything to prolong conversation with him and figure out a way to get time with him outside the bookstore.

He asked how long I would be in Moscow. But before I could answer, someone poked me in the back. I turned and looked.

"Young man!" said a middle-aged woman in line behind me. "Are you buying a book or reciting a medieval epic?"

"Babushka, kindly wait your turn," said the salesman. "I'll be with you in a minute. He's a foreigner." Every Westerner still held minor celebrity status here even after the Iron Curtain's lifting.

The woman rolled her eyes. "Just get to me before you close!"

"I'm afraid we're out of *Wings* right now," he said to me. "It's gaining in popularity…in certain circles." He again smiled, revealing that crooked eyetooth.

"Oh," I said, unable to get up the nerve to ask him on a date. "Well, thanks anyway. It was really good to—"

"I know a Russian bar," he said, interrupting. "Not the new Western kind, but old-style. Maybe I could show you? Probably interesting for a foreigner."

A bar? Was he asking me for a date? I nodded vigorously, and he said to meet him out front in half an hour.

I don't know what we talked about as we strolled down alleys and crossed boulevards to the bar. His name was Naum, that much I grasped; but, as for everything else—whether we talked about historic buildings or literature or the price of mushrooms in the market—my consciousness was somehow on automatic pilot. Every time our elbows touched, and once even our upper arms, I felt a twisting in my stomach. Twice—while stare-tracing the outlines of his beard, the way a few red hairs curled back under his ear, a few gray ones bristled longer than the others—twice I stumbled on uneven sidewalks, and he reached out to prevent me from falling: strong grips that held onto me a little longer than necessary while I regained my balance. I reached the bar nearly breathless.

The bar was little more than a stuffy room crammed with men standing around chest-high tables and drinking beer from glasses. Men in suits, men in shirtsleeves, some well-groomed, others scruffy. Russian men are not known for their frequent bathing or use of deodorant, and I was struck by the room's strong scent of male body odor mixed with beer. I inhaled deeply. Arousing.

We made our way to the bar—just a small counter, really—where Naum ordered two beers and something I'd never heard of: *voblya*. I watched blankly as the bartender held out a flat dried fish the size of a hand. Naum lifted it by its tail, I took the beers, and we maneuvered to a corner table, squeezing between other guys standing and drinking.

"You know *voblya*?" Naum asked, dangling the flat fish.

I shook my head.

"Ah." He opened his mouth and slowly, deliberately swiped his thick long tongue up and down one side of the fish. Then Naum took a gulp of beer. "It's salty," he said. "Salted fish. Goes great with beer. Try it." He held the *voblya* in front of my face. I stared at it. This was how Russian men got their rocks off? Licking dried salted fish? No wonder Communism fell.

"*Voblya* used to be low-class food," he explained. "Common. But now it's a delicacy. And men always share." He pointed his chin at one of the other tables where I saw a group of five men passing around one *voblya* and licking.

"Come on," said Naum, "stick out your tongue!"

A wave of disgust rose from my stomach, and I took a step back.

"Come on!" he said, snickering at my obvious discomfort. "Don't American men know how to use their tongues?"

Suddenly, national pride was at stake. I had to step up to the plate and hit a homer for Uncle Sam. I stepped forward, took a firm grasp of his hand dangling the *voblya* (I couldn't help but notice that his knuckles were coated in fine, blond hair), stuck out my tongue as far as it would reach, then licked the fish up and down. Hmmm...not exactly salted peanuts, but not so bad. I swirled my tongue all over the *voblya*, showing Naum exactly what an American tongue could do. I took a swig of beer. "There!" I said, swiping my lips with the back of my hand.

"Bravo!" Naum said, as he took another lick and swig. We then took turns, lick after lick, gulp after gulp. His side of the fish, my side.

Naum undid the collar button of his shirt, the top two buttons. Blond hair nearly sprang out in curls. To my surprise, Naum rubbed an index finger up and down my spine. What's that word from romance novels? S*woon*...that's it. I nearly swooned. "Another beer?" he asked.

I nodded quickly.

He set the *voblya* down on the table and squeezed his way to the counter. While he was gone, I watched men lick *voblya,* guzzle beer, stand with arms around one another, teeter against one another's shoulders, even slap one another's chests. I could get used to this.

"So," Naum asked, setting two full glasses on the table, "you have a girlfriend back home?"

Had I been wrong in the bookstore? Had he misunderstood why I was interested in Kuzmin's gay novel? Or was he just trying to confirm his suspicion about me? I shook my head, "No girlfriend."

"What?! A cute boy like you?"

Hmm. "How about you?"

He shook his head. "What!" I said, "A handsome man like you?"

He patted me on the cheek, playfully and affectionately, lifted the *voblya* by its tail, and held it up for me. I wasn't sure whether the side of the fish facing me was mine, but...hell, what did it matter? I'd lick anything this man dangled in front of my face.

By this time, even more men had entered the bar, and the crowd had been gradually shoving Naum and me closer, so close that his hip now pressed against mine.

"How old are you?" he asked in a soft voice.

"Nineteen."

He shook his head. "Still a boy."

I stood up taller, squared my shoulders in standard military pose. "I can do anything any man can do."

"Really? So you know how to take it like a man, huh?"

I wasn't sure what he meant, but said, "I can take anything you can dish out."

He nodded. "I might just make you prove that."

I wanted to kiss him then, to lean in and shove my tongue through his lips. But nobody else here was kissing. Was this even a gay bar? Not having been in one in the U.S., I certainly couldn't identify one in Russia. "And how old are you?" I asked.

"Thirty-six."

"A weak old man," I teased.

At that, he slammed down his beer on the table, threw his arms around me, and clamped me in so tight a bear hug that I couldn't breathe. "Weak, eh?" He lifted me. My feet left the floor. "Old, eh?"

Other men around stopped their conversations, looked at us, chuckled, and called out, "Show the kid what a real man can do." "Get the kid a diaper!" "Still sucking milk from his mother's tit, that one!"

"OK!" I managed to whisper. "You're not weak!"

"And?" he squeezed even tighter.

"You're not old!"

Naum let me go; the crowd resumed its chatter. I breathed deeply in, coughed, and reached for my beer, realizing I had a hard-on.

Naum must have realized too—under the table, he brushed the back of his hand against my erection. Slowly, back and forth, while staring into my eyes. He wasn't smiling, but gazing deeply. "Lick this," he said, holding up the *voblya* with his free hand. And as I leaned in to lick one side, he leaned in to lick the other. During a simultaneous side-to-side tongue swipe, our tongues briefly touched. I felt as though I'd stuck mine into an electrical socket.

"You like that?" Naum asked, his expression still serious.

"Yes," I said, matching the look on his face. "I love that. And I want more."

He set the *voblya* down on the table, stepped in close, so close that I couldn't distinguish his fishy-smelling beer breath from my own. Our belt buckles touched. "I live with my mother," he whispered, "but she's away at our country dacha for the summer." He tilted his hips forward; his hard-on pressed against mine. "Come home with me. Spend the night."

My heart racing, all I could do was nod.

We didn't speak much on the trolley ride to his apartment building, a drab gray apartment block built in the early '60s under Khrushchev. I could barely contain my mix of excitement and nervousness. Finally, I was going to be with a man. A gorgeous Russian bear of a man. Would I know what to do with him? Would he like me?

The stairwell of his apartment building smelled damp and moldy. As we started up to the third floor, I felt a punch of panic. This guy was so strong, he could hurt me. What exactly did I really know about him? That he worked in a bookstore, that's all. Here I was in a foreign country and going home with a stranger. Was I insane? I should wait to get to know him better. I had all summer, after all. What was the rush? Yes, yes, I'd tell him I changed my mind, that I'd forgotten a dinner appointment, that my roommate expected me, that—

"Here we are," Naum said. He undid three locks and opened the door. The smell of bleach and fried onions.

OK, I told myself, this was an apartment building. There were neighbors all over the place. If things got out of hand, all I had to do was yell, and somebody would—

90

Naum shut the door behind us, turned all three locks, then faced me, reached up to my face, and cupped my cheeks, running his thumbs gently over my eyebrows. He kissed my forehead. "Thank you," he said. "Thank you for being my guest." Then he kissed each of my eyes, licked my nose, and slid his tongue down to my lips. A tender kiss started as a light brush of the lips, tentative, then slowly sucking my upper lip between his, softly running his tongue along it to send tingles up and down my spine.

I reached my arms around him, held him close. No more fears.

Naum rested his head on my shoulder and licked my neck. "So this is what Americans taste like," he said. "Much better than *voblya*."

We laughed, holding each other, his fleshy chest and belly against my flat pecs and stomach, our hard-ons growing, our hands rubbing up and down each other's back. He ran his hands along my sides; I did likewise along his. I'd always excelled at follow-the-leader.

"Shall we go into the kitchen for some dinner?" he asked.

"I'm not hungry," I said.

He caressed my cheek with one hand, reached for my hand with the other. "It's been so long." He led me down a short hallway to a small room crammed with bookshelves, a dresser, and a narrow bed. "You're young," he said. "Now tell me the truth: Have you been with many men?"

I hesitated, then shook my head.

He ran a finger along the rim of my ear. "If anything's uncomfortable, you tell me, OK?"

Such a sensitive stranger. I whispered, "I want you so much." I hugged him, kissed him hard, opened my mouth for his tongue. He thrust it in and filled me. I moaned.

I pulled back so we could unbutton each other's shirts. *Damn!* He was so beautiful, with curly blond hair covering his chest and belly. He grinned as I ran my hands over him, squeezed his chest, bent to suck his hard nipples big as ruble coins. He groaned, rubbed the back of my neck, pressed my face closer. "Harder," he murmured.

I sucked in more of his chest.

"Let me feel your teeth."

I nibbled, sucked, and chewed while he ran hands along my hairless shoulders. He pulled my face up for a deeper kiss, then licked my bare chest, my button nipples; he dropped to his knees and undid my belt and zipper, yanked down my jeans and briefs. He lunged at my cock, swallowed it in one gulp, moaned while grabbing my ass, squeezing my cheeks. Barely able to breathe, I filled my hands with his thick blond hair, and his mouth bounced up and down on my cock, so fast and with such a hunger that in less than a minute I was gasping, "Now! Now! Now!"

I came deep in his throat.

He held me in his mouth for a few moments. My head whirled. Dizzy, I fell back onto his bed. He climbed up beside me, hugged me as tightly as he had in the bar. "My fiery young American man."

We lay for several minutes, me with my eyes closed; him running his fingers along my chest and belly, twirling my sparse pubic hairs. Gradually my strength returned. We kissed more, lying on our sides, hands exploring each other, Naum rubbing fingers between my ass cheeks, me feeling the hair of his shoulders. Then I rolled him onto his back, licked his neck, tasted the salt, again sucked his pecs hard the way I now knew he liked, bit the nipples.

Kneeling over him, I nuzzled my face in his blond chest fur, nipped at it with my teeth, nibbled down his belly. Down, down, down to where the blond curls turned wiry. I licked around the base of his uncut cock, so thick and smelling of sweat. I Popsicle-licked him and he mumbled, "Yes, yes." Then I licked the hood, worked my tongue under it, swirled, licked down to his light-fur-covered balls, took them into my mouth one at a time, filling my mouth with those museum-quality Fabergé eggs. I worked his cock with my hand, then took it back into my mouth, sucked it in as far as I could, and Naum began to thrust, holding my head firmly still. The thrusts were slow at first, then fast, then faster until I could feel his fingers pressing hard into my skull. I tasted as he shot.

I held him in my mouth as he'd held me moments before. Swallowing, I crawled on top of him and murmured, "So this is what a Russian man tastes like. Better than *voblya*." We shared another laugh. I lay on top of him, my head on his chest, his arms around me, and in a moment he began to snore. He held me like that, on top of him, his breath tussling my hair…and I fell asleep.

When we awoke again, aroused in the middle of the night, we kissed, longer this time, then shared the joys of 69. (Yes, numbers truly are international.) Then he said he had to get something from the kitchen. He waddled out of the room, his ass bobbing up and down. He returned quickly, holding a jar. "*Smetana*," he said. Sour cream.

Sour cream? What is he going to do with—?

Before I could ask the question, he dipped a finger into the jar and drew out a white gob, then deftly lifted my legs and smeared the sour cream between my cheeks. "Naum," I said, suddenly scared, "I'm a vir—"

He bent down and thrust his tongue between my cheeks, lapping up the sour cream. My God, it felt so good!

He lifted up his face to look at mine, his beard smeared with white cream. He smiled to reveal that crooked eyetooth again. Reading my mind, he said, "I'll be gentle."

More sour cream, and this time he slipped an index finger inside me. Oh, God, yes. This. This was what I'd been wanting for so long. A few deep pokes and swirls of that cream-covered index finger, and then a second finger, and then a third.

"I'm ready," I murmured, wanting him like I'd never wanted anything in my life.

He grabbed a condom from somewhere between mattress and box spring, slipped it on, and then slowly, gently eased himself into me. A sharp twinge; another, a whimper; he pulled out; he started again; the twinges felt less intense; then I moaned with pleasure.

Naum hooked my knees over his shoulders, bent forward to kiss me. His tongue in my mouth, his cock in my ass, my legs and arms around him—he filled me completely. He thrust first slowly, tenderly, rhythmically, then more quickly with shorter strokes, and all the while my cock rubbed against his hairy belly. Soon my head was snapping from side to side, and I screamed his name, "Naum! Naum!"

As I began to come, he pulled out of me, yanked off the condom, and came all over my belly. "Naum," I whispered, "Naum." I couldn't find the words. He fell onto me, and we both fell asleep again.

We shifted position many times during the rest of the night—on our sides facing each other, cupping each other front to back, his head on my shoulder, my head on his. When we awoke, Naum had to get ready for work, and I had to get myself off to class.

We washed and kissed, dressed and fondled each other through our clothes, and before I had time to question what would happen next between us, Naum murmured, "I want you every night."

We kissed, just our lips this time, little pecks as if blowing kisses with our lips barely touching.

That evening, I went back to the Ostinkino to get my clothes. My roommate slapped his thigh and hollered, "You found Russky pussky!"

"No," I said. "I found something better."

"What? Impossible!"

"Yeah, well, whatever."

Night after night. Week after week. Naum, my Russian bear, taught me many things throughout the summer—ways men could enjoy each other, uses for caviar I'd never imagined, the power of tenderness to arouse, passion as source of international harmony, the true meaning of that '60s adage: Make love, not war.

The day before I left Russia, during a private, bittersweet goodbye, Naum handed me a copy of Kuzmin's novel, *Wings,* and said, in that romantic way Russians have about them, "You gave my heart flight."

We e-mail now, Naum and I, several times a week. We're planning his first trip to the United States. He says the only sight he wishes to see here is his own ecstatic smile reflected in my eyes. Sure, he's over-the-top, but I have to admit to enjoying his adoration. Is this love or just lust? I don't know, and I'm not sure how to tell. I guess I'll need to make love with him a couple million more times before I can figure it all out.

The House of Saved Husbands
R.G. POWERS

Clean dew evaporated in the soft, rotund late-morning sun. Ernest came around the corner, hemmed pants and Pendleton soaked with the sweat of working in the heat. Cutting a cord was draining, and his arms ached. Those thick arms, laden dark with hair, shimmered in the afterglow of the chore. But now there was wood for a harsh winter coming. Soon the colored, dripping leaves of autumn would freeze into winter's most brilliant quietude, waiting for the springtime sun's shafting beams to dip low again and restore life with undeniable grace.

Humid winds rushed as rust-orange, auburn-brown, and burnt-yellow leaves tumbled quietly across a forest floor worn earthy by perennial ground fires. The elderly summer fixed their colors, peacocking them to the towering growth above. Pulpy columns dripped sap, storming shade across the watchful mountains. A slight breeze brushed by the needles, tickling their prickly nature.

Mr. Jameson was coming today with supplies for Ernest. Today was a good day for him. He sat on his dilapidated porch in his tired redwood chair, listening to jumbled forest sounds. The faded clips and clops of Mr. Jameson's horse played in echo down the mountainside. The sounds of nature hypnotized him into a comfortable silence. He thought about how he had always been alone, how it never used to bother him, and how now he needed more than a drunken night and a knothole to fill the immense chasm that had sunk his belly with longing. He breathed a low, deep sigh and rubbed his hairy stomach, as if the rubbing would fill the emptiness. A soft ground fog wandered by, evaporated into nothing by the skillet-hot sun.

Dust fired from behind Mr. Jameson's buckboard in all directions as tore around the bend, as if he were running away from demons and toward angels, perhaps warriors of Valhalla. He worked the reins taut; his thick, hairy forearms and beard-lined face beading with sweat. Dust choked the fresh mountain air as the wobbly wagon ground to a stop. He brushed back his hair, straightened his collar, and unbuttoned his shirt a few buttons, as if readying himself as a gentleman caller. His chestnut-brown chest hair reflected in the autumn sun. His tight jeans stretched as he stood, showing a bit of a belly over the waistline as he towered over his friend, perhaps like Zeus in love with Ganymede. He straightened his hat, rearranged himself in his trousers, and nodded.

"Well, hallo, Roy." Ernest looked at him, trying not to look too hard, yet not being able to keep his eyes off this man that he would never have, not even drunk or bound by rope.

"Hallo, Ernest. Looks like ya worked up a good sweat already." He hopped down, the buckboard creaking with age.

"Choppin' damn wood."

"Good day fer a picnic—damn good." He took off his hat, combing his hair back with his hand.

"If heat's what yer lookin' fer."

He shuffled the dirt with his foot. "Done new writin' fer the last week?"

"So t' speak. Come 'n' sit up t' the porch a while—I'll get 'em. You wanna beer?"

Roy's face lit up, happy as always to have something that might loosen his mood.

"Shore—good day fer beer."

Ernest smiled. "Damn good day fer beer."

He trotted inside to his rollback desk, pulled four folders out, and stomped into the kitchen. He looked frantically for the right glasses, careful not to make too much noise, and found them dirty from the last time they drank, only a week ago. He quickly washed them and returned to Roy.

"Brown Derby—good beer. Thanks."

"You gettin' that fergetful? You bought it. By the way, how's yer Mary?"

He turned and studied the forest, as detached from the subject as his friend was. "Bored 'n' complainin' all the time—no different. She says I'm out too much. Says she gave up worryin' 'bout me 'n' all, 'cause the last time I came I passed out here all night."

"Pity—good-lookin' woman." Ernest was clearly fishing for something, and it wasn't Roy's wife.

"You said it, not me." Roy looked away, noticeably disappointed. "How's things round here? Brought ya more beer, paper, a couple boxes of food, an' a bottle of some strange Spanish stuff—Anis del Toro, 'think."

"Yer a good friend, Roy—thanks. Hope ah kin sell that junk."

"Writin's yer thing—only few people got it."

"Come agin? I'm jus' some hick mou'tain man."

"With a downright odd sense o' truth."

Silence sat a spell in the sweet cool aroma of a lazy pine forest.

"Ya know, Ernest, ya ever think 'bout movin' inta town? Lot nicer there." A mile closer, a few feet, a foot; he would settle for anything that might bring this man closer to him—anything. He thought he would promise the gods that he would not even think of trying to touch him if Ernest would only move closer, so he might see him more often—he would promise not to even look at him, so long as he might hear Ernest's voice, and drift into that perfect moment where he fell into silence, and imagine love resounding in the low rumble of this handsome, gentle man, this creation of the muses that sang though his heart and the hearts of all those who read him.

"Yeah, did—hate people, though. They cloud ma' thinkin'. Most all folks do that, 'cept you."

"Why's that?" He looked up like a boy asking for his manhood, not realizing that manhood must be either taken or won.

"Yer…just dif'rent, 'guess." He turned his tired head back, staring thoughtfully through the myriad pine needles that lingered above. A baby-blue sky floated weightlessly across his vision.

"Stay for lunch? 'Ave makin's fer sandwiches."

"Yeah, sure. Thanks, Ernest." He thumbed his glass as he always did, unconsciously reacting—if he kept one part of his body moving, he might keep running from the torture he was fated to experience with the rest of it.

"No problem." Ernest disappeared into the cabin.

Roy looked deeply into forest. It gave him a disturbed tranquility. Something he had felt all his life was coming to bear, and he felt like there was no other place where he could be as happy as where he was at this very moment. It could not be, not after what had happened with his wife. How could he tell Ernest and still remain a man?

Ernest reappeared by and by, with a hearty lunch. He carried a tray of ham sandwiches and sliced cucumbers between his thick, powerful hands.

"Need any other fixin's?"

"Naw thanks—just great."

They wolfed down lunch as if they were hyenas gnawing a prize catch. Ernest popped the last bit of a sandwich into his mouth, rubbing his satisfied belly. Roy rubbed his too, content, like a cub full of milk.

"Better?"

"Lots. Ernest, ya ever fish over t' Crawford's Peak?" he inquired.

"Yea—they ain't that big, though."

Breaking branches echoed behind the old rotting cabin.

"What 'n the hell?! C'mon!"

Ernest led the way with a start. About a hundred feet behind the old landmark, under an evergreen, writhed a paining mass of fur.

"Ch-rist, what're we gonna do?"

"Shoot it, 'guess."

"No way, Roy—it's only got a broke leg. We're helpin' it."

"Bully." Roy pulled out a flask and took a swig. He dealt with death only slightly better than he dealt with love.

Ernest knelt down and gently but firmly grasped the injured cat. It wrestled with him, snapping at him, trying to get a good piece of him. Roy tied a blue handkerchief from his pocket around the mountain lion cub's muzzle, taking up Ernest's task as Ernest found sticks for a splint. They brushed slightly in the exchange. Roy thought he was going to faint—not from the scent of death but from the scent of lust, the animal lust he tried to hold down and control now. But he, like the animal, was out of control. "Goddamn it, Ernest—git this fucker tied up!" He was furious with his feelings and lashed out by grabbing the cat tightly and pinning it hard to the ground. Ernest undid his shoe-strings and wound them around the sticks, then tied the makeshift contraption to the wounded leg. He looked at Roy with satisfaction.

"See—what's wrong with helpin' another animal?"

"Just ain't nat'ral. Things gotta die when they's gotta die. 'Sides, ya ain't no animal." He was embarrassed to be so transparent and hid his face with a turn.

"Sure am. We're all part animal."

"Killin's fer things that just ain't right no more."

"Even people?"

"If they's gone an' done somethin' t' call fer it."

"What—like havin' compassion?"

Roy finally caught on, annoyed. Ernest ran to fetch a tarp, and Roy imagined that it was Ernest whom he was pinning to the ground and taking care of. He imagined it was Ernest who had to prove his manhood by wrestling free; but failing, he would have to be taught to be a man by some far more severe method, a method whose very thought, nature, and unspeakableness excited him with hope. Ernest raced back, and they rolled the lion onto the tarp. Roy grabbed the tail end, and they lugged the heavy beast into the living room of the cabin.

"Chained up he won't do no harm—least fer a while." Ernest rearranged himself.

"Ernest, yer playin' with fire."

"That's bullshit."

"Take it how ya sees it. I'm just sayin', ya know, yer messin' with a storm o' trouble—*del fuego.*"

Ernest squinted in skepticism out the window. Playing with fire was what warmed him to the strong yet yielding forbearance of nature. He hugged nature with the love of a boy for his mother and father, a boy whose life did not depend upon nature but whose very life was woven into nature, no matter how many others chose to cut themselves off from it. It seemed to Ernest that Roy was so cut off he couldn't even help another animal, much less himself. Perhaps that was the reason Roy and his wife had so many problems?

It had already turned into early evening by the time the mountain lion was bandaged up. A heavy, warm autumn shower was forming in dense, billowy gray clouds. These few minutes of silence stretched out into what seemed like hours.

"Stay fer dinner, an' git drunk?"

"Ma' wife's cookin', but I'd like t'."

"All the same, 'guess."

Roy rose and knelt down by the powerful cat, stroking its coarse fur, cautiously feeling its warmth. Ernest went over to the liquor cabinet and picked out some Irish whiskey. He returned to his seat by the once-roaring fire. He dumped more logs on the just-stoked embers and threw a shot back slowly, savoring the mellow flow of his coming intoxication, and feeling a little relieved. A few more shots loosened him up a bit more.

"Come t' think of it, she ain't gonna mind—I'll stay. Hand me tha' bottle."

Handing the bottle to Roy, Ernest stared into the whipping flames of the fireplace and scratched himself, moving to the side what was growing in his trousers against his will. The lazy cat groaned. Roy chugged straight from the bottle, filling his empty stomach with warmth. As he swigged he glanced out of the corner of his eye and absorbed an image he would spend the next week— weeks, lifetimes—dreaming about.

"Woodshed's almost built—only a few planks lef'."

"Yeah, saw 'er—lookin' good. Maybe put the cat in there." Roy thought about the animal, the trouble it could unleash at any moment, and thought about himself, about what might happen if he were unleashed.

"What ya want fer dinner?"

"What've ya got?"

"Guess canned's good—too crocked to cook." Ernest smiled in his inebriation.

"Sounds good—how long 'fore it'll heal?"

"Few weeks, 'think."

"Maybe less trouble 'n it sounds—nice animal, s'pose."

"Yeah."

Tumultuous clouds building energy broke rain in thunderous roars. Rain shot down in bullets, spattering on the roof like pebbles. Mountain winds bent their air-cooled paths in a confident, howling rage.

A now-empty whiskey bottle had rolled into a corner by the fireplace. The men lounged a little lower in their lazy chairs, chuckling and punching each other playfully in the arm. Perhaps, after a while, they might feel more comfortable touching each other, Roy thought, and might hug when he left, or kiss and stay together a lifetime.

They examined the fire a spell in silence, strong flat hands thrust under loosened belts. The purring lion's flashy eyes squinted the last light for the evening, as it curled up contented. They had fed it dried venison, almost a pound, and thought it might be good for Roy to come back from town to bring a few pounds of beef for the husky cat tomorrow.

"Rain's a-comin' down." Ernest almost couldn't pronounce the words without a slur—not from the liquor, but from a distant hope that if he slowed down his words, theoretically time might slow down, and he might have a few more moments of torture with the one he loved so powerfully.

"Yup."

"Want dinner? I'll make it." Ernest slapped his buddy's knee.

"Naw—too damned drunk," Roy said, in a low rumble.

"Me neither—spend the night? Kinda figured ya would."

"Too drunk to go home now, she'll kill me—shore."

"This's the house t' save husbands from their women." Ernest laughed heartily.

"Yeah—damned right," Roy joined in, cackling in bold, deep tones. Ernest moved a little closer. It felt good to have his buddy near. They sat blissfully, feeling good in their drunkenness, feeling good next to each other. Thunder shuddered the frail panes of glass.

An inarticulate emotion grew in Roy now, a lie he could no longer conceal, a truth he did not want to be known, a life that he did and yet did not want to lead, and an eternity that seemed he had waited an eternity to avoid. "Um..." He couldn't. Not now—not ever.

"Yeah?" Ernest just wanted to hear his voice, just the low sweet rumble of him.

"I..." Roy broke off. "I..." He began to weep, turning his head from him, and broke down.

"Jesus, buddy. What's wrong? Hey, what's wrong, buddy? Is it you and Mary?" Ernest didn't even want to hear her name, as the jealousy was at times overpowering. But he wanted to help Roy; Roy was the thing that kept him alive.

"Uh—" He sniffled, then cried again. "She...I...I've been kept up in town at the Scudder's."

"Did ya have a fight 'er somethin'?"

"Naw. We had a divorce kinda—she kicked me out. So I took up lodgin's at the hotel."

"Jeez, buddy." Ernest was ever so close now, and he had his arm on Roy's shoulder, rubbing it. He didn't even know when he'd put it there—it just happened. But he couldn't very well remove it now, when his buddy needed him the most. He could not afford to be abandoned now. "Well, buddy. You'll get back t'gether." He patted Roy on the back, as if burping the tears out of him as a mother would burp her child.

"Naw, we won't—I can't tell ya why." Roy dried his tears, worried he might be seen as some kind of Nellie, some kind of coward who couldn't even satisfy his wife, much less any other woman.

Ernest leaned in so close he could smell Roy's face, wet with tears and the scent of sweat from earlier in the day. "Roy. We've been friends now for a long time. Why won't ya be getting back t'gether?" He was fishing for a life that did not exist and was sure fate would slam him now with words like "She didn't put out enough" or "She doesn't know how to suck on a man good." He wanted to smash his fists though a wall, or beat his love into his arms, forcing him to love and feed off his love for him, forcing him down on him, taking him inside him.

"Awww…buddy. No," He brushed Ernest's cheek with the back of his fur-covered hand, and Ernest shuddered. "Oh, ah'm sorry." He was sure Ernest was disgusted with just the thought of a man touching him, much less the feeling.

"Oh, no." He tried to conceal his palpitation. "It felt kinda good. It's OK."

"Ah'm sorry ah lied to ya."

"'Bout what?"

"'Bout not tellin' ya earlier."

"It's OK, Roy. We've all got probl'ms."

"Not like these."

He was not going to get into an assuming frenzy again, and so he passed over Roy's last statement, which could be perceived either way, and let it go, as he should have several years ago when they had met.

"Got new Whitman."

"Ha, yeah? What have ya got?" Roy tried to draw the conversation further away from intimacy, desperately wanting it now more than ever. He was happy, though, for now he had an image to think about, an image to play with while stroking his member before sleeping through the cold, rainy nights at the hotel. Ernest's soft beard, his strong hands, his thickly haired barrel chest, his softest smile, his meaty package that was concealed behind his worn jeans—all these musky images were part of Roy now, for he had been to the land of masculine men in his dreams and smelled the heady scent of this warrior; he had breathed in his breath, he had felt his covered flesh against Ernest's covered flesh, and so he was happy.

"'To a Locomotive in Winter.'"

"Sounds good—do it," Roy said. Ernest spat out the poem with a wild tongue. The words tumbled out in a nearly flawless rumble. When he finished, he sat pensively as they glared at the waning flickers of finger-length laps of light.

"Always liked locomotives." He eyed his buddy, wondering if he had understood the idea behind the poem. He put a hand in his trousers and scratched himself.

"Yeah—the part 'bout the body was real descript've." He thought about the heaving of the iron beast, the chugging water in its belly, the burning coal in its heart, and the barreling down the tracks toward a destination without doubt or fear built into its very nature. "Hey, every time ya do that it makes me wanna…it's like sneezin'." He laughed insecurely and shoved his hands roughly into his trousers, not so much scratching himself as stroking his meat. Ernest nearly dove into the mountain of man that stood as a leviathan before him.

"How many ya think you'll get done this week?"

"Wha'? 'Bout four 'r five."

"Great. Publisher'll be happy to git 'em."

"Look at 'em embers—pure light is what they are. Glowin' somethin' fierce."

"Yaw—" He paused for what seemed like an hour, but was only seconds. "Like yer eyes."

"Wha'?"

"Ya know what ah meant."

The poetic mountain man laughed nervously, looked down, ran his fingers through his hair, and looked into Roy's eyes, serious. "Yeah. I know wha' ya meant." This was not happening. He was not going to be given what he had been denied for so many years. He would die alone—no, must die alone, for it was always what he thought someone of his caliber was born to do.

He stood in the heat of the room, and an immutable fire burned deep within his heart and pulled Roy toward him. Roy laughed.

"Hey there, whatcha doin'?"

Ernest wrestled him to the ground.

"Ya wanna wrassle, huh?" Roy yelled. "I'll show ya, ya bastard!" Roy, slightly bigger than his foe, turned him around and over, pinning him to the ground with his pelvis, grinding his thickening meat into Ernest's soft, tightening buttocks.

Ernest did not like this and reached around, flipping Roy over in passionate heat, and glared at him with the eyes of a mountain lion. "Goddamn, Ernest—jus' a game."

Ernest tore open Roy's Pendleton, the buttons flying, and pressed his hairy hand against his prey's heaving chest. "Not anymore, G'ddammit!"

Ernest pinned him to the floor, and slowly moved his lips toward his buddy's. Roy moved up a bit and closed his eyes, slightly opening his mouth. Ernest took the sign and slowly pushed his lips against Roy's mouth, staying there as if drinking up 10,000 Arabian nights. He began to rub Roy's belly and kiss his mouth, moving his tongue inside, feeling their warm beards connect, the most natural feeling he had ever felt. Too much and too soon, Roy pulled back.

"Jesus, Ernest. C'mon, buddy." Ernest grabbed Roy and buried his face in his furry neck, inhaling the intoxicating scent of his beard, and bit him. "Damn it! Ouch. Hey there!" He laughed insecurely and rubbed his buddy's back as Ernest slowly went to town on his neck; licking, suckling, and burying his furry face deep into this man's, his man's bearded neck.

"Please, Ernest—*please*! Goddamn it—Ernest!" Roy pushed him back—feeling the man's taut erection against his, two members of the same clan rubbing each other sensuously—and looked into his eyes.

"Please, buddy. I know. I know. It's OK now, but be gentle. It's OK. We know, we know, and it's OK." He pulled him closer kindly, smiling as if someone else's shoulder had taken the weight of Sisyphus's rock. He kissed Ernest gently, deeply, the way rustic men sometimes kiss, drunk or sober.

Ernest began weeping blindly as he kissed Roy back, letting the tears roll down his face as he kissed away his fate, the years of loneliness, the years of tear-filled nights of emptiness and lies. He kissed away his self-doubt, self-criticism, assumptions, and bitterness. He kissed himself across this man whom he had longed after for so long, and at once a deluge of emotion swept him into bliss. He could not rationalize this away; he could not find excuses. It was what it was; it consumed them as surely as waterfalls fall, and trees topple, and lives come and go like fog through time. He kissed Roy again and took his breath into him, then gave him his own breath in return. He removed the rest of Roy's shirt, which he had torn at so passionately, and then removed his own as he straddled the man's rough-haired stomach. Roy looked up at him as a boy who waited for his lesson in love, but they would have to learn from each other and test each other and reward each other.

Ernest kissed down Roy's face to his chest, where he bit his nipples playfully.

"Hey there, buddy. Oh, damn. Damn, buddy." Roy was at first afraid of the feeling, but then he gave into the pleasure of it, sure that Ernest knew what he was doing, knowing that what he was doing felt better than anything he had ever felt with a woman. The sensation in Roy's nipples shot like electricity to his trousers and pulsed his meat with a fire that he wanted to bury deep in the deepest part of his buddy.

Ernest buried his face in Roy's navel, tasting the sweat of the day on his musky body. He moved down, breathing in the scent of Roy's crotch and the manhood that lingered behind it; it strained to burst forth and take him with the patience of a saint and the power of warrior. He unbuttoned one button, then another. Roy lunged back, pressing his full belly outward, and clapped his hand on the back of Ernest's head, pushing it further against the stiffness in his pants. He grew confident, and pulled Ernest's head up by the back of his hair. Looking deeply into his eyes with a squint he said, "Ya wan' it? Ya want 'at, dontcha?" He palmed the fat tool in his pants. "Ya always wanted it, buddy. Why'd ya make me wait so long?"

Ernest could not believe what he was hearing. He tore open the man's pants and ran his beard roughly over his dangling, thick balls, slathering them with his tongue and nibbling at the sack.

"Damn—Goddamn!"

Roy moved his hands up and down Ernest's head, mussing up his hair, then moved them around his own body as if exploring it for the first time, twisting his nipples like knobs, rubbing his belly, as if anxiously waiting for every drop of his mountain writer to be inside him. Ernest's head moved up his purpled shaft. Roy examined it, as if it had been the first time he looked at the beauty of his own body. A thick piece of meat, short at five inches but as round and thick as a bottle of beer, pressed up against his buddy, beckoned to be taken inside those warm lips and softest beard.

He navigated his cock over Ernest's beard and studied him with lust, as if he would have what he wanted at any price. He pulled Ernest's face up to the head of his cock, feeling his warm lips and tongue ride the shaft to the top. And fast as a tree trunk rushing down a watery logging flume, he pulled Ernest down on him and buried his cock inside his buddy's wet logger gullet. He gasped and lunged, burying his cock in Ernest's face, pushing his meat deep inside, rubbing his fat rancher's tool down the man's throat.

Ernest gobbled the meat with every breath he could muster and gulped proudly without a worry or fear. He suckled the meat at first with powerfully deep, strong strokes, but then more gently, as if toying with what would end up in his beefy belly. Ernest suck-led the head, slowly looking at Roy with a cockiness, then took his tool all the way down. He slathered the sweet slickness and held it there, suckling as if trying to gulp the very life from it. He gripped the bottom of the shaft and took it down his gullet again, teasing and swallowing Roy's juicy rod, choking the member down his throat and savoring the juices. He shoved his large hand under-neath Roy's ass and playfully massaged the sweaty-haired crack, fiddling with his hole. Ernest loosened Roy's sweet hole and took his tool completely down his throat as he sank his finger up to the knuckle in Roy's ass. "Oh, fuck, don't do that—fucker—don't—not so—oh, shit!" Roy writhed as the man he loved controlled his pain and his pleasure.

Ernest worked another finger up inside Roy and massaged his prostate. He lunged his fingers deeper inside and twiddled them across Roy's prostate gland, in time with his cocksucking strokes, while burying his face deep on Roy's meat. Ernest sucked deep and hard one last time and shoved his fingers to the hilt. That was all it took.

"Oh, Jesus, man. Ya gotta…ya fuckin' gotta—oh, damn, god-damn, get off, get the fuck off—I'm gonna, I gonna, I'm gonna—Fuck! Oh, fuck! Yeah, yeah, yeah!" Roy let loose and pulsed uncon-trollable rhythm after rhythm of come down Ernest's gullet, his cock buried to the hilt, and growled as if it would never end. He squirted his load into Ernest, pumping every last drop while his lover eagerly choked on his cock, trying to get more of it down his throat. Roy let another shot go, this time with his hand on the back of Ernest's head, controlling how much Ernest would get in his mouth to taste and how much he would force down his throat into his hairy belly. His rhythm slowed down, his cock pulsing in shuddering heaves as his bulbous nuts, soaked with sweat and come, snugged up to his body and relaxed, spent from releasing every last drop of what they were designed to hold.

Roy looked down at the big man who was sucking his softening yet still-pulsating cock. "Gaaaaw-dammit." Ernest's beard and lips were slathered with his come. Roy brushed some of the hair below his lower lip and fed it to Ernest slowly, letting his thumb explore the inside of his warm lips made hot from the friction. "You sonnabitch. How long didja 'ave that planned?"

"Shut the fuck up." He pulled him close by his ass, where his fingers still controlled Roy's every movement.

"Heyyy—ouch! OK, OK! Whatcha wanna do?"

"What I always wanted, and jerked off daily thinkin' about... *this*." Ernest shoved his fingers deep again and got up on his knees, pushing his crotch against Roy's face. "Here." He yanked the buttons of his jeans open and released his fat piece of uncut meat, stuffed it into Roy's mouth, rubbing the snout over his tongue. Roy sucked in the thickness like a starved man, hungry as all hell for this man's seed. Ernest shucked back the foreskin, then shoved his meat down Roy's throat, feeling Roy's throat slowly loosen around his sensitive head. He slowly worked his cock farther down Roy's mouth, hearing garbled words like "I love ya" and "Always wanted ya in me," but he paid no attention; that would come afterward. What he was after was right here in front of him. He withdrew his wet cock and dropped his fat nuts into Roy's mouth, to be hummed by the man who was never supposed to be but somehow had become his. Roy sucked his nuts softly and groaned as he pumped his buddy's thick shaft.

Ernest dug his hand deeper between his thighs, burying his fingers farther inside Roy's hairy hole, and with his other hand explored the pelt of the man-sucking man. "Awww...man." He garbled "Ernst" from his filled mouth and suckled harder. Ernest dug in deeper, gently spelunking his hole like a miner who'd found a mother lode. Roy wriggled and adjusted as best he could under the unfamiliar pressure.

Ernest suddenly backed his hand out of Roy's meaty ass, rolled his prey over, and spread his hairy cheeks. He rubbed his sensitive cock head between them, then entered. "Please, be carefu—arghhh! G'ddamm't, Ernest!" Roy pleaded.

"Ya wan' it," Ernest responded, sinking his cock another inch, and then another, as Roy writhed under him to get away. "Say ya wan' it, fucker! Ya know ya do!"

"Ouch, goddamn!" Roy yelped. "OK, OK, buddy! I want it. I want ya all, buddy—fuck!" Ernest shoved in another inch. "All o' ya! C'mon on, fucker—c'mon! Give it all to me, buddy—I'm yers!" Ernest grabbed his waist and jackhammered his last few inches into the writhing bear below him, fulfilling his lust. He roared from the depths of his belly, waking the cat, who growled and rolled back to sleep.

Ernest stroked his way into Roy's heart through the most intimate part a man could offer another, the most sensuous, rustic place, where most men dared not go—a place that defined manhood, and brought out his masculinity the way nothing else could. He had become a man, a rustic man who had to answer to no one for his pleasure, nor for this crime, which seemed heroic.

"C'mon, fucker," Roy cried out. "Ya 'eard me. Ya said you'd make me wannit, now give it to me—Come on!" He clamped down tightly as he backed up and Ernest almost lost it. Ernest began pistoning him with a dangerous force that might have ruptured something but for his diligent, exacting thrust. He rubbed Roy's prostate with his cock head, buried himself deeply to show his prowess, then pulled out. He repeated this in a maddening rhythm that curbed Roy's loudmouthed orders down to a low, consuming groan. Roy arched, chortled a few rough tones, and groaned again in rhythm with Ernest's powerful thrusts. Ernest grabbed him and rolled him over every which way, pounding his prostate from every direction and contorting Roy's roundness to suit his member's every whim.

"Awww, awww, man, oh, yeah," Ernest grunted, finally turning Roy face up. "Yeah! Goddamn it, Roy, yeah! Yeah!" Roy clamped himself down on Ernest as he shot again, all over his fur-lined stomach, then turned his tool upward to squirt a few lines on his master, his servant, his Poseidon. Ernest pounded his way inside this man to the hilt, arched his back, threw back his head, and growled. He shot every last moment of his disarrayed life in thick loads of come into his buddy, bucking with every wave of seed that pumped from his soul and up his buddy's tight hole. His nuts sucked up and cuddled inside Roy's hairy crack and he fell over on top of him, tongue-slurping his mouth and snuggling his head in Roy's stubbled neck.

They growled a playful growl at each other and embraced in the warmth of the firelight. The cat purred a low, sweet tune and rolled over, turning its face toward the fireplace. Ernest grabbed a blanket from under the couch and started to cover them.

"Wait. I gotta go back t' town."

"Yer not goin' anywhere. Not anymore. Ain't nowhere to run but t' me, buddy."

Roy looked at Ernest a moment and thought of what the townspeople would say, then pulled himself out of those thoughts. He didn't have to think that way. He could live any way he wanted, and that was not the business of the townsfolk. Ernest and he could live together, surrounded by the forest and streams and wildlife, apart from the chatter of the town and the prying eyes of people who didn't need to know of this chaos that Ernest and he, as lovers, called manly love. He curled up to the big man who had taken and given his manhood. He cuddled up to Ernest, and they glowed in the aftermath of their inebriation.

"Firelight's still glowin', like yer eyes."

"Far's ah c'n tell, it'll be thataway fer a long time t' come."

The rustic, ember-lit room dimmed slowly. Through the window, from outside the cabin, two men could be seen nuzzling next to a glowing fireplace. They hugged each other like boys experimenting for the first time, and they snuggled on the bearskin rug like men who had loved each other since time began.

Outside, the rain quieted, having drenched the rich soil. Freed in the wind from millions of pine needles, droplets dove erratically into the sweet, resplendent ground. Far above the clouds, a ring captured by the moon's momentous beams foreshadowed more rain to come. A solitary cabin sat in the gathering stillness. There would be no spring today, but spring would soon arrive, riding on august winds.

The Centurion
JAY STARRE

The Roman 15th Legion was stationed outside Ravenna in Italian Gaul for the winter. Antony wound his way through the well-ordered camp as light snow fell. His legs were bare below the hem of his military tunic, but the thick blond fur on them kept him reasonably warm. He was used to it anyway. He was a tough soldier, or at least imagined himself to be, even though he was very young.

He was also in love—hopelessly and madly. Rufus, his centurion, had called for him that night. It was Rufus who was the object of the younger Antony's affections. Antony would die for the burly centurion. He would also suck his cock or take it up the ass if he had the chance. Antony shivered as he recalled that massive frame, tall and imposing, with muscles padded by years of good eating as a successful Roman centurion. Rufus was awe-inspiring—and Antony's cock was definitely inspired as it rose up stiff against his tunic just thinking about the man.

"Wait in there. The centurion is occupied for the moment. You can warm yourself by the brazier," a soldier ordered Antony as he entered Rufus's quarters.

The camp was more or less permanent, and the officers' quarters actually had solid stone walls and tiled roofs. There was even a fireplace Antony could hear roaring in the adjacent room just beyond the curtained doorway. Antony was left alone, and in his nervousness his heightened hearing picked up conversation from that other room.

"I love a hairy pair of butt cheeks, but how tight is the hole between them?"

Antony was sure his lust-addled brain must be playing tricks on him. Rufus's voice was unmistakable; the deep timbre could be heard above the chaos of any battle. But what was he talking about? Antony couldn't help himself. He crept up to the doorway and peered through the flimsy material into the room beyond.

A naked man was on his hands and knees on the floor in front of the blazing fire! The flames illuminated a fur-covered body, muscular but fleshy, thighs spread wide, a hairy ass writhing suggestively at the feet of Rufus the centurion. Antony held his breath as he peered at the man's face. The sandy-brown beard around lush lips, the blunt nose—it was Milo, his fellow infantryman.

"Let's see that hole, soldier. If I'm going to fuck it, I want to see it first." Rufus stood behind the soldier, his feet planted wide apart, his hairy calves and half his thighs visible below his tunic.

Antony stood fascinated as Milo's tongue licked the thick flesh of his lips so lasciviously that Antony actually shivered. But then Antony's eyes moved to that bare ass and the big thighs spread so far apart that the ass was almost on the floor. Antony could see the crack from where he stood, a pelt of soft brown hair swirling over the large butt mounds and into that crevice. Then he saw the hole, a reddened orifice pouting and twittering.

Antony emitted an audible gasp—his undoing. The centurion in the other room moved so quickly, Antony's gasp was still lingering in his throat when a beefy paw wrapped around his neck.

"What have we here? A spy? Antony Millites the infantryman is spying on his centurion? Get on your knees beside your fellow soldier and follow his example!" Rufus snarled in Antony's face.

The older soldier's features were twisted in mock anger, but they were handsome nonetheless, and Antony couldn't help staring into them adoringly. The soft-gray eyes were hooded by raven brows, the thick mane of equally raven hair pushed back from a broad forehead. The nose was long and straight, and the mouth was full. A thick black beard curled along the jaw line. Rufus was bearded, unlike most Romans, and many of his men emulated his appearance out of admiration and love. Both Milo and Rufus sported small beards.

Antony almost didn't hear the order spit in his face. But as the hand on his throat moved to his shoulder, his senses returned. "I'm sorry, sir! Forgive me for intruding, but you did order me to attend you. Forgive me, please!" Antony sputtered as Rufus dragged him into the room toward the sprawled Milo.

But then Rufus laughed, a great guffaw that rang to the rafters. "Settle, Antony. I was merely teasing you, man. I am in the mood for a little entertainment on a cold winter night, and Milo here indicated you would be amenable to a good fuck."

As he spoke, Rufus abruptly thrust his free hand up under Antony's tunic. Fingers closed around Antony's throbbing erection, eliciting a small, unmanly shriek from the startled soldier.

Milo was laughing too, and Antony's face was flushed bright pink around his own stubbled beard as he attempted an answering laugh. The centurion's hand was pumping his hard-on as Rufus continued pulling him toward the fire and his naked fellow soldier.

"Well, man? A fuck or no fuck?" Rufus grinned.

Antony bleated out a reply. "Yes, sir! Yes! I mean, *yes,* I want you to fuck me."

"All in good time. I want to see you fuck Milo first. I love to watch a soldier get it up the ass."

Antony was stunned, but fingers still pumped his dick and a rough hand was yanking on his tunic. Antony pulled his soldier's clothing off as if in a dream, his manhood thrust forward into Rufus's thick-knuckled paw and his knees weak with disbelieving lust. Rufus wanted him! Rufus wanted to fuck him!

Rufus's massive forearms pressed against Antony as he stripped, one down on his cock and the other around his waist squeezing one fleshy ass cheek. The forearms were covered in swirling black hair, and above them black armbands surrounded the centurion's giant biceps. Those arms fascinated Antony, even while his body vibrated with the intimate feel of the officer's hands on his cock and ass.

"Come on, man! Get down there between Milo's thighs and pump him full of that juicy cock of yours. It's a fair size, and it's dripping spunk already," Rufus was chortling. He was usually very stern during training and battle, but otherwise he was a genial officer. It was obvious he was in a fine mood.

Antony felt those hands release him and he stumbled to obey orders, these orders like the welcome music of a lute at suppertime. He sank to his knees behind Milo with the crackling flames of the hearth wafting over them. His own blue eyes, a gift from Gallic ancestors, were bright as he took in the sight of all that manly bulk. Milo was a big soldier, with as much fat as muscle— an eager one at the dinner board. The sight of all that hairy flesh excited Antony. He trembled as he reached out and cupped two handfuls of soldier ass. By the gods, that butt was hot! The flames of the fire had heated them up, and they wiggled and bucked under Antony's touch. Milo moaned as his hole bloomed outward. Antony's cock leaped up and dribbled a trail of pre-come excitedly.

"Don't worry, Milo. I've got some grease for Antony's big pecker. It'll slide up your hole like a thrust spear gutting a German barbarian."

The centurion's crude words only increased the two kneeling soldiers' fervor. Antony ran his fingers through all that silky brown hair and slid them toward the crack. Milo thrust his ass up to meet the exploring fingers. Antony all at once was in the crack and then stroking the hair-ringed but satiny, hairless slot.

"Fuck my ass, Antony. Ram your cock up it hard," Milo groaned, his face buried in the thick fur of the bearskin rug beneath them.

Big fingers coated with a generous gob of pale lard thrust down into Antony's lap, wrapping around his cock. The clean odor of fresh pig fat assaulted his nostrils as he squirmed under the centurion's stroke. Antony jabbed at Milo's fluttering asshole and lunged upward into Rufus's lubricating fingers. His own finger stabbed far up Milo's slot, eliciting a loud grunt from the prone soldier.

"Now for a good soldier fuck. Ram him, Antony. Shove that greased pole up his ass button!"

Orders from the centurion were never disobeyed. As Rufus's hand guided his cock to the reddened hole his finger was already massaging, Antony whimpered and shoved forward. His finger was still buried deep in the hot fuck tunnel when the head of his uncut cock followed.

The slippery lard melted in the heat of hole and rod. Antony felt his shaft slither far up Milo's guts, his finger wiggling around beside it to stretch open the obliging hole. All three soldiers gasped.

The centurion leaned over to aid Antony in the penetration, then released the base of Antony's fat cock and stood up. As Antony began to plow the greased hole in front of him, in rhythm to Milo's deep grunts, Rufus straddled Milo's back and shoulders, facing Antony. As Antony panted, shoving his cock in and out of Milo's steamy bowels, his centurion stripped in front of him.

Antony was staring at the object of his total adoration. Rufus was naked. A dark pelt coated the giant limbs and torso. A pair of huge balls dangled down between massive thighs, full and potent. Above that manly sac, a tower of fat cock rose up to slap against a hairy belly. The hood had slid back to reveal the plum-colored head, bisected by the deep piss slit, which oozed a glistening drool of precome. The massive slabs of the centurion's pecs and shoulders loomed dominantly over Antony. Scars crisscrossed that giant body, scars from innumerable battles fought on Rome's behalf. But those scars were beautiful to Antony's adoring eyes.

The blond soldier pumped deep into Milo's welcoming butt-pit, shoving his cock to the balls as he leaned forward to inhale the clean scent of the centurion's furry body. He squirmed around the steamy butt hole massaging his hard rod, wiggling it way up into Milo's guts as he leaned even closer. The hairy thighs were inches away.

"Yes, man, take a deep whiff of a man's crotch. Get in there and feel my hairy thighs with your face before you suck your commander's balls and cock."

The centurion's husky command rang in Antony's ears as he swiftly complied. He leaned into Rufus's thighs, feeling all that silky fur caress his cheeks, nostrils, and lips. The fat nut sac rubbed against his forehead and scalp as he buried his face in hefty flesh. The power of those thighs was unmistakable—they quivered against Antony's face. The soft hair tickled his nose and lips. He ran his own hands all over Milo's writhing butt cheeks at the same time, feeling the lush muscle grow slippery with sexual sweat as Antony continued to thrust in and out of the soldier's accommodating asshole.

Two big paws grasped Antony's shoulders and shoved his face deeper between the fur-coated thighs. They parted and Antony nuzzled up into the inner thighs below the balls. Ass crack loomed over him as Antony rolled his head backward and searched upward in Rufus's butt crack from below. Rufus half squatted over the kneeling centurion, his feet planted wide apart and holding Antony by the shoulders. Antony opened his mouth and stuck out his tongue to explore. The centurion's booming laughter rocked out above him as he rooted around in the furry depths. His nose met the distended lips of a fur-rimmed butt hole first, inhaling funky soldier butt. His lips and tongue followed as he pressed upward between the warm thighs and tickled centurion ass.

Antony rooted around like a pig in a truffle field as he rammed his cock in and out of Milo. Rufus laughed from above and clamped his massive legs around Antony's face. Rufus laughed again and squirmed around the tongue bathing his butt lips before he pulled Antony back out of his furry crack and forward.

"My balls and cock need some attention, soldier."

Antony gasped in air, shivering with the taste of the centurion's butt hole still on his lips. He was delirious with ecstatic lust. He gazed upward to see that hefty sac dangling just within reach. Antony nuzzled up into it, rubbing his face and cheeks all over the hairy balls to Rufus's low sighs. Then he stretched his jaw wide open and sucked them in both at once, bathing the sac and its precious contents in spit and rolling them around in his mouth. The root of Rufus's rod rubbed against his forehead as he sucked nuts, and suddenly Antony wanted that fat spear in his mouth.

He released the juicy balls and attacked the cock in his face. Reaching upward with mouth gaping open and tongue hanging out like an eager puppy, Antony sucked and licked the length of the giant cock. Rufus laughed contentedly, his thighs pressing into Antony's chest as he rubbed his big meat all over Antony's face and head.

Antony felt the shaft with his lips and tongue. It was huge. How could he get that monster meat in his mouth? He would try, though! A soldier of Rome, he did not know failure. The heat of the shaft pulsed along his open mouth and lips. He moved higher, with those big hands on his shoulders pulling him toward the bobbing head. Suddenly the slippery cap was sliding over his lips. He opened wide, practically dislocating his jaws as he sucked the thing in.

"Very nice. Few can take that big cock down their throats. Bob on it, soldier, and imagine how it is going to feel tearing into your sweet asshole."

The blond soldier gurgled over the fat meat and imagined it riding up into his tender anus. His butt hole quivered nervously, but a shiver of anticipation opened it up and he leaned into Rufus's waist and swallowed half the heroic pole in a mighty gulp. He slammed his cock deep into Milo's ass, the soldier beneath him moaning nonstop at the rough fuck he was enjoying.

"Time to fuck. I'll grease up your hole good first, Antony, but then you're going to have to relax that sphincter or you'll be torn in half."

The centurion's words sent a wave of delicious fear vibrating through Antony's sturdy body. It was the same thrill of terror he experienced in the moments before battle. His entire body quivered and his cock slammed in and out of Milo's tormented asshole. His lips slid off the steaming shank he suckled on, and the furry thighs straddling him stepped over his body.

"Spread them wide. Keep fucking too. I want you to feel this fuck-spear while your cock is wrapped in warm manhole. This will be a treat you won't soon forget," Rufus promised in his deep timbre.

Antony knew the centurion never failed to keep his promises. Antony pressed his body atop the sprawled Milo, pushing the soldier's legs wider apart with his own. The squishy asshole surrounding his cock opened up like a yawning pit and Antony rammed deep inside it and held his cock there. He felt Rufus behind him, and then a pair of fingers, hot and slippery, suddenly plunged far up his own asshole.

"Oh-h-h! Yes, yes, sir!" Antony blurted out, the fingers up his ass twisting and jabbing mercilessly. He needed the lubrication, though. His nervous hole gaped open just as the fingers were yanked out and the head of an enormous poker replaced them. Antony squealed, then clamped his mouth over one of Milo's muscular shoulders as cock began to invade him like a conquering army.

Antony could do nothing but take it as Rufus spread his ass cheeks open with two powerful hands and steadily fed fat cock up his asshole. The pole was well-greased, and Rufus's fingers had coated the insides of Antony's hole, yet the sheer size of the cock was impossible to negate. It slithered deeper and deeper, relentlessly, as the centurion hissed and panted while stabbing ever farther up Antony's guts.

Antony closed his eyes and wailed. The huge cock stretched him deeper and wider. He felt his ass lips quivering around it, his prostate rubbed mercilessly. When he seemed stuffed full, it only kept on coming. Antony knew there was only one thing to do. He arched his back, pulled halfway out of Milo's warm butt oven, and altered the angle of his ass channel. Suddenly, the giant cock slid all the way home in one deep plunge.

Antony wept and laughed at the same time, split in half, full of the biggest cock in the Roman world. That fat thing pulsed and throbbed, hot and hard way up inside him.

"Time to fuck. Hold on, soldiers!"

The centurion's bark brought both soldiers out of their reverie. They had been floating in mutual cock up the ass. Now they were going to get truly fucked, by the one man they knew with absolute certainty meant what he said.

Rufus's raucous laughter rang in their ears as he began to fuck. He pulled halfway out of Antony's tender hole and then rammed right back in. He leaned over the sprawled soldiers, mashing Antony between furry flesh, and jammed his cock up the blond's ass, forcing Antony's cock all the way up Milo's hole. The centurion slammed into the prone soldiers, fucking them all over the rug to the tune of his own wild laughter.

The soldiers moaned and whimpered, lost in the feel of cock possessing them, mashing and massaging their innards. Their own cocks drooled and pulsed. The centurion transformed into a mad bear above them, possessed as surely as their assholes were.

Inevitably, both fucked Romans came first, unable to resist the cocks stuffing them relentlessly and deeply. Milo screamed out as he spewed into the skinned beast beneath his belly. Antony soon repeated that shout as he too erupted, creaming Milo's squirming asshole.

"Good men! Release those armies of come. Let it go while I fill you with my own man-milk! Here it comes! Come—up—the—ass!" Rufus bellowed.

He pulled out just as his come sprayed all over Antony's heaving back and ass. Antony had never felt anything so welcome as the centurion's cock marking his naked body. When the giant man enveloped both well-fucked soldiers in his mighty arms, they nestled contentedly in front of the dying flames of the hearth and fell asleep.

Always after, as his legion marched on, or camped, or fought, Antony kept the memory of that magical night in his heart. The centurion favored him again, and Milo too, but Antony treasured most and would never forget that momentous first fuck of the centurion.

The Gorgeousness of Men's Hair
SHAUN LEVIN

I'm a barber; I cut men's hair and trim their mustaches. I love my job. Everything about men's hair is a wonder to me. I've taken care of thousands of men, and I remember every one. I don't forget a man who's been in the palms of my hands. These men trust me with their bodies. I can tell you this: No one sees them from as close up as I do.

I trim everything: sideburns, mustaches; I trim schoolboy fringes and the beards of Hasids and mullahs; I trim Nigerian students who live in the houses on Mecklenburgh Square; I trim Japanese tourists who stay in the B&B's along Guilford Street. Fathers bring their sons; friends send friends. I trim the hair in the noses of men. I love their noses and their hairy nostrils. I love men who come to me once every two months with thick dark hair in their nostrils, hair that whistles when they breathe, hair that sprouts out like tusks, and they put their heads back expecting to be trimmed.

I'm a good barber. I've been here 15 years; 10 years ago this place became mine. I've been here long enough for men to know me and become regulars; they come to me and to nobody else. "Marco," they say to me, "Marco, you're the only one to do the job." They say they don't want to think what would happen if I had to shut down. They know they're in safe hands. Some have been coming for years.

I've seen men go from manes of thick hair to no hair at all; men who've gone from long black hair to short gray hair; men who at 60 let their hair grow halfway down their backs, and still they come to me. They come for a shampoo, a trim, a clip of the hair in their nostrils. I've seen men who, when they first came in, sat down with naked nostrils, and now they have thick hair in need of regular trimming. There is a wonder in seeing men come of age. The passage of time manifests itself in the hair on the bodies of men. And when they're oblivious to the lush hair growing in their nostrils, I'll say to them: "Would you like me to see to the hair in your nose?"

Men can get embarrassed. They don't like their bodies to be scrutinized. They don't like to be told their bodies have lives of their own, that their skin and orifices are vulnerable and in need of care. And when I mention the hair in their nostrils, some feel a thing of shame has been exposed in them. Then they do what men do when they cannot walk away. They smile. I gently press on the bridge of their nose, spread their nostrils to clip easily at their hair, and they know they're in good hands. They trust me. Who else could they go to? Who else is dedicated to them like I am? Who else would love them even more because of who they are? It's my pleasure to cut the hair in the nostrils of men.

I know all there is to know about men's hair. I know that young men with thick nasal hair are a promise of lush body fur. These men mature into perfection. I cut their hair until they cannot let anyone else care for them. I take care of the hair on their bodies, from head to toe, and devote myself to them until they trust me. They rely on me to trim the hair on their heads, in their nostrils, in their ears. Everywhere. And why me? Because lovers don't touch them the way I do. Lovers don't take the time to care for the hair on their bodies. They don't wash the hair between their thighs, comb the hair on their chests, trim the hair in their ears.

I'm here to love the soft hair in men's ears. To love the brittle hair in men's ears as they get older. To love the spikes that grow back after each trimming. Men who've been coming to me for years will, after I've done their heads, tilt them to the side, ear facing up as if listening for distant noises, and smile. And if they don't know how to ask, if they cannot overcome the shyness about the tufts of hair in their ears, I will hold their ears, one at a time, like an embryo between thumb and forefinger and trim the insides. Soft, brittle, spiky: It will be my pleasure. Everything about men's hair is a pleasure.

I'll tell you one thing: This is about love. This is about my love for the hair in men's ears when it turns from downy blond to coarse brown, when it grows back like needles. This is the hair I will leave until last. The last thing I snip at is the hair in men's ears. That is, if the rest of their body is smooth and they don't need a trim to the hair on their backs, shoulders, chests, around their cocks and arseholes. To these men, men with hair everywhere and in their ears, I will say: "If you were my lover I would lick the hair in your ears. I'd say: Come to the room in the rear and I will lick inside your ears. Let me run my tongue across the bristles, lick the wax that nestles there like amber." I say, I say to those men who've never been here before, men who come at first for a simple short back and sides, I say to them: "I have a room in the rear where I will trim the hair on your body. Come with me."

When they do, when these men come with me to the room in the rear, I lick the hair in their ears, feed on the bushes in the nostrils, crop the fur on their chests, comb the hair that grows like reeds on the banks of the strip between their balls and their arseholes. I will do anything for these men, and all they need to do is lie naked on the leather-padded table before me. I have asked men, men who sit in the barber's chair with their elbows out to rub against my cock, I've asked them if they'd like to come to the room in the rear to have the hair on their bodies trimmed.

And then they keep coming. One man comes from Norway and talks to me about furniture while I trim the sweetcorn fur on his back, crop the mohair that hides the pink-red hole of his ass, comb the bush under his arms. This is the man who *designed* the room in the rear. I was combing around his cock five years ago, holding it out of the way, when he said: This place needs to be empty. No sofas, no coffee tables, no mirrors, no fireplaces, and no armchairs. All these things need to go. Now the room in the rear is simple and red. Walls, leather, fake burning coals for winter, all red, except for the old ceiling fan he installed last summer. The ceiling fan is gold.

Some men come to me like animals, the way an animal returns to the drinking hole that has quenched its thirst. I have men coming to me with hair on every inch of their bodies, and they stand before me naked and expectant. These are the men who book evening-long appointments and tell lies to those who ask where they're off to. Our meetings are secret because they are sacred. One man comes from Rome in his frock, another from Beirut, a general in the Lebanese army. These men are taken into the room in the rear to be cared for. I close the shop, take them into the room, and say: "Make yourself comfortable."

Sometimes I will watch them undress. Sometimes, when they are familiar to me, I will watch them reveal their bodies, knowing what awaits me, and still I will be surprised at the wonder of their naked bodies, still be in awe of the way hair curls from their armpits; the way hair grows thick between their thighs; the way hair spreads down the bridge of their feet to their toenails. I love the way hair grows softer over muscle, and on the inside of arms, and on the stomach. Everything is a delight to comb and trim and care for.

And if they are strangers, if this is their initiation and they are uncertain how to undress before me, I will say: "Let me help you with your clothes. Let me show you how to be naked before the one who adores you. This is how to be naked." I will face them, like I have for years, and help them lift the Vatican robes above their heads, unbutton olive-green uniforms or three-piece suits. I will brush the hair on their shoulders and their chests. I will smooth the hair on their stomachs and at the base of their cocks. I will smile, and they will lie naked on the padded table, ready to be cared for.

Have you smelled the leather on the padded table? It was taken from two old barber chairs. This place has been a barbershop for over a century. This red leather has been preserved with Brylcreem and Old Spice. Men come to smell it. They come because they smell beer shampoo and because I have condoms for sale at the counter. This is not a brothel with bowls of free condoms lying around. I'm a barber, not a whore. What men do while I snip at the hair in their nostrils or trim the hairs around their arseholes is their own business.

Let's get something straight. The hairless '90s are none of my business. If men want to turn their bodies into waxed legs and endure the cruel pain of sugar, it's none of my business. That is not my business. My business is with men who want the hair on their bodies to be nurtured, looked after, and adored. These men stand before me and they are noble stallions, a breed unto themselves. They know they're adored. This isn't about sex. This is about the gorgeousness of men's hair. These men are the true Dionysians. The Bacchae and the satyrs.

This is a praise song to the gorgeousness of men's hair. This is not about sex. When men are being taken care of they don't mind who touches them. When men are adored they forget who they are.

Women know this; they use it to kill men. Samson sleeps between his lover's thighs while she snips at his locks. And then, poor Samson, his head hacked of hair in the days when hair equaled power, poor Samson crumbles with the Philistines. And mad-eyed Judith. What about her? Swinging Holafernes's head like a handbag before she plops it on a platter in a pool of its own blood. Don't tell me you need more proof than that. Women only kill the men who love them. Those who can bear the difference relish the hair on men's bodies. And men? What about the men who love men? Aren't they the ones who've turned the '90s into a decade of hairlessness? And I'll tell you why. They too cannot bear difference. They cannot bear to be so different from women and so similar to aging heterosexuals.

I worship difference. You want to know who fucks me? Who fucks the barber who bathes in the hair from the bodies of men? I'll tell you who fucks me. Every man who lies before me on the bed in the red room in the rear fucks me. Any man who comes to me and pays me to take care of his hair, he will be the one who fucks me. I am devoted to these men and they will fuck me if they wish. I am a barber, and I am here to serve. I am not a whore. I am in love. Constantly.

And what's in it for me? What do I get in return? I get to take care of men. I get to trim the hair in their nostrils, in their ears, around their arseholes, on their balls, between their thighs, at the base of their cocks, under their armpits, across their chests, over their shoulders, down their backs. I cut men's hair. It's my living and my life. I'm not mad. I know what I'm doing. I haven't stuffed pillows or made pincushions from the hair I have trimmed. I haven't kept hair in bags or glass jars, but I have bathed in armfuls of fur and covered myself in a man's hair while he fucked me.

And who taught me? Who taught me to cut men's hair? Who introduced me to the world of men's hair? Let me ask you this: Who taught you to walk? Who taught you to sing? Who showed you the worlds you discovered on your own? I'm a barber, like my father and like his father. This is all I know. This is where I was born. This is where I sat, dribbling, watching two generations at work until the old man died and my father went to live in a commune in Devon. This is what the '90s have offered the hard-working classes. Everyone gets to embark on a spiritual journey. And I get to inherit a barbershop.

If you look in from the street you'll see I've changed nothing. What you see is how it's always been. This barbershop smells of loyal aftershave and hair oil. By the sink there's a glass jar with balls of white cotton wool to wet the napes of men's necks before they're shaved. The walls have the original wood paneling, the mirrors are still from basin to ceiling, the magazines are on the low table while you wait. This is, and always has been, a respectable establishment. There are men who drank grappa with my grandfather, who were here at my birth, who enjoy my touch because they trust the generations I carry in my flesh. I will do anything for them.

What I will not do is give pain; this is not a torture chamber. I don't care if a hundred years ago barbers were extractors of teeth.

I will not pluck or wax or depilate; I will stroke and caress. Trim, crop, clip, comb, and snip. I will brush. I will kneel down to smooth out the hair on your chest. I will watch over you as you lie on your back; I will ease your legs open to trim the thick hair on your inner thighs. I will hold your cock to the side as I clip your pubic hair. And if you want to put your fist around your cock while I'm combing your balls, while I'm trimming their hairs to a soft fluff, that is up to you.

I have heeded the words of my father: Find something you love, son, and do it often; keep noticing what you love to avoid a life of regret. When they gave my father's cancer six months to kill him, he took everything he desired and went to live close to the soil. Now he sends me bell peppers in five colors and tells me to cut down on the spinach if I want to love longer. "Give up raw button mushrooms," he tells me. "But most of all, son," he says, "devote yourself to what you love." And I do. I have always loved men's hair. I have always noticed the gorgeousness of the hair on the bodies of men. I have my father to thank for that.

My father's body led me to this. His work and his flesh. Lathering our bodies in the bath; me a baby splashing between his legs, held against the hair on his skin. And older, a little older, facing each other—him sitting so we're chest to chest—I see what I am not and learn that difference is the face of love. I learn that devotion is the way to possess what is before you. Kneel before the Lord and he is yours. Don't attempt to be reborn into what you are not. To become the object of desire is to be left without anyone to love. And even later, when I'm strong enough to stand on my own two feet, my face level with my father's hips, he lets me lather him from stomach to shin.

Don't misinterpret. Just because the bathtub was the birthplace of passion doesn't mean my desire is distorted. When I was old enough to be in the bath alone, old enough to play with rubber ducks and battleships, my father would read to me from the Bible, dry me at the end of chapters, wrap me in red towels, then I'd sit on the toilet seat while he added hot water to the tub. He'd lie there for hours, singing, and in later years when they gave him his dead-line, he'd read Wordsworth and Ginsberg to my stepmother or lis-ten to her, naked on the bath mat, read letters from their guru in Devon. Their flesh has branded me with the choices I'll make until I die. My burden is their list of priorities. It's up to me to keep let-ting go.

Amongst the men who come to me I have my favorites, and they know who they are. I say to these men: "Let me take care of you. I expect nothing. I am at your service." Amongst these favorites I have my favorites; these men love to fuck. They will, if you adore them, if you touch their bodies as you would the bodies of gods, they will fuck you for the offerings you place at their feet. This is not just about sex. I am a barber. I am a professional. This is more than sex.

You can't be close to the bodies of men without knowing who they are. You can't have a man's cock in your hand without being given his story. Each story repeats the original one planted in you. Each story you encounter—if you stop relying on surprises—reproduces and rephrases the glory of the original. Each story is a reincarnation of the first until it disappears into the light. Some stories are echoes of Genesis; others are so close they will fill you with the dread and excitement of death.

There is one favorite amongst my favorites. The chosen peo-ple have their chosen one. He is the prophet. Of all the men who come to me, he is my favorite. This is George, my farmer-archi-tect from just outside Athens. George, who brings me bunches of sage and oregano flowers from his garden. George, whom I've known since I was a boy, when he'd come to my father for a hair-cut. See him walk down Marchmont Street, a trail of scented herbs in his wake, beads of sweat on his forehead and in his mus-tache, a growing wetness in his armpits. Nothing changes in the world of fantasy and expectation, except to elaborate and expand. I have been waiting for George, and the memories in my skin rise to meet him.

I am at the door alone—customers gone, lights off—and

George walks in, grinning. We're old friends, and we hug, our palms pressing into each other's backs. His cotton shirt under his jacket sliding over his skin, fabric rustling against the lush fur and soaking up sweat. "How's your father," he wants to know, walking with his arm around my shoulder to the room in the rear, the damp smell of his armpit slouching up my neck and over my face. "He's fine," I say, and help George off with his jacket. Make yourself comfortable. George and I have learned to do without the pretense of coffee and trust-building small talk; we're not here to tell word stories. He leans against the table and takes off his shoes, then his trousers, his socks, boxer shorts, then airs his cock, which glistens with sweat and is almost hard. George peels the sweaty base from against his balls, pulls at his foreskin, unbuttons his shirt, unwraps his chest and shoulders. This is George before me. Naked. And I can forget who I am.

"Tidy me up, Marco, my friend."

And his flesh opens to welcome me.

I brush the hair on his shoulders with my fingers, like a mother will do to the fringe of her son as he walks off the football field, sweating. I loosen his shoulder-hair, flattened by his shirt and jacket. His eyes are muddy pools beneath an undergrowth of eyebrows. The heat and sweat from his legs and his cock rise up through the matted fur on his stomach and chest. I will be honest with you; I have nothing to hide. I can smell the shit from someone else's arse on George's cock. I know this for a fact: George fucks his boyfriend at the airport before he comes to London.

But when he's here he comes to me first, and often, like today, straight from the airport, the smell of his lover's arse on his cock, dry come on his chest. Did the father not comfort the prodigal son? How can the son then refuse the body of the father? Shem's eyes were riveted to his father's drunken cock. Come, George, let me smooth the hair around your nipples, like this, and stroke your arms, and turn you to face the table. This is Adam and Eve and the soft black body hair of God Almighty. This is the holy altar, the godhead. This is the hairiest-of-all George: thick hair, thick flesh, and a cock so thick you'd think he was twins. This is not just about sex. This is what I do. I am a barber. Look it up. I care for the hair on the bodies of men.

Warm shoulders under my palms as I ease George onto his stomach. I will start at his arsehole and work my way up to his neck. Any man who comes to me will need to bare his arsehole, that hairless bud on the bodies of men. You've read your Swift. You know what makes the Yahoos special: Hair from head to toe, except for the smooth, delicate ring of their bumhole. This is where fantasy is born, between arsehole and nostril. The hair on George's head is not part of this, neither that on his legs, though they are perfect, coated with thick soft black hair and curls to touch, to imagine untreated wool.

"I have missed you, George."

He lifts his arse and slides up onto all fours. My palms on the cheeks of his arse, his thighs wide enough for me to reach the thick hair on the slopes that run down to his arsehole, and I want to say, "George, I could stand like this forever with my hands on the mounds of your arse, my tongue this close to that coat of thick fur. I will lick the flecks of shit from your crack." But I am a barber, and my job is to trim and clip. George comes to me because no man can look after him the way I do. There is no one before whom he will get down on all fours to be scrutinized, to have his arsehole— lush with fur and smelling of shit—handled and parted and fingered with care.

"Three month now," George says. "That feel good, my friend."

I am combing the hair on his arse with my fingers. I am trimming the fur that shelters his arsehole, that covers his arse cheeks, that gathers like moss at the base of his spine. Snipping hairs with flakes of dry shit, then brushing them onto the floor, cleaning around his arsehole with balls of perfumed cotton wool. George on all fours is a call to prayer, an echo of the humility of Christ. I am the whore at his feet, here to wash every pore and hair on his skin. Everything is egg-shaped. From behind, his body is a series of ovals:

the soles of his feet, the cheeks of his arse, the two halves of his back.

"Do my balls," he says.

Closer, the flesh cradling his balls is a stork's blanket. I only use metaphors to keep myself from disappearing into the thing itself. The thick dark hair of his scrotum brushes against my nose, his smell keeps my eyes shut. This is the vision by which I am blessed. This is my burning bush, my mountain of the Ten Commandments. George from behind on his hands and knees—hairy arsehole newly trimmed, furry balls dangling like the essence of goodness—is a sheer fucking delight.

If only fingers were scissors. If only flesh was as sharp as steel. If only George would let me, I would trim the hair on his balls with my teeth. In the silence of the ritual, going over the hairs on George's balls, my face up against his arsehole, smelling perfumed skin and traces of morning shit, I am the enlightened believer, the doubting Christian, the pagan rabbi; every thought is a blessing. With the tip of my silver scissors, the ones handed down from before my grandfather, sharpened and oiled and tuned like a harp, I snip, I snip, I snip. Thank God for this bounty of fur; without it, the end would be imaginable from the outset. I am at the beginning and I have nowhere else to go.

"Touch them," he says. "Touch them with me, my friend."

"Oh, George."

"Feel, Marco," he says. "Feel how smooth my arsehole, my balls."

And I want to say, "George, don't you know? Don't you know by now it's the hair I love, not its absence. When I touch your hair like this, when I run the tips of my fingers over the trimmed hair around your arsehole, across your balls, it's the memory of the thick fur that I love. The memory of hair as thick as the abundance on your shoulders, the lush mound at the foot of your cock, the mat on your chest that protects your heart from damage. George," I want to say, "I wouldn't be doing this if it were irrevocable."

I stroke his back as he lowers himself onto his front, my other hand on his cock to make sure it lies flat against his stomach. His body is before me, more than six feet of muscled flesh and hair. I comb and crop to the music of scissors, rising with the waves of hair that grow away from his spine, mats of hair parted by vertebrae where no hair can grow. The spine is the one part of his body unguarded by fur. The spine and the palms of his hands and the soles of his feet. And his cock. This is where the heart manifests itself on his skin.

Can I bear to notice every hair and every clearing on George's body? Can I bear to arrest time and see my fingers work like a tongue in the hair at the base of his cock and across his chest? My body is a tongue lapping at George like the wafer of Christ; his hair sticks to the roof of my mouth. Can I bear to tell you all this? Can I bear to be watched as I disappear?

Stop.

Share something with me.

I don't want to feel ashamed of myself. Don't sit there untouched. Don't let me kneel here, every orifice in my body agape, and then have you smile, patronizing me. Love me for what I love. Love me so that I can tell you everything. Everything. Everything. Can I tell you exactly what George does to me once I've trimmed his body, three hours after the moment of undressing?

Now he offers the other side of himself. This is his cock, with veins the color of olive oil; these are the pubes I have mentioned; this is the stomach, these are the hairs of his chest that grow tougher with each visit. What began as a thread has become the ropes of a ship. When he comes next time, all this will be thicker, coarser. I need to believe in a next time. I need to believe each visit is a prelude to its successor. Everything is the past and the future and now we are so close to the end. I have trimmed the hairs on his arsehole, I have trimmed his back and his shoulders; now his stomach is before me, a crater and a slope, an exposure as trusting and as threatening as his arsehole. George will not tolerate violation; he is there to be worshiped. His pubes must be trimmed to within an inch of his cock, his stomach and chest hair clipped to match his back. We are almost done now.

I am beginning to fade; I am losing my grip on the present.

"Now," George says.

"Yes, George," I say, and watch as he lifts his arms, palms open like a Mohammedan facing Mecca, to put his hands behind his head. How lush the hair in these caverns, pearls of sweat clinging to clumps of hair thicker than the fur at the base of his neck, denser than the hair that is the greatest treat and the closest to the place of birth. I pat the sweat from his armpits with cotton wool, as you would a wound before the bandage, and because his eyes are closed and because he is smiling, I dab his sweat behind my ears.

When the hunting dogs come sniffing, they will take me for George.

"George?"

"Mm?" he says, reluctant, his eyes still closed, his breathing calm and deep.

"Can I lick now?"

"Mm?"

"Can I lick now, George?" I say. "Let me lick your armpits."

Which is when he opens his eyes to look at me, to put a hand behind my neck, to draw my mouth to his armpit. George watches me, watches like mothers watch babies drink the milk from their nipples, as their thighs open in memory. I drink and I nibble, George's hand resting firmly on my head, then he lifts me by my hair and moves me to his other armpit. He is not laughing. My tongue in his armpit does not tickle. George trusts like a cat trusts, untroubled by questions of loyalty, groaning to himself until I am ready to trim the hair in his arms.

"Finish soon, Marco," George says.

"I will," I say. "I will, George."

I know that the body can bear only so much attention before it erupts. And how much more will I be able to bear before I turn into a joke? How much longer before they look and say, "Marco, what the fuck are you doing, mate? You're ridiculous." But when George holds onto my wrist and leads my hand to his cock, my touchstone, nothing else matters. The small scissors from the side of the table and I trim the bush that fans open as George puts his hands behind his head, watches me from the corner of his eyes, eager to fling me across the padded table and fuck me. It's been like this for years; there is a right and a wrong way. Nothing must be rushed.

We choose which gods to worship; it's their job to comply. Not everybody knows this.

It is autumn outside. No rain, but the cold finds its way in. The electric coals are burning, their light reflected off the walls. This room is earth, blood, fire. Everything is food and warmth and unquestioning care, and I'm sweating like a pig. My whole body could be oil the way my cock slides against my thigh. But I will not undress while trimming the hair on the bodies of men. This is George's armpit, its sweat drying on my lips. This is the hair in George's armpit I'm snipping, not like Delilah to kill, not to kill, not to belittle, not, like her, to take-take-take; I am here devoted to the gorgeousness of his hair.

I have slipped off my shoes, and I am in my bare feet, rubbing George's clipped hairs between my toes. He cannot see my cock is hard, my arsehole moist from sweat and longing. He cannot see the sweat on my face mingled with tears. How do I let him know that he is more than just himself in my body? Thank God the flesh gives nothing away. George is safe, smiling at silence, his armpits wide open. Snip. I am letting go. This is my weakness, a gift, a love that drives me to my knees. When a man lays his naked body before me, I bend. When a man invites me to explore and glorify his flesh, I forget who I am. I am there to beautify, to mold and make perfect. I am there to serve and receive. Stick your cock inside me, George. Fuck me soon, George, or there'll be nothing left of me to take you in. Restraint keeps us separate from the gods. Our desire keeps other men mortal.

I kneel before George. Brushing the clipped hair from his armpit, I bring my nose to the birthplace of the divine. No wonder this is where hair begins to grow on the body, to protect and to draw attention to the home of the spirits, the healing powers. I don't care if you want to call them lymph glands. George has an entire day in his armpit: sweat from fucking in the airport toilets, sweat from his journey on the Underground to Marchmont Street, sweat from the heat in this room, from the garlic in last night's meal. Across the dark fields of his shoulders to his neck, my lips are against his stubble.

"Kiss me, George."

"Poor, Marco," he says. "Poor, pretty Marco."

His palms on the back of my head and his mouth is a spring. His fat tongue laps at the insides of my mouth and slides along my gums. My hands rest on his chest, the hairs sprouting out between my fingers. There is one more thing to do before George fucks me: to move my lips from his mouth to his nose; to circle the insides of his nostrils with my tongue; to let him know I have not forgotten. The salt in his nostrils draws out every flavor.

"Enough," George says. "Enough, Marco."

"Wait, George," I say.

But he is grabbing my hair and whacking my cheek against the mattress—the leather is warm, damp from his sweat—and pressing his elbows into my back. George clenches his teeth and growls at me.

"Take them off," he says.

"George," I say.

"Take them off, Marco," he says.

There is no time to prepare, no time to relax my arsehole; his cock is hard against my crack; I think he might come before he's inside me. This is not the first time we have ended in anger, George forcing his way into me.

"Why, Marco?" he says. "Why you must to do this?"

"Fuck me, George."

I am so wide open now he must press my body against the padded table to stop me from collapsing. I don't want to hold on to anything. I don't want these thoughts. I don't want this to keep repeating itself. If only I could always be filled like this. If only I could always have a body pressing against me, gripping me to it.

But how angry the deities get when the mortals submit. Look how furious he is at being created, how envious to have the act of creation taken from him. All he's expected to do is fuck, to put more and more inside me, to give me what he is to make my own. *Trust me, George, I can hold onto entire worlds.*

Sweat sticks hair to our skin. George clamps me from behind and breathes hot air into my ears. I want to sob. I want to stay curled up forever. And I know—as he pulls out of me and I turn to lick the sweat from his cheeks and forehead, and I kiss him, and our bodies are covered in his hair—I know I will sleep the night on the floor. I will sleep like this until I have stopped disappearing. George pulls away, ignoring my cock, unconcerned about kisses. I am no longer part of his body. I watch him in the glass shower, spikes of water sketching charcoal patterns on his body. I will not mention his ears. I will let the hairs in his ears grow until they are footpaths to the ground. And then, when they are long enough, I will climb them like the angel did at the end of his wrestling match with Jacob, I will climb them until I am inside him, back in the body from which I have sprung.

Mass Tourism

SIMON SHEPPARD

Nope, he hadn't expected the action at the Colombo train station. He'd been waiting for the train—which was, unsurprisingly for Sri Lanka Railways, late as fuck—when he went to take a piss. The men's room stank, of course. Public bathrooms in South Asia always stank; he'd quickly learned to breathe through his mouth.

The place was smallish, tiled, the floor flooded. Some skinny old guy was washing his feet from a tub-type thing in the center of the room, splashing everywhere, and Marc winced as the filthy water on the floor splattered his sandals-clad feet. Par for the course. Ick.

There were eight or nine urinals ranged around two walls, all but one of them occupied. The universal language of tearoom cruising, restroom Esperanto: nobody zipping up and moving off, instead hands in motion, heads swiveling, eyes cast diagonally down toward other men's dicks. "We are everywhere" and all that. Well, maybe not "we." Marc understood enough about cross-cultural hoo-ha to know that some, maybe most of these men didn't necessarily think of themselves as "gay," much less "queer." Maybe some were married, on their way home to the wife and kids. Maybe some really were straight, just exhibitionists who got off beating the meat where other guys could see. Whatever. He still had to take a pee.

Eight pairs of eyes following his progress, he walked to the tiled pissoir. On one side, a cute 20-ish boy with very dark skin. On the other, a middle-aged man he never would have clocked, straight-looking as hell, caramel-colored face, mustache, kinda tough. Both had their dicks out, both stroking away at hard meat. Marc started to piss, but his hardening cock made things difficult. He gave himself a couple of tentative strokes. His dick, unsurprisingly for someone who hadn't gotten laid since he left New York nearly three weeks ago, got hard in a jiffy. He looked over at the boy to his left, who remained staring straight ahead, dark shaft gripped tightly in his hand. His other neighbor, the middle-aged man, was more forthcoming. He looked at Marc's hard-on, then up at his face, then down to his cock again. Then he smiled, white teeth bright beneath dark mustache.

Marc felt uneasily thrilled at being an object of desire. It wasn't that familiar a feeling for him; he'd always been a big guy, ever since he could remember. He'd been a cute fat boy with an unruly shock of blond hair, the kind of kid who was a moving target for pinches on the cheek from old ladies wearing too much perfume. He was a less cute teenager, miserably closeted and dateless. It wasn't till he'd hit his early 20s that he came out and accepted himself, kind of. He still had his belly, and in the years since he'd been a cute kid, his tummy had acquired a dense covering of blond fur. He hated it.

But Liam didn't hate it. OK, Liam was, like Marc, on the heavy side himself, and Marc had found him wildly attractive. Still, they'd been in love with each other, more or less, so when Liam lustfully stroked Marc's belly, rubbed his cheek against it on the way to giving him head, it had been somehow suspect. Liam had persisted in calling him "sexy" and "hot," but Marc never trusted his judgment. It was as if Liam had had an ulterior motive, one that Marc had been too obtuse to puzzle out.

"Stop putting yourself down," Liam had said to him more than a few times, but somehow Marc never could. He'd wanted to see himself through his boyfriend's eyes, or so he believed, but every time he looked in a mirror, he winced. Finally, just months before he left for Sri Lanka, Liam got him a copy of a book, *Bears on Bears,* in hopes of improving his self-image. Marc obliged him by growing a beard, and Liam responded with gifts of flannel shirts and blue jeans. Then Marc got his job with WholeWorld Guidebooks, and he and Liam agreed to put their relationship on hiatus. When he left for Sri Lanka, though, he took his beard and bearish wardrobe along—strange as it seemed, the bear thing actually did make him feel better about himself. Not great but better. He hadn't really thought about what he'd do with flannel shirts in 90-degree heat.

As he stood there in the railway restroom, cock in hand, Marc became increasingly uneasy. It wasn't just that he was supposed to be researching restaurants and hotels, not cocks and balls. It wasn't even his vulnerability as a foreigner—Lord knows that if the cops were going to bust a scene as blatant as this one, they'd have done it long ago. It was, he realized, that what was happening was all come-on and no payoff, all sizzle and no steak. Or, rather, no rice and curry. And, he reminded himself, he had a train to catch.

He zipped up and went back to the crowded platform. The train for Nuwara Eliya still hadn't arrived. There was only one smallish free spot on the benches alongside the track. Rather than sit down, he put his backpack there—no sense getting the bottom dirty by putting it on the concrete platform—and stood alongside. He was dying for a cup of tea, but he figured if he went to fetch one at the station canteen, the train would choose that exact moment to show up, and any hope he had of grabbing a seat would be gone.

It was the smile that first got his attention. A young man sitting on a bench on the opposite platform—a handsome young man—was smiling. A beautiful smile, in his direction, though not directly at him. No, wait, it *was* at him. The dark-skinned man wore blue jeans, a button-up white shirt with shades hanging from the neck, had a shock of glossy black hair, a neat little goatee, wide dark-rimmed eyes, and he was smiling. Smiling directly at Marc. At Marc.

Marc smiled back.

The young man shifted in the bench, maybe thrusting his crotch out just a tad, and raised his hand in a half-wave. Marc nodded back. His cock, unsurprisingly, began to swell. The young man gestured. Huh? Marc gestured back. This time it was unmistakable: The handsome young man was gesturing him over. Marc hesitated for perhaps a tenth of a second, then swung his backpack over his shoulder and headed toward the front of the station, en route to the adjoining track, the platform where the man was.

He walked through the crowded station, tense about ambiguity. Even the best of guidebooks, even the one he was writing—and the WholeWorld Guides always did have a section titled "For Gay and Lesbian Travelers"—didn't cover cross-cultural cruising. He thought back to the week before, when he'd been in Sigiriya. He'd finished up checking out nearly a dozen hotels and had settled into the place he was staying, a rustic place whose proprietor, to Marc's delight, had a pet mongoose. He'd finished an early dinner—the inevitable, ubiquitous rice and curry, but a good one—and decided to explore a path that, he was told, led through the fields to a nearby lake. He was heading down a little dirt road beside a row of huts when he realized he was being followed. At first he was tense about being robbed. Though farmers and kids were coming and going, who knew what could happen, even in plain view? He stopped in his tracks, and his pursuer did too, maybe 15 feet behind. Marc took a closer look.

The guy was a Tamil, maybe late teens, early 20s: a skinny, dark little guy wearing nothing but a pair of raggedy shorts. Black hair covered his legs and chest, and he was hellaciously cute. He was also smiling, beaming really, at Marc. Back in the States that would be a cruise for sure. Here, it could mean anything from "Hey big guy, I want your dick" to "What an odd and amusing foreigner you are." Who the hell could tell?

The two of them stood there in a field in Sri Lanka for a longish time, until Marc took a couple of steps forward and the boy responded in kind. They were a just a few feet from each other.

"Hello," Marc said. He'd forgotten the Sinhalese word.

"Hello," said the boy.

"How are you?"

Uncomprehending stare.

"What is your name?"

"No English."

A little girl walked past them, stared, and giggled. The boy said something to her and she continued on her way.

"Your sister?" Marc asked, knowing full well it would be futile. He scrutinized his new friend. The boy was, like most Sri Lankans, slightly built. As he frequently had for the past two weeks, Marc felt very tall, very heavy, and very blond.

"You're a cutie-pie, aren't you?" The wiry boy smiled wider, maybe responding to the tone of Marc's voice. He reached down and fiddled with his crotch for a second, though to what aim, Marc couldn't tell. Maybe he was adjusting a hard-on, maybe he just itched. In any case, the tattered shorts were too baggy to give a clue. There was, however, a dark stain right at crotch level. Precome? Pee? Something quite else? It was all very mysterious. He wished he knew the Sinhalese for "I will give you the best blow job you've ever had," but he still couldn't even remember how to say "hello." There was only one thing to do. He screwed up his courage and touched the boy, placing his hand on a dark, thin shoulder. Not a flinch, so he let his hand trail downward, over a thicket of dark hair, heading for a nipple.

The boy said something indistinct. It might have been "no," it might not. Marc jerked his pale hand away, feeling immediately ashamed. His chagrin was probably overblown, since the boy might in fact have been coming on to him, though maybe he hadn't been. Anyway, the spell, such as it was, had been broken. The boy half turned away.

"Goodbye," Marc said. The boy wordlessly continued on his way. The lake, when Marc reached it, had been beautiful in the gathering gloom.

The young man on the station platform invited him to his place, and Marc figured he could always take another train. They left the station and caught a *tuk-tuk* toward the wealthy district of Cinnamon Gardens. As they rode through the crowded streets, the young man explained, in perfect English, that his parents were on vacation on the south coast, in Bentota, and he'd been catching a train to join them.

The young man, Ramesh, asked Marc about the purpose of his visit. When Marc said that he was writing a travel guide, Ramesh seemed fascinated.

"It's actually less interesting than it sounds," Marc said.

The young man's house was luxurious, worlds away from the shabby farmers' huts at Sigirya. Once they were in his bedroom, the boy seemed a bit awkward, though no more awkward than Marc himself. But cock sucking, it turned out, was a universal language, and soon handsome Ramesh's handsome, dark cock was hard in Marc's mouth.

His dick still between the kneeling American's lips, Ramesh took off his shirt. Marc's hands traveled upward over the young man's lean, hairy torso.

"Take your clothes off," Ramesh said, gently pushing Marc off his cock. "I hardly ever have sex with white guys."

I'm not exotic, Marc wanted to say, *just big.* But it wasn't the sort of thing to say under the circumstances. He stood up and reluctantly took off his shirt.

"Mmm," Ramesh said, "hair on your shoulders. Very nice."

Well, whatever you say.

The handsome Sri Lankan ran his hand over Marc's hard crotch. "Yes, nice," he said. He squeezed harder. "Nice." He unbuckled Marc's belt, unzipped the fly, and slid Marc's shorts partway down the American's beefy thighs. A stain of precome spread across the front of Marc's boxer briefs.

Ramesh smiled and slid his hands over Marc's bulky torso, bending over to take one of the blond's big nipples in his mouth as he stepped out of his own jeans. Then he dropped to his knees and nestled his face against Marc's damp crotch, reaching around to the blond's big butt, pulling down the back of the boxer briefs, grabbing hold of Marc's fleshy, furry ass.

"Oh, fuck!" Marc said. He'd been so horny for so long that he was afraid he'd shoot off in his underwear. Ramesh, still kneeling, pulled down Marc's undershorts, and Marc's prick, as chubby as the rest of him, sprang forth. Ramesh nestled against it, face in the blond bush of pubic hair. He wrapped his arms around Marc's big waist and licked the blond's pale cock head. And then it happened. Marc, unable to restrain himself, shot off, strands of come falling on Ramesh's glossy dark hair, on his shoulders, his goatee, his handsome face. Everywhere.

"Sorry," Marc said. "Sorry sorry sorry."

Ramesh looked up and smiled. "I'll take it as a compliment," he said, "especially coming from a man of the world like you."

Marc reached down to pull up his half-mast shorts.

"Stay naked and we can sit around for a while," Ramesh said. "Listen, I'd like to fuck you, if that's all right. Or you can fuck me."

Marc was an eager bottom who knew an irresistible offer when he heard one. He shuffled over to the bed, sat down, and pulled his clothes off.

"Can I make you some tea?" Ramesh asked.

So they lay around, drinking tea and talking about their lives, until the touch of the Sri Lankan's hand made Marc's cock hard again. Then Ramesh reached into his bedside table, pulled out a rubber—did his folks know he kept condoms?—and unrolled it over his stiff, dark cock.

"You want me on my back?" Marc asked.

"I'd rather I lie back and you ride me," Ramesh said. "I want to feel your weight on me."

So Ramesh lay back on starched white sheets as Marc straddled him and guided the young man's cock toward his hole. Just the touch of the lubed-up dick head sent a delighted shiver up Marc's spine. He relaxed, sat back, and felt foreign dick inside him. Except, of course, that *he* was the foreigner.

145

Ramesh was a responsive lover, not just lying there but using his hands on Marc's meaty, furry chest, rubbing Marc's belly, a dreamy look on his face. Marc felt like he was being petted. It felt great.

Unsure of whether it would be all right, Marc leaned over to kiss the dark man's lips. It was just fine. Ramesh kissed back hard, tongue on tongue, and thrust upward into Marc's butt. He knew just where to hit; clearly, he'd had more than a little experience. If Marc were to write him up for the guidebook, Ramesh would get the highest rating.

The lingering kiss at an end, Marc sat back up and, his hand's on Ramesh's hairy chest, rode the dick inside him till the dreamy look on Ramesh's face turned into something more wide-eyed, more urgent. They were both dripping with sweat. Marc reached down for his own husky, throbbing dick, gave it a few desperate strokes, and shot off all over Ramesh, just as the Sri Lankan pounded his own orgasm home.

As they lay, wiped up, in post-sex closeness, Ramesh, his head nuzzling Marc's furry chest, said, "You can stay the night if you want. My parents won't be back for days. I'll phone them, tell them I'll be there tomorrow."

"That's sweet," said Marc, and it really was. The young man was sweet. "But I have work to get done in the hill country. I really should get going. Maybe when I get back to Colombo…"

"Maybe," said Ramesh. Distances.

When Marc, toting his backpack, was heading out the door, Ramesh asked, "You need help getting back to the station?"

"No, that's fine."

"If you can wait a little while, I'll go with you."

"No, that's fine, Ramesh. Thanks." What was it? Why did Marc still distrust, at least a little bit, anyone who found him hot?

Ramesh grabbed Marc around his sizable waist and kissed him gently on the lips. "I'll look for a copy of your book," he said.

"Thanks."

"You'll remember me?" It was an odd question, poignant, real.

"Yeah, I will," Marc said.

And he would remember. He was taking notes.

velvety revolution
LOUIS ANTHES

The Story, which the author said Shakespeare would have laughed at, used too many sheets of acid-free paper. The Writer, Tim Haddock, who worked for the government from timetotime, abandoned all sense of economy, concision, brevity—according to the unfriendlyreviews. The Publisher, who agreed to promote the book, had just declared chaptereleven, so the infrastructure for a particularly cumbersome grammar of experimental English utterances fellapart. If you ask me, it was a quiet, velvety revolution in the life of a man for whom a future of technicalwriting beckoned as he haplessly cruised a secluded beach.

"I'm over here!" shouted the would-be novelist's reclined boy-toy, peering over secondhand Foster Grants. "You're late."

"How can you read through your mother's glasses?" Tim asked, standing armscrossed nerdlike above two Barbiegirl beachtowels.

No answer.

"So?"

"Well, ah, I'm on chapter five. Pity."

"And?"

"Ya know, ah, the dialogue... The whole thing's queer." The young man sniffled and hid behind his sunglasses. "Where did you come up with that?"

"It's reversed."

"Oh, reversed. I see."

"Does that change it for you, Nick?"

"What, Tim?"

"The whole thing. I mean, is it sort of different now that I told you the process?"

"The process, right." Nick put on more cooking oil, unsparingly. "No, not really."

"No or not really?"

"The latter, I guess."

Tim looked up and away and toward the foamyshore. "Right."

"OK, now that I think about it, it's a no."

"What's a no?" probed Tim, interested that his friend was interested, at least intermittently.

"The process."

"The process is a no?"

Nick cackled. "No, silly," he said, tossing sand at his friend's hairylegs. "I mean the process you revealed hasn't changed my feelings about the dialogue."

"So, it's good?" pushed Tim, dropping his cellphone on the Barbietowel already laidout for him.

"I said 'odd,' not 'good.'"

"No, you said 'queer,' not 'odd.'"

"Suppose so."

"You did," growled Tim. "What makes it so?"

"Not process."

"Mere result, then?"

Turning to sun his postpubescent bony shoulders, Nick mumbled, "Huh-huh."

"The mere result is what makes it so?"

"It's what makes it queer, as you said—"

"No, you said that."

Nick laydown his bleachblond head, alongside Barbie's. "I did, sorry."

"Don't you get the depth?" Tim earnestly inquired, wincing as his tone ascended.

"Honey, still waters run deep, but you're running in circles." Tim turned the reddestred. "C'mon. Whattaya talking about? Reversed? What's that mean?"

"You sounded like you knew," sighed a disappointed Tim.

"I was trying to get you happy." Two youngchiseledswimmers jogged by in matching tangerineSpeedos. "Twins, yum," Nick confided to Barbie.

"Forget it," Tim barked, fumbling his beachhat, then throwingit on his phone.

"Fine," Nick leakedout, thus saying the mostbitchything probably since they had met, which was one month ago tobeprecise.

If only Nick had been Tim's sugardaddy, as I might have been, or had promised to makehimastar, then it all would have felt like someoneelse's fault, as he removed his Hawaiian swimtrunks and walked away. Instead, Tim combed the wetsand and seaweed, feeling that he had to change, repeating to his nakedself, "The fault lies not in the stars." That was his firstdecision. What he likely never perceived was his seconddecision to go for a skinnydip in the June sea. He probably didn't decide to do that. He just did it.

As he walked, first quickly, then slowly, a fiercestream of his piss hit the surf gently lapping his lowhanging balls. His nipples got erect, and he dove, goatee first, hands joined behind his tailbone. The author, Tim, sank while his body swam freestyle. Two bathers, admiring each other, splashing water between playful gropes, apologized for bumping his trim hips, which kept coolly heading for stillbutdeeper waters. Sealeveled and unraveled, he skimmed the afternoon tide, finally floating backside-up on the wind and waves marinating his wounds. He licked his lips, and from the corner of his smile, he dribbledspit like a child trying to eat a first spoonful.

Quietly approaching Tim's calm body, I trod water just behind his head and steadily began lettingout the beer I had been drinking allday. "Please keep closing your eyes and try not to move," I suggested gently. "Now, can you feel that?"

There was a short pause. "The sudden warmth?" he asked, chuckling.

"Yes?"

"Yes."

"Good. Are you getting relaxed?"

"Yes."

"Very good." I drewcloser, a noselength from his buzzcut, and lowered my voice. "I don't think we know each other."

"Probably not."

"I was watching you earlier. Tim, right? You were...discussing things with a friend."

"Yes."

"Are you unhappy, Tim?"

"Well, I was. Not now." A noisy motorboat momentarily cut him off. "Your voice is nice. It's like the desert."

"Hmmm." I took that as a compliment, especially since there was waterwater everywhere. "Thank you."

"Sure. And you are?" Andyouare. Well, that deserved an answer, but I didn't want to give one, yet.

"Tim, can you just let go, out here, listen to my voice, and forget about everything you left behind, back there?"

He sighed, deeply, and spit some ocean out in an arc to oneside. "Whatever."

"Good." I paused, then repeated, "Good."

"Tell me about your voice."

"The accent?"

"Yes."

I raised my hands and caressed his wet, bushy chest, as my chin droppeddroplets on his forehead. "I'm Corsican, but I learned English in Edinburgh when I was younger. I visit here every summer, so I use my English."

"Huh-huh," Tim purred. "I've never been to France."

"Corsica's not France." A wave rolled him back, toward my

broadshoulders, which yielded as my legs rose beneath his fleshy bottom. "There's no such thing as France." My firm belly pushed his spine upslightly, lifting his hirsute sixpack in the air as his firmpecs trickled water. My feet extended just beyond his, my wrists grazed his fingertips, my nose kissed his scalp. I guessed he was about onehundredeightycentimeters headtotoe. He would have said I was sixfive.

"Your scruff's like velvet," he murmured coyly.

"I keep my beard neat and short, and the sea leaves it supple."

"Tell me about your eyes."

"I've been told they're like black pills floating on blue pools." He smiled. I added, "I guess your mistress's eyes are nothing like the sun." He smiledevenbigger.

"What color are her lips?"

I protested, "*His* lips. They're not coral, like yours," I halfjested, yearning to savor his rubyred seafood on mytongue. "Stolen from Willie the Shake."

"Indeed. So, what do you do?"

I thoughtabout his question forasecond, hoping he was not going where I thought he mightbe. "I do men," I answered sternly. "And do you know what you do?"

"Not anymore," he said, manifesting vulnerability and honesty.

Myhands folded hisarms across hischest. I movedup his tits, to his neck and backdown his sides, then massaged his shoulders and slowly twisted them, turninghimaround. He saw my face for the firsttime, as we began treading water. I moved in, tilting my head to the left, lipsonhislips, sucking seasalt, moaning deeplyintohisthroat. His toes dangledonmyankles. My arms surrounded his frame like a vise, and, as I exhaled, he tookmyair greedily; as I inhaled, I squeezedharder, blood rushing to his groin. Mouthtomouth and beardtobeard. He giggled. "What is it?" I asked.

"Beach sex never worked for me. I don't think I could take you here." I thought, *You'renottakingme.* He elaborated, "Too much sand."

"True," I admitted. "You asked me what I do. Well, I do it over there," and I pointed toward the shore. "In that condo there, second floor, room 22. There's a job for you. Why not come by?" He stared at the building, and then his eyes drifted to his beachtowel, which was alone.

"Shit, I think Nick took off."

I kept silent, waiting for him to act, but nothinghappened. "So?"

"Let's at least get out. Are you set up close by?"

"Right there," I repointed. "Not far. You'll see me."

"OK," he said, and he began swimming back. His swimstrokes were precise and disciplined. Though I could swim, I could hardly follow his pace, and he got out first. When I arrived, I noticed that where NickandNick'stowel had been were Tim's book and two words scribbled in sand for everyone to see: A BEAR? The questionmark was a curlicue hovering over a sadface circle. Tim bentover to reach for his cellphone, which had been under his abandoned beachhat, and standingup again, he typed some textmessage in about twentyseconds. I wrapped a towel around my waist and slippedon sandals, in a hurryupandwait way. Then, he donned his trunks and walked over.

"My name is Orso. You asked earlier," I said, trying to keep his eye ontarget.

"Orso...interesting name. Hey, look. I think I have to head back," he said calmly. I showed a pokerface.

"Sure."

"I'll take your number, and you can have mine too," he proposed, at least revealing some interest, yet at the sametime, his eyes made me feel studied and secondguessed. His unraveling was unraveling. Maybe he wasn't upforit. "Sorry for the drama," he apologized, as he tookout his phone to punchin digits I spoke. I just memorized his. Afterward, he said, "Well, Orso, maybe later, huh?"

"No problem," I returned, smiling out of half of my mouth. And just as we were about to go our separateways, his phone played a danceclub tune, and he responded dutifully.

"Hello? Yeah. Yeah, I got the message. Wha...? What about those twins? Yeah, he's right here. Ain't saying. So what? I think you're being...are you going to let me finish? You're way off. Maybe. I don't know. No way. What do you want? Fine. Fine. No, you're right. Yeah. Yep. Later." He sighed and looked at the settingsun dominating the horizon. Then, "I think that, ah...I think I need to go grab a drink or something."

My eyebrow arched. "Let me buy you a beer," I offered.

"No, that's OK...aw, I left my wallet at home, 'cause Nick brought the cash."

"It's OK. I invite you for a drink." Tim and I looked at each other for a fewseconds, and then I said, "How about it?"

"Your English is quite good."

"You should hear my Scottish," and we both grinned.

"Lemme grab the towel, book, and hat," he said cataloguingly. He walked over and picked them up, and rereading A BEAR? he moved his foot to quickly erase Nick's message. When he finished, only the sadface remained visible.

"Thing is," he explained, walking closer, "I don't have ID on me, and they card all the time 'round here."

"You?"

"Yeah, I'm 35, but some think less," he stated matteroffactly while putting his hat on.

"Thirty-five, huh. Anyway, I have scotch at my place." And a genuine smile lit my face, since I was only toohappytooblige Tim.

I walked behind Orso to the woodenboards that led up to the condoentrance. He didn't turnaround once, so I stared at his back the wholetime. It was the blackest pelt, sweatbeads pulling fur into parallellines curving away from his spine. *Thirty-fivehuh,* I thought, and wondered what his number was. Fiftymaybe? As we climbed the stairs to the secondfloor, he looked back and smiled in that same halfsmile he made just before Nick called. That sandmessage was really embarrassing, which it was meanttobe of course, though it was in a way Nick had not intended.

"Here we are," Orso said, opening the door to number 22. He walked in first, removed his sandals, and invited me to pour myself a scotch. "Ice?" he asked, moving about his kitchenette.

I answered, "No, thank you. Just straight up."

"There are glasses next to the bottle, by the open window." I walked over and took in the view of the beach slowly emptying of sunsoakers. "Do you think you could pour me one, please?"

"Sure." I had noticed that Orso was watching me when I was arguing with Nick, but I wasn't interested. I had also sensed that he was followingme into the water, which I ignored, thinking that if I swamout far enough, he would backoff. The fact he didn't intrigued me. Also his voice felt warmdrystill.

"Some pretzels? Or do you prefer chips?"

"No, pretzels are fine. Thanks." And as he approached me at the window, I handed him his drink. "Here."

"Thank you. A double," he commented.

"I need one."

"Yes, I see that." He took his arm, a handlength longer than mine, and placed it on my swimmer's shoulders, inviting me to rest my feet on the rolledup futon.

"Listen, Tim," he began, "I have a proposal for you." *Howformal*, I thought. Everything he was doing was aimed at gaining my confidence. "Are you up for it?" I put the towel, book, and hat on a nearby table.

"Depends," I answered.

"I propose an exchange. I agree to seriously read your book—you are a writer, after all. It's what you do, right?" he asked, picking up the copy that Nick had leftbehind on the beach.

"Well, I have also worked for the government from time to time," I informed him, trying to sound unpretentious.

"I see. The story seems rather, er...long," he observed, leafing through the pages.

"Honestly, working for the government has made it hard to

write clearly and concisely. You should read what the unfriendly reviews said."

"Oh, my." He put the book down.

"Yes, the Shakespearean humor was especially savaged."

"I see."

"Looks like technical writing for me. Anyway," I interjected, trying to get him back to his proposal.

His large, gentle hands petted my belongings as he spoke, then one of them found my thighs. "Yes. So, I agree to read and talk with you about your book later. In exchange, you agree to stay here until midnight."

"That's it?" I skeptically replied, borrowing his halfsmile.

"Well, no. Not exactly. I ask that you also follow two rules," he said sternly, as when he told me *I do men.*

I sneezed. "OK. And?"

"Well, let me continue."

"I'm listening," I reassured him, taking a healthyswig from my glass.

"Good. You can say no, obviously, and if you feel unhappy in any way, we can stop, but all I ask is that you express your unhappiness by kindly leaving the way you came. The door's unlocked, and it'll stay that way until you leave, sooner or later."

"What are the rules?"

"So, you're interested?"

"I'm still here," I said sarcastically.

"Yes, you are," he laughed. Taking his hands from my things to my thighs, he stood and faced me. "First, you may not speak unless spoken to." He scanned my face, which hardly moved a muscle. "Good. Second, you do whatever I tell you to do." He crouched down, sticking his face in mine, penetrating my pupils. I stopped breathing forasecond, then blinked.

"It's ah, it's ah..." Hunting for words, I searched his apartment. There were no signsofviolence hanging from the walls. Just photographs (presumably of friends), a full bookshelf, liquor, TV and radio, and plain furniture. "It's ah...interesting, but..."

"But?" He stoodup again.

"Orso, look. I don't know you."

"Not yet."

"And—"

"And?"

The words stopped again. "Well..." Why was I hesitating? I felt suddenlyshy, in a way I had not felt in a longtime. Then, I realized I was vulnerable. He smelledit. I grabbed a pretzel. "Can I have a minute?"

"Of course. I have to take a shower anyway. Please help yourself to another drink."

"Thank you."

Walking toward the bathroom, he said, "I'll even make it easier, Tim. If when I'm done, you're still here, then I know you've agreed." He turned the faucet on. "If you're gone, then, well, I'll know you haven't." And he closed the bathroomdoor behind him.

I tiptoed to the exit, checking if it was unlocked, which it was. I doublechecked. It was. Orso began singing, quite well infact, in a lowhum. I thought, *Whatcouldgowrong?* He didn't seem interested in torturing me, and he was playful in the water. I sat back down on the couch, realizing that my inability to act was a decision. I ate another pretzel, but started feeling really hungry. I spotted a digitalclock. It read sixohfour. My book was soggy; the cover split. Would he really read it? There was still polish on my pinkietoe from Nick's party lastweek. Two rules? Thefirst could really be covered by thesecond. Whatif I broke them? I should have asked. Whatif he's making this up as he goes? Whatif he's unconvincing, a turnoff? I lifted my headfullofquestions and spotted what looked like a closet, slightly ajar. Curious, I stood, turned, and then the shower stopped. I sat back down and finished my drink.

He said "good" upon opening the door and seeing me still there. "First, turn off the sound of your phone, and set its alarm for midnight. Does yours do both?"

I spoke "yes" calmly.

"Do that." He approached, drying himself, and unplugged the clock. "How long have you been seeing your friend?"

"Nick? We met a month ago."

"It's serious?"

"No. He's slowly recovering from serial monogamy."

He faced me. "Come here." My stomachrumbling, I advanced and kept my eyes fixed on his. He stepped forward and placed bothhands on my shoulders, turning them and guiding me into the steamybathroom. He removed my trunks. "I'm going to shave your nuts and then you're going to take a shower." He grabbed a razor, changed the razorblade, put it down, and massaged shavingcream on my thighs. Without speaking a word, he placed his slipperyhands beneath my armpits and lifted me up on the sinktop. He stepped back, squatted, and took my ankles, placing each on eitherside of his neck. "Pull back your sac." Taking the razor in his hand, he began. "Turn the sink on." Twominutes later, he finished, and removing my ankles, he stood and grabbed me by the neck. "Now, shower up. There's a clean towel on the rack there, and a robe behind the door. Do a good job. Take as long as you need." He left mealone.

Sliding the showercurtain back, I started the water, which sprayed instantly hot. The air was still humid. I steppedin and soaked. There was a soapbar, and I began to lather my hands, rubbing everywhere, enjoying my body. My balls felt smooth, loose. I remembered shaving myself totally when I was first going to clubs yearsago, taking Nair to my hair and stubble, trying to pass as boyishly as possible. I stopped when it got boring. And now, deeplines circled my mouth. Tiny crow'sfeet framed my eyes. But I had kept my definition by swimming regularly. And I let the bodyhair grow. After I was satisfied I had rinsed all the sandandsalt, I gulped some water and swallowed. A towel lay neatlyfolded on the rack. I dried off and slipped into the robe, emerging from the room renewed.

Orso was sitting on his sofa, naked and cool, drinkingsmoking. He waved for me. "Here. Sit down," he directed, pointing between his legs. I complied. He bent over and diddled my cockandballs.

Pulling away, he sat back and began stroking himself, the precome glistening in his hand. His other hand took the back of my head and pushed it between his legs. I opened my mouth and took his foreskin between my lips, my tongue licking his glans, driving down. Orso repeated "yes," taking his cigar from his mouth and flicking ashes in a small tray near my things. My palm slid along strands of his softleghairs, until my thumb rested against his asshole. He grabbed my arm. "No," he warned. I was losing control, lurching deeper, gagging. He stood, placing his hand on my scalp, holding my headstill, now stuffing me, his belly pounding my brow. I pulledback, he forced me close, overwhelming my throat, moaning, retreating to shortshallow thrusts. "No, not yet." He pulledout and kneltdown. He took me by the chin and kissed me, like in the ocean, playing with my tongue, breathing into me, for me, forcing air from my lungs with a powerful, relentless hug. Then, he offered a shortsoft kiss.

"In the closet, there are two shelves. On the lower one, there's some Elbow Grease. Get it and bring it here," he instructed through his teeth holding the cigar. I stared at his redhotstogietip three inches from my nose, understanding what he meant. I walked over, searched, and then grabbed the rightjar. Maybe I should speak unspokento? I returned as he asked. "Open it up. Good. Now put the lid on the TV and take off your robe." I smiled and turnedaway, doing what he wanted, but rolling my eyes. Was he convincing sofar? "Bring the jar here." I quickly moved to the sofa and he put twofingers in the whitegoo. He turned me around and began playing with my ass, still smoking. He stood behindme, reached around my head, and told me to drink some scotch. He pried me apart, rammingme. I almostchoked on my drink. I handed the glass back to him, and he put it down and rested his cigar in the ashtray. Taking out his fingers, he smearedon more grease and reprobed me with threefingers, sitting backdown, massaging me as he jackedoff. "You're fucking tight." Forbidden to respond, I just closed my eyes, imagining a longserene shit. Every so often, he pulled out and started yanking my testicles. Then, he found a rhythm—stopping, greasing up, and restarting on my hole, until he felt like my balls were lonesome.

"Get on all fours."

And I did, with my rear filled. Orso now slid fourfingers in, past his knuckles to his thumb. He grabbed my shoulder, pinching it slightly. Twistingpushing his hand in deep, he kneeled behind me. Then he paused. Leaving his hand still, he turnedaway and said, "*The Folly of Ants.* By Tim Haddock." He resumed fisting and asked, "Minaret Press, are they still in business?" I abruptly withdrew his hand, and was about to answer, when he slapped my ass, telling me, "Don't move." He got up, walked infrontof me, and pushed my face on his prick, ordering me to take it in my throat. He asked again, "Are they still in business? Answer with grunts."

"Uh-uh," I hummed.

" 'Uh-uh,' is that a no? Harder."

"Huh-huh."

"Yes, it's a no? So, they're not in business?"

"Uh-uh," I repeated.

"Slow down, Tim. I don't want to yet." I pulledup a bit and pushed my tongue tip in his pissslit, then traced his thickestvein with my nibbling lips. "Like that, yes." I kept at it as he moaned. "Chapter One. Revolution." Was he reading my book outloud, mocking me? I didn't get his tone through his accent. "Don't go too slow." I refocused and found my former tempo.

He read:

It is one thing to have a conversation with someone. But, it seems something else to exchange words as your breath caresses the face of your listener, while your hands, moving to the rhythm of speech, barely graze his chest. Such a sensual exchange cannot be truly called a conversation. Yet, insofar as talking does not transcend the desire to talk, it must remain on the threshold of what it is and what it might be. Spoken words are human currency. They bring us into relations of exchange, but they also create the conditions for our emancipation. The more our bodies physically sense them, the more we want to revolt.

I thought, *Itsoundedsoqueer outofhismouth.*

" 'Want to revolt.' Hmmm. Tim, am I revolting?" Was that supposed to be a fuckingjoke? "Answer me, am I revolting?"

"Uh-uh," I grunted, deciding to playitsafe.

"No? Are you sure? I think I'm revolting. Harder."

Until I got what he meant, I just wanted to do what I thought he wanted. "Huh-huh."

"You don't understand, do you?" he asked, sounding severe.

"Uh-uh."

"No, you don't. You're not revolting!"

Did he mean I wasn't A BEAR? in Nick'swords? Or did he mean I was not revoltingagainst? He yanked back and looked at me. "You're not revolting, are you?"

At this point, I felt unhappy, turnedoff. I stoodup, slightly dizzy, gravity pulling my blooddown. I faced him, scowling and feelingmocked. He silently handed me my towel, book, and hat, and I took them reluctantly. After standing motionless foramoment, I finally said, "I have to go," but he didn't react. I turned my back and went for my phone, then relooked him over. He was smoking there, unexpressively. I dressed, put my hat on, and headed forthe beach.

It was almost empty, now that the sun was hiding behind distantclouds. It was good stretchingout my tired legs. The sand felt cool beneath my feet. As I strolled, the towel hanging from my shoulder, I passed two strangers pickingup, and one asked theother, "Should we wait for her highness, or can we eat right away?" Maybe Orso was a bitteroldman, seeking revenge on my youngerbody. But then, I thought about the water, the rules. His generally reserved manner had earned my trust, tobehonest, and he had not seemed angry, except sortof toward the end. The part he had read to me was about transcending spokenwords. Was he using my words to say something about me? Perhaps I seemed too passive, too willing to submit to his spokenrules. It could have been that I wasn't revolting in any sense atall.

When I gotback to the room that Nick and I were renting, I

discovered that the closet was open but halffull, the CDstack that had been on the bedroomtable had shrunk, and most of the jars and bottles in the bathroom had disappeared. Thenandthere, I accepted feeling vulnerable. I was happy that Nick had acted. I didn't mind not revolting. On the bed, next to a single velveteen pillow, there was a note written in pencil, alongwith some tensandtwenties. I let down my towel, book, and hat on the mattress.

Dear Tim,

Sorry to go like this. I'm taking the bus for the city tonight. Here's a couple hundred for my share of the rental. I was really upset on the beach. You were nagging me with those artsy questions. Maybe your book is over my head. On top of it, you went swimming with that hunchback. There's still some food in the fridge. Hope you're happy.

Love,
Nick.

P.S. While I was waiting for you on the beach, your friend walked over and saw what I was reading. He said he read it before and liked it. Whatever. Do what you want!

I dropped the letter back on the bed, grabbed my phone, and dialed.

"Yes?" he answered.

"It's me."

"I'm over here," stated Orso.

"Right."

Fake Fur Collar

R.E. NEU

I'd been a beat cop for seven years, so nothing surprised me anymore. When Sgt. Mike D'Angelo, my boss, told us all to head to the locker room and strip naked, though, it came pretty close.

"Whaddaya think's up?" Officer Fitzgerald asked me, his hands clasped in front of equipment his little finger could have hid.

"I dunno," I said, scratching the steel wool on my chest. "I can't think of many cases that call for naked cops."

Pulaski stepped out of his boxers, and his enormous balls swung like Nina Simone. "Maybe *Playgirl* called looking for centerfolds. 'Men of the Philadelphia Police Department.'"

"You think?" I replied, not believing this for a second. "I always wanted to be in *Playgirl*."

"You'd have a better shot with *Field & Stream*," Fitz joked. "Only an animal lover could stand that hairy ass."

While he was talking, Mike came in and snuck up behind him. "That's where you're wrong," he barked, and Fitz jumped like a chilly Chihuahua. "You can put your clothes back on. Steve, meet me in my office. You got a new assignment."

Fitz went beet-red. "That's not fair!" he squawked, shaking his fists like maracas. "Why didn't you pick me?"

Mike jerked a thumb toward Fitz's crotch. "We're playing hard-ball," he grumbled. "Not miniature golf."

I put my uniform back on and followed Mike to his office. He took a seat at his desk and grabbed a sheet of orange paper from the multicolored stack on his desk. In the Marines he had been stationed in Japan, and he returned with a love of sushi, an appreciation for bonsai, and a bad case of origami.

"Steve, there's been a flood of counterfeit hundreds surfacing on the West Side. I think I got it traced to a place called the Bear Cave, but I'm gonna need your help to get the evidence."

I watched the muscles in his meaty arms bulge as he folded the small square. "The Bear Cave?" I replied, my stomach catapulting into my throat. "Isn't that a gay bar?" I didn't need to ask, since I'd gone there a couple times. OK, a couple dozen times.

Mike didn't look up. "Yup," he said. "More precisely, a 'bear bar'—for hairy gay men. Which is why I need you in particular. Their 'Mr. Bear' contest is tonight, and I figure it's a good time to check the place out. I'll get a couple guys to mix in with the crowd, but I also want to get backstage, to look behind the scenes. With 50 thou a week on the table, though, this could get dangerous. I need another hairy guy there to watch my back."

Shit, I thought, I'd been watching his back for years. His front too. "We're going to enter a beauty pageant for gay guys?"

"Yup. We're gonna hunt for a counterfeiter while prancing around nearly naked in front of a couple hundred burly, sex-crazed homosexuals. Not only do we have to be astute detectives, observing everything and missing nothing, but we also have to be charismatic, witty, and just goddamn sexy."

The room started to spin, and my life flashed before my eyes. Was this some bizarre joke? Was I on *Candid Camera*? He betrayed a hint of a smile, and I thought maybe I was right.

"On the plus side," he said, standing a tiny paper bear on the corner of his desk, "we can win *trophies*."

At 9 o'clock that night Mike showed up at my apartment, and we drove his old Chevy pickup to the bar. The contest was at 10, but we had to get there early to sign up, plus I wanted to knock back a couple beers to try to relax. While I'm not exactly shy, I don't spend a lot of time scantily clad and entertaining whole roomfuls of men. I prefer to do it one at a time.

The Bear Cave looks like your average gay bar, with lots of wood, polished brass, and one-way windows to watch clueless passersby. The only odd note is the posters. Covering every square inch of wall space are photographs and drawings of naked, fur-coated men, glistening with sweat and oil and contorted into positions Madonna wouldn't try. This is what Boston Market would look like, I thought, if they sold Italians instead of chicken.

When we walked in, every head spun our way, lusting after the meaty forms beneath our taut black T-shirts, and when we got in line to sign up, all the other guys hightailed it out. I figured Mike and I had the thing locked up, and they obviously agreed. While I wasn't exactly in Mike's league, I'd never gotten any complaints about my looks. Hell, when you're 6-foot-2 and can tear cookbooks in half, you don't get many complaints at all. You'd have to be crazy to compete against Mike, though.

Mike was big as a barn, with shoulders so broad he had to turn sideways to get through doors. He was also smart as a whip and had the unassuming charm of a cowboy, which was what got me trailing after him like a puppy. I tried to be content with our friendship, but I found myself living for the occasional weekend we spent together fishing: two wonderful days soaking up his magnetism like a sponge, mooning after him like a schoolboy, and trying to stay focused on his eyes whenever he pissed off the side of the boat. It took all my self-restraint not to throw myself on top of him and suck him so hard that light wouldn't escape.

Mike bought us a couple Buds, and we played some pool while

we waited for the pageant to start. Ten minutes before showtime, something big and at least partially female barreled through the crowd and dragged us off by our collars. We were finally released backstage, in the presence of either a drag queen or a frighteningly ugly woman named Nosquiza LaSharmán. With a wide-screen forehead and frilly gypsy dress, she looked like the lost love child of Stevie Nicks and Dick Butkus. Someday in the next millennium, an exasperated paleontologist will try to reconstruct her skeleton in the spacious rotunda of a natural history museum.

"Here's the dressing room," she sang, circling both above and below Mariah Carey's range. "Make yourself at home, but touch the makeup and I break your face. At 10:30 I'll go warm up the crowd, then I'll introduce you guys. You come out in Speedos, we talk for a while, and then the audience votes. Got it?"

I nodded obediently. She wasn't somebody you'd want to meet in a dark alley. If God had made her instead of Eve, in fact, we'd all still be eating apples in Eden.

"Now change into these," she said, shooting us small elastic swimwear. She eyed Mike up and down, though mostly down. "I'm going to rustle up more contestants, but if you need a hand—or any other part of my anatomy—just yell."

We took off our shirts and shoes, and I tried to grab a few surreptitious looks. I had a mental slide show of Mike in various forms of undress, but I'd replayed it several thousand times and desperately needed new shots. My eyes wandered from his sturdy shoulders to his barrel chest, with pecs the size and heft of Ford fenders, to his stomach, lean and flat as a washboard. He worked out every day, so he was pretty damn solid. His chest was woven with wiry curls that sprang up when his shirt came off, his back tufted like grass, and his legs were furry as mink, with a seam that ran down the backs from his ass to his ankles. Every square inch was covered, but if I ever had my way with him, I'd leave him flatter than the industrial carpet at the mall.

When he hooked his thumbs into the waistband of his boxers, though, I knew I couldn't take much more. This was a scene I dreamed about daily, but I already had a hard-on that could have dented cement. I was going to slide into swimwear the size of a rubber band, and he had to wonder why I looked like the next in line at a gang bang. I reluctantly turned my back and tried to think about baseball, but even the bats started to swell.

"Shit!" he barked from somewhere behind me. "This thing is damned small."

"I wouldn't worry about it," I said over my shoulder. "Gay guys wear less than this to church."

He chuckled but kept wrestling with the spandex. "This can't be right. Does this look right to you?"

Now, a guy this handsome could stretch the thing over his head and nobody would say a word, but he wanted my OK, and I couldn't come up with an excuse. I tried to think clean thoughts, but when I turned around and saw him in shorts that concealed less than Saran Wrap, my dick started to bounce like a '57 Chevy. "Whoa!" I said, the room going bright as all the blood drained from my head. "You look fuckin' *hot*!"

I think he was startled, but I wasn't looking at his face. "Huh?"

"I mean, yeah, that looks good. There's no way you can lose this thing."

"Thanks," he said, his grin returning. "I figured we'd take the top couple spots. Besides, I don't think we got any competition."

Nosquiza plowed through the curtain, a Woody Allen look-alike following her like a baby chick. "Don't grab those trophies yet, boys. I found one poor soul stupid enough—er, I mean, *brave* enough—to take you on." She flung a pair of Speedos at him, but since she'd been staring at Mike they smacked Woody in the face and crumpled to the floor. "Put those on quick," she murmured, not moving her eyes. "I want you on me—I mean, on *stage*—in five minutes."

Nosquiza turned to her makeup mirror while Mike and I double-checked our outfits and Woody reluctantly stripped. "I still think we'll take it," Mike whispered as the newcomer bared spotty pink flesh. "Hell, I got more hair on my knuckles than he's got on his whole back." Woody spent more time adjusting his

Speedos than he did getting into them, and when he turned around he was smiling broader than a doomed contestant should. Instantly I knew something was wrong. My eyes slowly slid down his spindly body to his shorts, where something the size and shape of a PVC pipe extension protruded from his groin.

Mike did likewise. "Do you see that?" he whispered, like I could have missed a zeppelin moored to my nose. "Look what he's packing downstairs!"

"That's not his dick," I said, with absolute confidence. I'd checked out our little friend in the mirror, and you couldn't have seen his equipment if you were standing on his balls and pointed north. "He's got something stuffed in there."

"Shit!" Mike barked. He examined his own crotch—which, while adequately packed, suffered by comparison. Next, his eyes slid over to mine, which didn't. "He makes us look like *chicks,* for God's sa—" He broke off mid word, his attention locked on my lap. "What the *hell* is in your shorts?" he demanded.

I swallowed hard. "Just my dick, that's all."

"Dick, my ass!" he barked, and Woody and Nosquiza spun around.

"Save it for the talent competition!" Nosquiza yelled, hurtling through the curtain.

Mike glared daggers at me. "I didn't realize how much you wanted to win this thing. OK, buddy. You wanna play rough, we'll play rough."

He grabbed his boxer shorts, bent them in a rectangle, and jammed them into his Speedos. Examining his reflection in the mirror, he folded and refolded the shorts. When he turned back to face me, he had a smug smile on his face and an uncanny rendition of Milton Berle's endowment stretching from groin to hip. Though I knew it was just plaid cotton, my own dick started to spring around like a hamster on a hot plate. I momentarily stunned it with my palm, but Mike grabbed my arm and wrestled it away. He knelt down to get a closer look, then shook his head.

"You *bastard,*" he growled, his stubbled jaw hovering inches from my groin. "You've even got *foreskin* on that puppy."

At around 11, Nosquiza called for us and we obediently trotted onstage. Woody went first, to a smattering of applause, me second, the noise distinctly ramping up, and Mike third, to whoops and woofs and whistles. Woody introduced himself as "Brick," though with his fuzzy pinkness he probably should have gone with "Fiberglass." Mike said his name was "Steel," and although it was always pretty low, now his voice shook the ground like an earthquake. *OK, let's play rough,* I seconded, and in a voice that made Barry White sound like Betty White I introduced myself as "Cement."

What can I say? It was either that or "Asphalt," and that sounds like what you get when you eat too many beans.

The pageant was something like *The Dating Game,* if the host was a drag queen and the three bachelors wore Post-Its. Nosquiza fluttered about the stage like a gay moth, quizzing us on our likes and dislikes, our hobbies and interests. Our answers were what you'd expect from a hairy, sexually active Miss America. Each of us won over fans, but by the time we reached the final question it was obvious Mike controlled most of the house.

Nosquiza went all serious, like Barbara Walters quizzing Angelina Jolie. "What are the qualities that make a man a bear?" she asked.

Woody went first, describing a hot, hairy body that he apparently thought was his. I had similar ideas on the subject, but since I didn't want to alienate anyone in the crowd, I hedged my description. "Masculine" became "male," "hunky" became "fit," and "hirsute" became "postpubescent." When I finished I realized I'd described Tobey Maguire.

Mike stepped forward and took a deep breath, like he was going to be there awhile. "What makes a man a bear," he said, "is on the inside, not the outside. A bear understands the importance of friendship, and he stands by the people he chooses to be his friends. So most important, I think, is loyalty." He slid his hands into his shorts, and with the adroit skill he learned in Japan he twisted and folded his "genitalia." When he finally extracted his hands and the Spandex thwacked back into place, a 10-inch fox terrier was sprawled across his groin.

Every hairy jaw in the room dropped open, including mine. "To be a bear, a man also has to know where he's going, and needs to learn from where he's been. So the second most important thing, I'd say, is wisdom." The dog vanished, and with a little more massaging, Mike formed an owl perched on the branch of an old willow tree. He illustrated strength with a mule and playfulness with a kitten, followed by independence and sincerity and compassion and resilience. I've always been an animal lover, but this was the first time I'd thought about kissing a frog.

The audience was too stunned to respond. One by one they rubbed their eyes, but when they looked again, they still saw a guy with an amphibious dick. "Last," Mike declared, "a bear needs to know what's in his heart—so he can freely and truly offer himself in commitment." And with a flip of the wrist he tied the whole thing in a knot.

The crowd went wild. Shrieks and cheers and shouts rang out, and I half expected them to hoist Mike onto their shoulders and carry him away. One lone voice of dissent rose up from their midst. "What's so great about that?" a gruff old guy with a gray goatee asked a neighbor. "I could do that with my dick."

"Oh, please," came the response from a dissenting cub. "We had sex once, remember? You couldn't make a Twinkie if I spotted you the cream."

Nosquiza put up a hand to shush the crowd. "Before we vote, let's ask the contestants who they like." She thrust the microphone at Woody first. "Who would you pick if you had to vote?"

Woody scowled at me like he was examining a cold sore. "I don't like Stucco at all," he declared.

"Cement!" I snapped.

He stared at Mike the way Jim Belushi would look at pork chops. "Steel, on the other hand, is pretty fuckin' hot."

"He is, isn't he?" Nosquiza purred. She tottered over to Mike, dodging the knotholes with her heels. "What do you think about Brick?"

Mike scratched the back of his neck. His bicep blew up like a balloon, so nobody really cared if it helped him think or not. "He's a good-looking guy."

Nosquiza did a double take but was too much of a lady to argue. Instead she sashayed over to me. "Cement, who would you pick if you weren't up here?"

By this point I was starting to lose it. Why would Mike pick that bony bastard over me? Hell, I'd worked with him for almost eight years. Was loyalty nothing more than a terrier in his shorts? I tried to pretend my feelings were platonic, but I knew the truth: If we were on *Ricki Lake* right now, I'd be wrestling Brick and screeching, "Bitch, you ain't *touchin'* my man!" "I don't mean to be rude," I said frostily, "but I don't even know why Brick is up here. His pecs are flabby, his legs are scrawny, and I think he's stuffing eggs in his basket. The only man he could attract is Colonel Sanders."

Woody went crimson, and if this had been a cartoon, he'd have morphed into a whistling teakettle. "Yeah?" he hissed, strutting over and sticking his face in mine. "You wanna piece of me? You wanna piece of me?"

"Buddy," I replied, "I'd rather suck Nosquiza's meat—and it's taped to her ass."

Nosquiza lowered her head like she was going to ram me, but Woody beat her to it, hurtling us to the stage in a crunch of splintering plywood. He fought like a chicken too, I thought, smacking my face with his hands and scratching my legs with his feet. Police training and 200 pounds of muscle gave me a distinct advantage, though, and before he knew it I had him flat on his back and helpless as a kitten. I straddled him across his groin, pinning his shoulders with my hands, and as our muscles reached an impasse and our chests heaved from exertion, I realized something long and hard and definitely plastic was jabbing me in the ass.

"Christina! Britney!" Nosquiza shrieked. "This isn't *Divas Live!*"

She grabbed my arm and pulled, but before I let Woody up I reached into his shorts and yanked out an eight-inch plastic dildo.

"See?" I yelled, holding it out to the crowd. "His dick is fake!"

The audience gasped and scanned all our Speedos, from Mike's padding to my real thing, which was now stretched out longer than PBS Pledge Week. "They're *all* fake!" somebody hollered, and other voices murmured their agreement.

A furious Nosquiza stomped over to Mike, peered into his Speedos, and plucked out the folded boxer shorts. "This is a serious violation of my penal code!" she snapped. Glowering, she hustled over to me, thrust her hand in my shorts, and wrapped her manicured fingers around my swollen dick. Before I could protest she yanked it—trailed by two beefy, bouncing balls—into the night air.

Nosquiza leapt five feet in the air and everyone stared in shock as my meat lurched up and down like a dashboard dachshund. "I think we have a winner!" she squealed to whoops of approval, but when I waved Woody's dildo over my head and $100 bills flew out, all hell broke loose.

The next day I ran into Mike in the locker room. He was changing out of his uniform and recapping the night's events with Captain Warner when I got out of the shower.

"Well, we got our man," he said, unbuttoning his shirt. "He confessed to everything once we confronted him with the videotape. Turns out, every Friday he went to the Bear Cave to replace the bar's real bucks with counterfeit cash. One of the bartenders pulled all the big bills out of the cash register, swapped them with our man in the bathroom, and replaced them before anybody noticed. With a little luck and some damn fine wrestling, Officer Ferrara pretty much solved the case by himself."

The captain clapped me on the back. "Good job, Steve," he said.

171

"But don't underestimate yourself, D'Angelo. Something tells me you had a hand in this too."

After he left, I unwrapped the towel from around my waist and began to dry myself off. I couldn't take it anymore. I looked at Mike—the warm eyes, the square jaw, the five o'clock shadow you could strip wallpaper with—and knew I wanted more than just friendship. It was time to fish or cut bait. "He's right," I said. "Our guy would never have signed up for the contest if he hadn't seen your hot ass in line."

Mike looked startled but mostly flattered. "Thanks," he stuttered. "Sorry I accused you of stuffing your shorts. Like a guy as hot as you would have to cheat to win." His eyes zigzagged down my body before settling on my groin. "And I've got to say…that's the biggest dick I've ever seen in my life."

My glance toward his endowment was met with an embarrassed look. I couldn't believe he was self-conscious after the demonstration he'd given. "Hey, it's not what you have," I assured him. "It's what you can do with it."

He grinned and dimples appeared that could hide Jimmy Hoffa. "Hey, how'd you like to check out a domestic disturbance with me? I hear there's a couple guys stark naked raising all kinds of hell."

"Sure," I said, shrugging my shoulders. "Where and when?"

"My place," he said. "In about 10 minutes?"

Papabear Bean

ADAM BEN-HUR

In my mid 20s I had a summer job at Brentano's Bookstore in the Beverly Wilshire Hotel on Wilshire Boulevard at the foot of Rodeo Drive—a very trendy neighborhood, not that I personally could ever afford to shop there. I had a small upstairs apartment on Almont Drive, right around the corner from the Academy of Motion Picture Arts and Sciences. I often walked the nine or 10 blocks from home to the bookstore and back, which kept me in pretty good shape.

Late one afternoon after I got off work, I decided it was time to get my hair cut, since it was starting to get in my eyes. I went to the barber at the hotel and asked if he had any time. He was a friendly, personable Italian man who had been a fixture at this shop for years. I always assumed he was gay. He was very chipper and said hello whenever we ran into each other. He was much too professional to make an advance or flirt overtly, but he had an outgoing manner, and I knew he liked me just as a person. He smiled and said he had an appointment coming down but it was only a trim, and he could see me in half an hour.

I wandered through the hotel lobby awhile. When I returned to the barber, he was finishing up a trim on a large-framed man with a

173

Southern accent who was apparently staying in the hotel on a business trip. Even though he was under the barber's protective covering, I could see that he was a big, well-built man, around 6-foot-4 and about 220 well-taken-care-of pounds. He must have been in his late 40s and had that kind of iron-gray hair sweeping up his temples that makes men look sexier than heck. He had the look of a professional coach, someone who probably played a lot of sports in college and managed to keep his physique. I picked up a magazine and began thumbing through it, occasionally looking up to get a glimpse of this attractive, broad-shouldered gentleman with the rich baritone and classic Southern drawl.

As the barber made small talk, it became apparent that this was the client's first visit to Los Angeles. He was curious about what to see and do over the next few days. As the conversation bounced around, I spontaneously joined in and suggested that he try to see the laser show at the Laserium at Griffith Park Observatory and try to get to the Getty Center. He smiled and appreciated my effort. As we warmed up to each other, the barber introduced me as Adam, and I discovered that the client's name was Beau.

Nice name, I thought. *That really suits him.*

As Mario finished the haircut, Beau thanked me for my suggestions. Then, unexpectedly, he suggested that I meet him for a margarita in the hotel bar, Don Hernando's Hideaway, after my haircut so we could continue our talk. The margaritas at Don Hernando's Hideaway were famous, and you could make a meal of the generous hors d'oeuvres served alongside them, which I did often rather than face cooking for myself at the end of a workday.

After my haircut, Mario slapped some lightly scented tonic on my hair—a watered-down, distant cousin to bay rum, not too overwhelming—and then I wandered over to the dimly lit tropical bar with pleasant expectations. Beau was sitting in a cozy booth in the corner, partially hidden behind a green tumble of exotic broad-leafed plants. A frothy margarita in a large salt-rimmed glass was already waiting for me on the pink tablecloth. I grinned and slid in across from him. He was quite a large man, with broad shoulders and big, hairy hands. A brilliant smile illuminated his clean, precisely cut features. Through bright sapphire eyes he radiated intelligence and masculine confidence. I was strangely excited by the situation and by the fatherly sense of appreciation he showed me. As I took a first sip of the crisp, chilled cocktail, he asked if I wouldn't mind joining him for dinner, since he didn't enjoy eating alone. He told me he had taken the liberty of ordering the chateaubriand, which is traditionally prepared and served for two people, and that he would feel awkward sitting by himself in front of a plate of food like that. I smiled and said, "Sure, I don't really have any plans tonight. Dinner sounds great."

"Thanks. I was hoping you'd say yes. You're a very refreshing young man. You didn't have to go out of your way to make me feel welcome here. But I appreciate it very much. Every meal I've had since I arrived here has been more or less a business meeting with a bunch of stuffy old financial men. I was hoping to run into a friendly native at some point." He twinkled at me and settled back.

He told me about his business enterprises and described his life in Gulfport, Mississippi, on the coast of the Gulf of Mexico. He was obviously proud of his Southern way of life but without the condescension you occasionally run into with Southerners. He was excited about being in Los Angeles but was looking forward to returning home soon to participate in the annual blessing of the fleet, a major social event in the Gulfport-Biloxi area. He mentioned he had a medium-size pleasure craft—if a 47-foot boat can be considered medium-size. As he explained it, everyone of a certain status in the community owned a boat. Throughout the summer, there were parties at the marina where you wandered from boat to boat, drink in hand, visiting with people late into the evening. He prided himself on making a creole shrimp dish that was the talk of the harbor and said that I would have to come out sometime, sail with him, and enjoy spectacular fresh seafood. It all sounded breezy and carefree, like a Jimmy Buffett or Christopher Cross song. He won me over completely.

Dinner arrived, along with another round of margaritas. I was feeling more and more relaxed with this Southern gentleman as we chewed our way through a perfect piece of beef. He pressed me for more details of growing up in Northern California and more ideas about what to do during his few remaining days in town. It was obvious he enjoyed my company. I felt great giving him ideas about fun things to do and surprised myself at how much cultural knowledge I'd absorbed during my relatively short time in Los Angeles.

Offhandedly, he asked me if I had ever been to any of California's nude beaches that he'd heard so much about. I brightened as I explained that when I was going to school in Santa Barbara, I had a guest cottage in Summerland up the hill from one of California's most famous and popular nude beaches. I described how I used to hike down the hill in the morning in just sneakers, cutoffs, and a T-shirt to a little trail that led past Pajaro Lane and Highway 101 to the nude part of Summerland's two-mile-long beach.

"You can spend all afternoon playing Frisbee with the surfers who hang out naked on the beach. You can catch up on your reading and soak up as much sun as you like and never worry about wearing a stitch. No one ever hassles you. The families with kids and clothes on stay up the north end of the beach close to the parking lot. Farther along you might run into nude couples. The surfers, free spirits, and single guys looking for adventure hang out toward the south end. It's a longer trek to get to. Then there's a rocky sort of no-man's-land that separates Summerland from Carpinteria, which you can only walk when the tide is way out." I didn't mention that it was this remote rocky area that was also the most likely place to run into some freewheeling tribal sex. Most guys can figure that out for themselves.

He smiled broadly, took a sip of his margarita, and leaned forward. With a subtle sweeping glance around the lounge to ensure privacy, he confided, "I'd be too worried about my big ol' pecker coming up hard on me to relax and have fun. You have any problem keeping a boner down around all that bare-ass skin?" He gleamed at me with an I'm-a-guy-you're-a-guy familiarity that set off a little wave of electricity in me. I returned the gleam.

This is cool, I thought. *I can relax and talk about sex with this guy. He's all right!* Suddenly, the idea of this handsome Southerner strolling nonchalantly along the beach or stretched out on an over-size multicolored beach towel in the summer sunshine with a big juicy boner lit my imagination.

"Don't worry," I assured him, probably without any real need. "When everyone is naked, it's really a different mentality than just flipping through *Playboy* magazine and getting horny looking at glossy pictures. Some of the guys do have sex in these little coves and natural rock shelters. That's for sure. I've seen it once or twice. I don't have any problem with that myself. But I think most folks are there just to get some sun and enjoy the ocean and the beach. It's a nice feeling, being out of your clothes."

"Yes, I'm sure it's very enjoyable," he agreed. "I'll have to give it a try. Why not?" he smiled. Another sapphire twinkle flickered across his eye.

Talking this openly about nudity and sex with a mature, handsome stranger was arousing the heck out of me. This father-and-son camaraderie touched a vulnerable nerve. My dad had never talked to me or kidded around with me about sex the way most dads do. Because he was a thought-controlled Baptist by marriage—my mom taught Sunday school—I think the subject embarrassed him. When I was 14, he tossed a book on my bed called simply *The Facts of Life* and said, "Well, you should probably read this now, but don't let your mother find it." That was it. No follow-up, no "Did you like the part about such and such?" which would have made it an endearing father-and-son conspiracy. I remember the book had a few spare black-and-white line drawings—nothing I hadn't already seen in full color in the family medical encyclopedia—and a lot of big Latin words. Pretty dull going.

My uncle Charlie, however, had the really cool stuff. Uncle Charlie was a big, happy, rambunctious Okie with a good word for everybody. He and Aunt Dolores lived in a ranch-style home in Niles, a rural part of the East Bay then as now. They served gin cocktails on weekend afternoons; their house was the only place I ever saw my folks get halfway giddy. My uncle Charlie told off-color jokes with gusto and brought out the good-humored earthiness in people. Aunt Dolores would pretend to be embarrassed by the whole thing for my mom's sake, but you could see she loved her big bad boy all the more for it. He'd been in the military service in Europe and had come back with a medal or two on his chest and a treasure trove of fully illustrated marriage manuals, pictorial sex guides, and just flat-out hard-core they-kiss-on-the-streets-in-Paris pornography. The real thing. In-and-out close-ups. Whenever we'd go for a visit, hunky Charlie Jr. and I would ferret out the books and magazines from behind his father's toolbox in the garage, hike off to the woods together, and just get punch-drunk silly over all the pictures. Your basic teen hormonal high. There was one book that especially attracted me, whose title translated as *Variations in Sexual Behavior.* It displayed every possible combination of men and women, doing everything imaginable, and it gave me my first inkling that there was a great big adventure up ahead. We'd strip down to our underwear, spread all the books and magazines around us on the grass, lie back, and jack each other off through our white cotton briefs. We'd usually climax three or four times in an afternoon.

"It's not necessarily arousing or lewd." I went on about Summerland. "It's just natural. Healthy, even. Sometimes you'll see entirely nude California hippie families playing in the surf with their kids and building sand castles and all the normal beach stuff, completely unself-conscious. It's kinda nice seeing people be that free."

I started to think back on some of my friskier afternoon encounters on that stretch of beach. As I fiddled with the stem of my margarita glass, one especially exciting episode came to mind...a spur-of-the-moment thing with a husky blond bisexual married naval officer up from San Diego for the weekend. He was extremely well-endowed and took my ass hard behind one of those big rocks in broad daylight. The poor guy was so fired up by seeing all those golden Santa Barbara folks naked on the beach, I think he would have screwed anything with a hole in it. After all of five minutes of "Do you come down here very often?" conversation, he had me bent over a boulder with his dick jammed so far up my tanned ass I thought it would bust out my belly button. Thank God for the coconut suntan lotion or I would have been seriously damaged goods. I had to waddle uphill home as it was. Swapping sex stories with buddies, I've always joked about that little impromptu beach skirmish as being "caught between a cock and a hard place." I mean, he had me right up against a rock, and sex doesn't get more raw and primitive than that.

I must have blushed. My new friend grinned at me across the table with a sexy flash of white teeth. He leaned forward again and said quietly, "A good-looking guy like yourself probably makes out pretty good on a nude beach, eh?" Either my smile or the sudden sweep of color in my face had given me away. Between the talk and the tequila, my neck was getting very warm under the collar. I loosened my tie, opened the top button of my shirt, and ran my hand through my new haircut, noticing it still smelled of a splash of barbershop spice.

I stammered some sort of modest "Aw, shucks" reply but he smiled and winked. *Damn,* I thought, *this guy is out-and-out flirting with me right here in Don Hernando's Hideaway.* Not that any hotel bar is ever exclusively straight—especially in Los Angeles, where you are assumed to be bisexual until proven otherwise. But most of the cocktail-hour crowd had wandered away, and only a few tables still had couples seated at them. We were safe and unnoticed behind our atmospheric screen of urban jungle foliage. "Flirt on, full speed ahead!" my inner naval officer commanded.

"I'll have to find that place next time I come out. Maybe you can take a day off and go up the coast with me. It's called Summerland, you say? That ought to be easy to remember. Hey, I've got a bottle of fine Southern bourbon up in my room. May I invite you up for a drink?"

He was pure Southern hospitality, one generosity after another. "Sure thing!" I replied, even though I don't really enjoy the taste of bourbon. Heck, he could have invited me up for a sip of yesterday's dishwater and I would have said, "Sure thing!" This guy had me by the balls—in a very pleasant way.

It dawned on me that I was being seduced slowly, gradually, smile by smile, by a charming Southern gentleman who was in total control of the situation. He probably knew from the moment we caught each other's eye at the barbershop that he could have me. I could feel the vein in my neck pulse and my cock grow warm and hefty in my tight-cut slacks. As we slid out of the booth, I was a little embarrassed that the outline of my sex was showing, but with a swift reconnaissance glance at my dinner partner, I saw that he was showing a lot more cock through his pants than me.

We rode the elevator up quietly to his floor. Walking down the empty hallway toward his room, he dragged an arm across my back and grasped my far shoulder with a wide hand. "You folks have a nice way of life here in California, that's for sure. But the tempo is faster than I care for. Everyone seems stuck on fast-forward. Even when people are talking to you, you get the feeling they are already thinking ahead to the next conversation, or waiting for someone more important or influential or better connected to walk into the room. You come on out to the Gulf, I'll show you what Southern is all about. People take everything slower there, and they savor it because they're not in a hurry. They work slower. They play slower..." Then more quietly, he said, "They screw slower..." and drawing me closer with a conspiratorial grin, "unless you need it fast, darlin'."

The mischievous gleam in his eye made it obvious he took pleasure in the kind of man-to-man talk you exchange with a guy only when you're headed for the hay together. My smile said I was in on it. Much of the past hour had unfolded with a father-to-son quality, inevitable considering the 20-year difference in our ages. But now that we were alone together, he made me feel like we were two equally attractive, available males meeting on the common ground of bone-stiff sex in a hotel room on the West Coast of America. *Why not?* my mind echoed back to me. *Why the hell not?*

As he opened the door to his suite, I slid my hands into the pockets of my slacks to adjust myself to the left, hoping to conceal how fully erect I was. He motioned me toward a stylish traditional wingback sitting chair and poured us each a glass of bourbon.

"Kick off your shoes and relax. This bourbon will hit the spot. It's fine, old-fashioned sippin' bourbon. I guarantee you it will go down smooth and put a fire in your belly. And if you don't mind, I'm going to get comfortable. It's been a long day. You're welcome to get out of your clothes yourself and relax a while, which I suggest you do before you burst the fly in the front of those ass-tight pants of yours," he chuckled.

Why did I even bother hiding it? This guy was way ahead of me!

"Sounds nice," I said, feeling pleasantly hazy from the citric margaritas and profoundly enjoying the sensuality of this man's company. Everything seemed to go into soft focus as I noticed the surroundings: a random scattering of new magazines across the luxurious bed, a change of clothes draped over the other sitting chair, a spill of miscellaneous pocket stuff across the Spanish-style writing desk along with hotel stationery, a lamp, and a red telephone. And Beau, the gentle giant from the Gulf, talking like a character from a Tennessee Williams play and undressing in slow motion in front of me.

Stepping out of his black dress shoes, he casually unbuttoned his shirt and undid his pants. His thick, muscular chest was covered with a dark pelt of curly hair, bristling with silver, gray, and copper lights. A pair of pronounced and extremely kissable nipples rose from two round medallions of pale crimson flesh on either side of his fur. A coarse vine of hair wandered up out of his boxer shorts across his white belly, emphasizing the carved outline of a still-powerful set of abs and pecs, somewhat softened by maturity. The ripcord muscles of his forearms flexed as he stripped down. The defined veins of his arms and hands stood out with each motion. *Football,* I thought to myself. *This guy had to have been linebacker material in his college days. No coach in his right mind would let a made-by-God body like that go unpunished.* I was mesmerized. Luckily, Beau took control.

"Speaking of ass, my young friend, I've been admiring that butt of yours ever since you walked into the barbershop downstairs. Couldn't help but notice. I like a firm, round, fuckable ass on a man—or a woman, for that matter. Are you fuckable?"

I liked his directness. It's very becoming to a man to be plain-spoken about sex. I handed it back. "Sure thing, Beau. But how about you bring out that big ol' Southern pecker you were bragging about so I can kiss on it for a while? You got me kind of excited at dinner and…well…I like the taste of cock on a big man like you."

"No problem there." He smiled, looking savvy, and stripped off the last of his clothing. Socks and boxer shorts fell to the floor with a soft whisper. He leaned his massive Zeusian body back across the plush bedspread, his big thighs sprawling apart leisurely. He pushed the magazines to the floor on the other side of the bed with one bearish, broad-armed swipe and motioned for me to join him. What must have been a full 10 inches of fat, curving pink dick rose proudly from his hairy groin and arched across his belly invitingly. "Come on over, son, and show me how a California boy sucks cock. I haven't had anything since I left Mississippi, and I'm afraid you've got one horny Southern daddy on your hands tonight."

That was all I needed to hear. I took one more sociable sip of bourbon—about all I could really manage of the taste—and then stripped down myself, turning my back to him as I pulled off my white briefs and set them along with the rest of my clothes in a neat pile on the wingback chair. "Whew!" I heard him exhale. "Damn, boy, that's nice! That's real nice."

Over the years, I'd been kidded or complimented enough on my ass that I finally stopped fighting off the praise and just accepted it as one of my better features. These were the days when we were all—men and women both—telling each other we wanted to be loved and valued for our minds, our professional accomplishments, and our myriad talents, not just for our bodies—as if a little heartfelt lust was somehow beneath us or bad for our image. Looking back, I'm not sure that my mind at the age of 25 was any more or less above average than it is now or all that remarkable or anything someone else ought to have found attractive. My ass, however, was truly outstanding. Sometimes it feels nice to be loved for your body alone. I smiled and said, "Glad you like it, Papabear."

Sliding forward across the bed, I brought my face down as close to his cock as I could without touching it. I inhaled the unmistakable salty aroma of sex, and it excited me. The tip of my tongue grazed the seam of his scrotum gently as he released a long sigh of pleasure from the deep bellows of his lungs. He spread his heavy thighs farther apart and settled back onto the bed with greater comfort, all 6-foot-4 of him lying naked and open to whatever pleasure we might find together in the refuge of a rented room. I rose up a little to admire the way his full heavy sac hung down and spread out underneath his cock, filled with two large weighty oval balls, with plenty of skin to spare. This man's stuff was impressive—like everything else about him.

My hands wandered up across his shaggy chest. My fingertips began to caress the meaty buds of his solid nipples, while my tongue dragged slowly across his scrotum and up the underside of his curving dick. His skin tasted sweet and earthy at the same time, mingling with the salt and citrus of the margaritas still lingering on my mustache. I let the journey from his scrotum and balls up to the swollen head of his dick take forever, reversing and starting over several times.

Through closed lips he began moaning quietly—a deep, rumbling, leonine purr of arousal, the sound of a dark beast of pleasure awakening in a secret cave. He wrapped both his hands around my upper arms and pulled me down closer. I've never had baseball biceps, but there was plenty of meat around my arms and shoulders to grab. His hands were magnetic as they explored my neck and shoulders and idly stroked the back of my new-mown hair. An electrical current swept up my tailbone and rippled across my spine in a humid wave. I was smooth living Mediterranean clay molding around the hard contour of his desire.

Some guys are more like machines than lovers in bed. They move abruptly and respond jerkily, and their touch has an oddly remote feeling to it, as if they were following instructions from some inner teleprompter. They're the ones who give "do this, do that" orders in bed, as if they were directing traffic rather than making love. Somehow they missed the chapter on 360-degree sensuality, on blending in with another human being, on letting the lead and follow move back and forth spontaneously like a dance. Or maybe their nerves were never wired completely to appreciate the sensitive side of life to begin with.

Beau, on the other hand, was wired for love.

As my mouth opened to slide over the head of his wide cock, he met my lips with a slow fucking motion, sliding toward the back of my throat. His cock felt heavy and warm as he began pushing and withdrawing at an adagio tempo, enjoying all the sensations of my moist lips and tongue wrapped around his hard, horny shaft.

"Damn, son, you are one fine cocksucker. Kiss on those big ol' balls for me again."

Letting his cock slip from my mouth, I wrapped my lips around one of his balls and lifted my head slowly away from his sex as if trying to separate it from the rest of his body. The pressure teeters on the edge of pleasure and pain but builds up the excitement, especially as I was massaging his cock at the same time. I sucked playfully on his testicle and rolled it around with my tongue, relishing the shape, size, and taste of it. Then I released it and took the other one in my mouth, all the while stroking his hairy stem, which was beginning to glide with a steady ooze of precome. He moaned with pleasure, a low growl of approval for what this frisky boy beast was doing.

I slid down behind his balls and let my tongue wander toward his asshole. He sensed my destination and lifted his powerful thighs toward his chest to allow easier passage to his ass. As I licked the steamy, hairy hole in the center of his round, cushioned buttocks, he grasped his thighs with his hands and pulled them up closer, offering me more of his already well-lathered asshole. I pushed my head farther up the crack of his ass, my broad chin pressing up against the division, my tongue seeking out the depth of his hole.

"Fuck, boy, I haven't had anyone rim my ass like that in years. Damn, you're great! I think I'm gonna keep you, for sure."

I smiled and looked up at him, light-headed with pleasure. I caught another sapphire glint from his eye and the flash of a satisfied grin. Then I went back down into the muscular crevice and continued licking and kissing his sensitive asshole while stroking his huge cock. After a while he lowered his legs on either side of me and shifted his position a little.

"Come up here on my chest, son, and feed me that young dick. You've got this old man horny as heck and I want to taste that hot dick of yours before I get you belly-down and fuck the hell out of your pretty ass."

I rose up and straddled his chest as he took my engorged cock in his mouth and began sucking it long and slow. His mouth was powerful. He put an unbreakable suction around my cock that I still can't forget. He was as hungry as I was. His wide hands grasped my hips and ass as he pulled my whole body back and forth across his chest. I braced myself against the headboard as he devoured me. I could feel the entire length of my yearning shaft disappear into his cock-starved mouth. I was fucking his mouth good, but as much as I wanted to release all my pent-up maleness, I decided I'd better settle down before I went over the edge. After I shoot my load, I usually lose interest in sex fairly quickly—and I wanted this interlude to last. Besides, I hadn't been fucked in months, and I wanted it badly. The idea of getting belly-down for this big handsome Southern man had fired up my curiosity.

"I bet you can fuck really good, can't you, sir?"

"You bet, boy. I can fuck like a goddamn farm animal—and have been since I was 13. We start young in the South. I've made a lot of people—men and women—very happy," he bragged. "I want to see this big fat cock of mine sliding in and out of your sassy ass. Do you think you can take all this?"

"Sure thing. I had a black buddy one summer with a 12-inch cock who taught me how to relax and open my ass for him and his service buddies. We tried out every position you can imagine. He managed to get most of that huge thing in me just fine. I learned to enjoy the feeling of being penetrated. It usually takes a minute or two for me to adjust, but after that it's fun and easy," I explained. It was pleasant remembering my buddy Taj, who was stationed at Holloman Air Force Base in Alamogordo, New Mexico. He was a tall, handsome black pilot who could really fill out a uniform. We had a lot of good times together until I had to move north to Santa Fe to take a job working on the newspaper there.

"All right, son. Sounds good. Why don't you get over on your hands and knees for me and let me grease this big ol' pecker up for you."

He reached for a small jar of Vaseline in the drawer of the bed table while I dutifully turned over on my hands and knees and offered him my young ass. Kneeling behind me, he greased his own cock first. Then he gently greased the outside of my asshole. Gradually he introduced a finger into my ass, digging deep into the dark channel. After the first exploratory probe, he added more grease and pushed two large fingers as far up my asshole as possible. I gasped but quickly met the two fingers with relaxation and reminded myself to breathe deeply. He reached underneath me and greased my cock generously. He positioned himself at my asshole and slid in slowly. I felt so vulnerable and helpless in this position, but I opened readily to his first full-body lunge. God, it felt so smooth and huge and awesome. I was completely filled up by him.

"Damn, boy, your ass is tight. This is going to be some good fuckin'!"

"Thank you, sir," I said. Regardless of any momentary discomfort I might experience, pleasing him was my number 1 priority. Having his huge, beautiful cock buried deep inside me made me feel intensely desirable. The physical sensation was incredible as his cock beat against my butt and his balls slapped rhythmically against my own pair of nuts. The psychological value of being wanted and used for sex by a handsome, worldly, masculine man, of taking his raw, mature masculinity into my young and willing flesh, filled me with a kind of fierce pride. I was profoundly happy and satisfied giving him such intimate comfort and pleasure.

"Oh, yeah, son, squeeze my cock hard with that tight young ass. Let me feel your ass squeezing the juice outta my dick. Attaboy!"

I tightened my asshole around his cock. There is an art to being the receiving partner of a butt-fucking team. My black buddy Taj had taught me to relax my asshole completely on his forward thrusts, opening as wide as possible to receive his sex as he pressed into me. Then, as his cock withdrew, to squeeze and tighten the ring of rectal muscle, grabbing and pulling on the shaft. This creates a very powerful sensation of being held and stroked.

"Oh, yeah, boy, you like this big ol' daddy dick shoved up your ass, don't ya?"

"Yeah, it feels great. Fuck me hard. I can take it, sir."

"You've been needing some hard cock thrown into your ass, haven't ya, boy?"

"Yes, sir. Please fuck me hard—*really* hard, sir."

Beau began to fuck faster and deeper, slapping my ass rudely with his big hairy hand as if he were riding a horse, but I didn't mind; the contact was exciting as hell. He could do anything he wanted to me. The Vaseline and precome and natural physical moisture and sweat had all merged and blended into a perfect gripping ride. I could tell Beau was getting close to the inevitable point of no return, and I braced myself for the impact of the oncoming full-body climax. Beau's cock was at the point of peak arousal and felt about as hard as a hammer handle pumping away at my rear end. I wasn't going to be able to stave off my own orgasm much longer, so I began to buck back with each of his champion-breeding thrusts. His groans of pleasure became ferocious. As his cock burst its full load of high-octane juice into my ass, he reached around my belly and jacked my dick off fast.

"Oh, God!" I moaned with pleasure. "Oh, God, Beau! I'm fuckin' coming!"

"Yeah, fire that fucker off, son. Show your Southern daddy you can shoot a man's load for him. Oh, yeah! Oh, yeah! Shoot that firecracker off for me, boy!"

After only four or five hard ball-busting strokes, my cock volleyed a major round of ammunition into his big strong hand and all over his fingers. I fell forward onto the bed, trying to catch my breath. Beau, still embedded in my backside, turned me over on my side and put his arm around me, holding me close as my passionate breathing gradually returned to normal. He stayed hard for quite a while and then slipped out of me as I began to doze off.

"Damn, that was nice, boy," he whispered close into my ear. "Lie still. I'll clean us up a little."

He went into the bathroom and returned with a plush white hotel towel bearing the Beverly Wilshire monogram. He stroked my body with it and then wiped himself off as I wafted in and out of consciousness.

"Would you like to spend the night with me?" he asked.

"Sure thing," I said. "Someone at work might notice I'm wearing the same clothes as yesterday, but that doesn't really matter to me."

"Don't worry about it, son. Tomorrow morning after breakfast, I'll take you shopping at the hotel men's store and pick up a new shirt and a pair of slacks for you. Would you like that?"

"That's really nice of you, Beau, but you don't have to do that for me. I can run back to my place and change. It's just a few blocks away."

"No, I'd like to do something nice for you. You've given me the first real affection I've had since I got to this crazy town. Let me show you some appreciation. Pick out whatever you want and I'll get it for you. Besides, I'd be proud to have a handsome California boy waiting for me out here on the coast next time I come out, so I'd better treat you right, haven't I?" He smiled and beamed another twinkling sapphire at me. The man's charisma had no end.

I got up to go to the bathroom as he turned down the covers. I looked into the mirror as I splashed water on my face. My skin glowed with the rosy after-burn of sex. I considered showering, but I didn't want to rinse the feeling of Beau off. Climbing into bed next to him, I felt warm and human and loved, completely at home in my skin. Like me, he was a cuddler. He wrapped his big nude body around me gracefully, like a robe of soft fur, all night long. I slept deeply and dreamed of islands and dolphins and ships and rippling seas and billowing sails and blue eyes until dawn.

We made love again at dawn, taking each other's cocks into our mouths and sucking the sweet white sexual milk from each other tenderly. He made me feel special. Whatever we did in bed together felt new and wonderful and meaningful, as if we were the first human beings ever to discover sex and each act and movement of physical love was our own invention.

After a third round of tender, ball-draining sex, we fell asleep again. When I woke up several hours later, I jumped, cursing that I was already late for work! With no time to scrawl a note with some numbers for the sleeping giant, I pulled my clothes on quickly and was heading for the door when the hugest pair of arms grabbed me from behind and pulled me tightly into a big bare chest. A boar-bristled chin burned into the back of my neck.

"Please don't forget me, son," the voice growled, dark with sleep, the musky breath scraping my ear.

"Don't worry, I won't. Gotta go, man. Bye!" And I sped down a blur of red carpet into a future of memories.

Sometimes you glance at a person just for a moment as they pass by and, mesmerized, you think about them the rest of the day and night. Or you spend a night with someone and you remember them the rest of your life, wondering where they are at this moment, what their life might be like if they found the one they were looking for when they found you. And you wonder if you can say now what you should have turned around and said then: "I will never forget you, Papabear Beau."

A Lusty Tale of Farson's Wood, or, Men Well Met

HANK EDWARDS

Garrick's thick, hard cock pressed insistently into Osric's spit-slick, hair-shrouded hole. The large, muscled potter leaned forward over the cool surface of Osric's armor and trailed his tongue along the smooth, glistening breastplate. As Garrick fully impaled the young squire, spearing into the man's arse, Osric grunted and closed his dark-brown eyes. Garrick looked down with tenderness at the man who was pumping into him with a quickening pace, his grip on Osric's ankles tightening with the intensity of his thrusts. Osric's full lips parted, exposing the tip of his tongue behind his even teeth, and Garrick noticed that his dark-brown beard and shaggy mane of hair had recently been trimmed. Garrick leaned down again and tongued a drop of sweat off Osric's exposed neck, smiling as the knight shuddered.

"Does it feel all right?" Garrick asked.

Osric grunted beneath Garrick's thrusts. "Yes—ugh—it feels very right!"

Garrick looked down along Osric's body and drank in the sight of him. As Garrick liked, Osric wore only the breastplate etched with the image of a large bear. William Halstead, the baron who oversaw this corner of the king's land, had chosen a bear as his symbol and ordered it to be emblazoned on everything that belonged to him: his robes, his flags, even the armor worn by his knights and squires.

Osric's arms, thick with hair and tightly corded muscle, were taut as his large, hair-speckled hands gripped the thin blankets on the table beneath him. The knight's own blood-gorged cock, shorter yet thicker than Garrick's own, bounced in time with Garrick's pumping hips. A strand of precome swung between the piss slit and the mat of dark fur that covered Osric's belly. Garrick licked his lips, anticipating the sweet taste of the man's load he would lick off the cool armor after Osric had spent himself. He watched the man's heavy, hairy balls bounce in time to his fucking, at times slipping down to skim the top of Garrick's own shaft as he drove it deep.

As Garrick arrowed into him, Osric could not help but compare him to Sir Edward. As a squire, Osric had not yet been fully knighted—that would come after he proved himself worthy in battle or through another act of bravery—but until that time he was in service to the baron through his mentor, Sir Edward. Edward had been a knight for many years and taught his student much about the strategies of war as well as politics.

He also, as Osric soon discovered, used his young squires for manly release when no women were available. Many times when he had serviced Sir Edward over the past two years, Osric had ground his teeth to keep from crying out as the knight plowed roughly into him from behind, unconcerned if his actions caused his young squire pain. Osric found that he enjoyed not the uncaring insertion of Edward's cock, but the feel of the man's lance inside him. It excited him to eruption each time, a fact he was usually able to hide from Sir Edward since his mentor would, upon satisfying himself inside Osric's battered hole, withdraw and stand back a few paces with his eyes averted until Osric turned and wiped his drooping cock clean. Sir Edward then would stumble drunkenly to his cot, for he was most every night drunk by this time, and collapse into a snoring heap. Osric would clean himself up and polish Sir Edward's armor before the dying fire and then fall asleep himself on his own cot set off in the corner.

Garrick's cock was slimmer and longer than Sir Edward's blunt, thick club, but the real differences, Osric had discovered, were not in the size of the men's cocks, but the way in which they made use of them. Garrick was thoughtful, caring, gentle, and versatile, whereas Sir Edward was a gruff, hard, uncaring man with cold eyes and rough manners, slamming himself into Osric with no pretense of concern for what damage he wrought upon his student.

"Kiss me, Garrick," Osric said, overwhelmed at being filled up so caringly by the potter, and sucked the proffered tongue into his mouth. The hair on his face twined with Garrick's rust-colored beard, scratching and entangling, mixing their colors together.

"I'm close," Garrick gasped into Osric's mouth. "How shall you have it today?"

"My mouth," Osric moaned. "On my face and in my mouth."

"As you like." Garrick pressed slowly, deeply into Osric's arse a few more times then withdrew to step around the side of the table. With the fingers of one hand wrapped around the base of his shaft and heavy, hairy balls, Garrick jerked himself to climax. A stream of thick white seed shot across Osric's face and gaping mouth. Garrick stood on his toes, raising his hairy body enough to stuff his cock deep down Osric's throat as his second shot blasted across the young man's cheek and down his gullet.

Osric sucked the remaining seed from Garrick's softening cock. As he milked the potter dry he relished the taste of the thick fluid drizzling down his throat and began to pull on himself, his cock a hard bone of veined red flesh aching to spurt its load up along his armor-covered torso. His hairy, muscular legs still hung high in the air where Garrick had left them, the muscles tightly bunched. The potter leaned over Osric, his cock still lodged deep in the man's throat, and slid three fingers into the gasping hole he had just recently vacated. Osric grunted around Garrick's cock, his vocalizations falling into a rhythm that matched the timing of Garrick's fingers as they slipped in and out of his hole. With a last, fierce grunt, Osric arched his back and blew his load. The thick white spunk splattered over his breastplate and Garrick's face and the potter opened his mouth wide to catch as much of it as possible. Osric's seed coated Garrick's nose and chin, dripping from the potter's face onto the silver breastplate and running into the etched lines of the baron's symbol.

Garrick gently slid his fingers out of Osric's swollen, reddened hole and lapped up the puddles of warm semen, his cock still held firmly between Osric's lips. The etched silver of the breastplate was smooth and cool beneath his tongue, and he closed his eyes as he worked.

After he had licked up all of Osric's offering, Garrick rose and pulled himself free from the squire's mouth. A strand of clear fluid clung to his foreskin-sheathed cock and stretched from Osric's lower lip, breaking as Garrick leaned down to gently kiss him on the mouth.

Osric opened his eyes and smiled. Garrick ran a hand along the man's cheek and smiled back, watching as the sweat on his lover's face began to dry in the heat of the fire and the cool breeze wafting through the windows. He shivered in spite of the coat of rust-colored fur that covered his torso and stepped toward the fire to grab his tunic.

"Don't," Osric said quietly. He lay on his back across the rough-hewn wooden table, legs lowered and his head turned to take in Garrick's body. "I like to look at you naked."

"Do you, now?" Garrick said, feeling his cock twitch as Osric's deep brown eyes traveled the length of his body.

"You know I do." Osric sat up slowly, his face glowing. "I've always liked to watch you move."

Garrick shook his head and smiled in embarrassment. "All right, then, fair is fair. Get out of the rest of your armor and join me in my nudity."

As Osric unfastened the catches and ties on his breastplate,

Garrick marveled at the man's thick stature, stout cock, and large, low-hanging balls. Osric sported a thicker coat of fur than Garrick himself, something Garrick found incredibly arousing. If seeing Osric dressed only in his breastplate could get him hard, seeing the squire completely nude and sporting that lascivious grin of his could make his cock stiff within moments.

As Garrick watched the man remove his armor he thought back to the day they had met and felt the same swell of longing as he had then. It had been just over a year ago and early in the morning as Garrick had set out from his cottage and taken to the forest known to all in the barony as Farson's Wood. The fog had been lazy about thinning that morning. When Garrick had stepped from the trees onto the narrow trail to town, he had not seen the armored squire rushing along the path until it was too late. Osric burst into view, the fog tangled in his beard and flowing hair, and Garrick had just a moment to let out a startled yelp before the man barreled into him. The force of the collision spun them apart, Garrick to one side of the path, where he twisted his ankle, and Osric to crash into a beech tree on the opposite side.

Moments later, as Garrick groaned, Osric staggered to his feet and across the path, falling to his knees beside the potter. He was apologetic, sweaty, and handsome, nothing at all like the other knights of the baron's guard. Garrick's first thought as the man approached where he lay holding his injured ankle was that he was going to die there on the path near his home. The baron's knights were known to be vicious and ruthless, killing without cause or provocation, let alone in an instance where Garrick himself had caused one of them to fall. But Osric proved to be different from the other knights. He helped Garrick to his feet and slung the man's arm over the cool armor covering his broad shoulders, then assisted him back to his cottage.

As they walked Osric explained why he had been running through the woods: "I'm on a mission for Sir Edward, the Baron's most trusted knight, and must return before noon."

Garrick squinted up through the fog at the faded sun, barely visible, and replied, "You should have time enough to make your way back, the sun is not yet halfway risen."

Osric nodded and was silent the remainder of the way to Garrick's cottage. The fog here had begun to lift, and he helped the potter sit in a chair outside the door, then inspected the pots lined up along the outer wall. "You do fine work, potter. But why do you live out here in Farson's Wood, so far removed from town? Do you not need customers to keep in business?"

Garrick nodded as he rubbed his ankle, grateful to find it just a twist with no permanent damage. "I do need customers and have a regular income from several businesses in town, which affords me the opportunity to live away from the bustle of the village. I like my solitude, and the clay and water are close at hand here with the river just over the rise."

The squire paused and listened to the birds singing and caught the low murmur of the river. "You have made a good home here, potter."

"Garrick," he said, and their eyes locked. Garrick felt a spark and saw a reaction on Osric's face that told him the young squire just might want the same thing that Garrick did himself: the feel of a man's hard, hairy body beside him.

Osric nodded. "I am Osric, squire to Sir Edward of Baron William Halstead's guard." He looked through the open door into the one-room home, his eyes taking in the rows of jugs, pots, and plates, the throwing wheel and stacks of wood for firing, the low table and narrow, hand-carved bed. "Have you no wife, Garrick?"

"Aye, true," Garrick said and dropped his eyes to his ankle. "None would have me, and I decided I was better off alone."

Osric turned to him, and Garrick raised his gaze to catch the man's eyes once again. The spark burned there still, he saw, and had grown hotter and more intense. "We are well met, potter, but I must be off," Osric said and pulled his eyes away. "Edward will whip me for sure."

Garrick watched the squire run off into the trees, the brightening sunlight winking off his armor as he vanished into the thinning mist. A week later, Garrick hitched his small cart to his mule and rode into town to drop off an order of jugs at the inn. On his way back through the village he saw Osric in the street and was surprised when the squire gave him a hearty hale. The man was on his own, out of his armor and dressed in a loose tunic and breeches. Lonely and looking for company, Osric offered to buy Garrick an ale to make amends for their collision. Surprised at Osric's generosity and friendliness, Garrick accepted, and several hours and much ale later, they stumbled out of the tavern and rode in the cart back to the potter's secluded cottage for some bread, singing loudly, with their arms around each other's shoulders.

The night was balmy, and by habit Garrick removed his tunic upon entering the confines of the stuffy cottage. Osric's eyes briefly roamed Garrick's body before he pulled off his own loose tunic. They sat across from each other, wearing only breeches and watching the sweat track down each other's chests as they silently ate the hard bread. Osric's small, round belly was slick with sweat-matted hair and Garrick wondered what the young squire's skin tasted like in the summer heat. Before long Garrick became aroused, the stiff member more than evident beneath the rough wool of his breeches. Osric stood to get more bread and when he returned to his chair sat nude and erect across from a surprised Garrick. Osric began to stroke himself as his eyes, bleary with ale, moved along Garrick's body.

"You have a fine body, potter," Osric slurred.

"As do you," Garrick replied, feeling himself somehow growing harder despite the many mugs of ale he had consumed.

"May I?" Osric asked and staggered out of the low chair to cross the room and fall on his knees before Garrick. He roughly pulled the breeches down Garrick's legs and swallowed the potter's cock whole in a single gulp, causing Garrick to gasp. They struggled to get at each other, so enthralled at the thought of finally realizing their fantasies they were reduced to stumbling and fumbling like unskilled boys.

Finally, Garrick fell on his back on the narrow bed and Osric turned his back and straddled him. He hovered over the potter's face and once again took Garrick's cock deep down his throat. Garrick swallowed the thick, sweaty length of meat above him and sucked hard. Osric climaxed first, spewing his load—buckets it seemed—into Garrick's mouth. Feeling himself hit the edge, Garrick pressed hard on the back of Osric's head, impaling his face, and emptied himself into the squire's mouth.

Osric drank down all of it, savoring the taste and milking Garrick for every last drop. Exhausted, they collapsed in a heap on the bed and spent their first, and only, night together. The following morning Osric awoke with a start and leaped from Garrick's side.

"I must be off," he said. "I was supposed to be back before nightfall."

He pulled his breeches on as he hopped to the door, turned back once to look in Garrick's bleary, sleep-filled eyes, and then was gone.

Later, Garrick learned that because he did not return the night before Osric had been punished, given 20 lashes by Sir Edward in front of the rest of the members of the Realm of the Bear and under the baron's watchful eye. They never again spent the night together, but two days later Osric returned to the potter's cottage, his face pale and drawn. Garrick tended to Osric's lashes, tears rolling down his face as he applied ointment and dressings, knowing he had unwittingly had a hand in the man's punishment. After the dressings were applied, Garrick held the man in his arms and quieted his moans. The fact that Osric had returned after such a beating said more to Garrick than the squire could ever have put into words.

Garrick shook himself from his reverie and looked at Osric now standing nude before him, on the cusp of becoming a full-fledged knight. "Come here," Garrick said, his voice low with desire. "Let me wash you."

"All right." Osric stepped into a low-walled wooden tub waiting in a corner and stood with his arms at his side. Garrick lifted a water jug from before the fire, tested the temperature, then poured it over Osric's head. He watched the water sluice away the sweat, dirt, and sex from the man's hairy body and felt his cock twitch with fresh desire. Osric made Garrick feel so much younger than his 42 years. It was amazing, actually, that they had come together at all, this 25-year-old squire to the baron and him, a mere potter.

Osric reached out and grabbed Garrick's cock. "Hard again?" he said with a grin.

"Does that surprise you?" Garrick poured another jug of water over the man and ran his hands along his body. He eased his fingers over the scars left by Sir Edward's lashing the previous year then down to the rounded swells of the man's arse. Moving slowly, Garrick massaged the firm, hairy buttocks then slipped a finger into the warm, wet hole between.

Osric gasped at the invasion and peeled open an eye. "Keep that up and I shall make you pay homage to *me* this time."

"Oh, you think so, do you?" Garrick teased and interchanged a few fingers, sliding them as far inside the man as possible.

"Oh," Osric sighed, leaning forward and closing his eyes. "I'm serious, Garrick."

"Oh, I know you are." Garrick removed his fingers and reached around to grasp Osric's freshly hardened cock before grabbing another jug of water. He doused the man again, then leaned forward to kiss him, their tongues sliding together as Osric stepped out of the tub and walked Garrick around the potter's wheel back to the small, low table.

Garrick's buttocks pressed up against the table edge and Osric leaned him back, raising his tanned, hairy legs. Moving down along Garrick's body, Osric ran his tongue through the man's bearded jaw to his neck, where he paused to suckle on the tender skin and leave a slowly darkening bruise in his wake. He slipped down to Garrick's nipples and teased each with his tongue and teeth, nipping and sucking at them until they became points of brown flesh that stood up hard and firm.

Sliding off to the sides of Garrick's body, Osric hungrily licked up the sweat that had gathered in the potter's armpits, sighing and moaning at the heady aroma and salty taste. Garrick groaned as Osric feasted on the sensitive skin beneath the sweaty, rust-colored hair of his armpits. More bruises came up beneath Osric's demanding mouth, something Garrick had become used to during the year he and Osric had been meeting. More often than not he would discover love bites all over his body following an afternoon spent with his squire. Osric liked to mark Garrick's body as a sign of possession: Garrick belonged to him, and no one else.

Moving lower, Osric felt Garrick's thick, long cock poking and skimming across his chest. He paused to suckle at Garrick's navel and tightened his chest, trapping Garrick's cock in the muscular furrow between. He began to move his upper body, stroking Garrick's cock with his wet, hairy skin.

Garrick sighed and dropped his head back on the table, squeezing his eyes shut as Osric's chest stroked him close to orgasm. "You would be wise to stop," Garrick grunted. "I mean it."

Osric smiled down into Garrick's navel, his tongue slipping through the hair of the man's stomach and around the smooth interior of the indentation. Raising himself slightly so that he released the hold his chest had maintained on Garrick's cock, Osric ducked quickly and swallowed the staff whole.

"Ungh!" Garrick gasped and his fingers clawed at the tabletop as Osric sucked his cock with a furious tempo.

Osric gripped Garrick's cock tight around the base and began to stroke in time with his sucking, focusing his suction on the soft head beneath the tough foreskin. After a time, Osric slowed his sucking and released Garrick's staff to move down to the potter's hairy balls, taking them one by one into his mouth and sucking strongly, continuing a tight-gripped stroking along the man's cock.

Osric loved the feel of Garrick's hardened pole in his palm, down his throat, and deep inside him. When he was with Garrick like this, engaged in sweat-drenched sex, he felt filled up and complete. Many times during his lessons or training he would become distracted by thoughts of Garrick and lose his place, struggling afterward to catch up. Osric knew what he did with Garrick was considered sinful and different from the acts Sir Edward visited upon him. Those times when Sir Edward used him in the absence of women were for release only; Osric's times with Garrick stayed with him, comforted him, filled him with longing for the next meeting. Osric felt more for this older man stretched out before him than he had for anyone his entire young life. He was willing to risk his life to enjoy these few hours of pleasure they shared in Farson's Wood, and if he must keep their meetings hidden from those around them, then that would be what they would do. He had found his true calling and, right or wrong, was determined to pursue it.

Moving his mouth even lower, Osric kept up the rhythmic stroking along Garrick's cock and teased the hairy hole just beneath the man's balls with his tongue. Garrick's arse was ripe with sweat, and Osric breathed deep, inhaling the odor and feeling lightheaded. He loved the smell of Garrick's body as well as the hardened feel of him.

"Oh, Osric," Garrick groaned. He reached down and spread his arse cheeks wide, allowing the knight in deeper. "Get your tongue up inside me."

Osric licked around and spit into Garrick's slowly loosening hole. He slid a thick, blunt finger deep within him and watched with satisfaction as Garrick arched his back and opened his mouth to gasp at the invasion.

"You like that, potter?" Osric asked teasingly. "Does that feel good to you?"

"Oh, yes," Garrick replied. He shimmied down along the table to bring himself even closer to the edge. "Get another up inside me."

Osric adjusted his hand and slowly penetrated Garrick with two fingers. He watched, his cock hard and aching, as his fingers moved in and out of Garrick's body. "Do you want more?"

"Yes," Garrick groaned. "Get your lance up there, squire. Joust with me."

Osric grinned and removed his fingers. Standing up, he spit down onto his fully hardened member, mixing the saliva with a generous amount of precome along the head and pulling back the foreskin as he eased up next to Garrick's body. Slowly, steadily, Osric pushed himself inside the willing tunnel of flesh, the entire length of him sliding into Garrick's arse. He wrapped one hand around Garrick's cock and the other around one of his ankles.

"Oh, God!" Garrick opened his mouth and closed his eyes. His hands gripped the table edge, and the tendons in his neck stood out as his body arched up off the surface of the table.

Osric pushed relentlessly forward, plowing deeper and deeper into the hot, dark recesses of Garrick's body. With a last deep thrust, Osric sank himself completely into the man and held his place. He remained buried within Garrick for several moments, relishing the feel of the older man's muscles tightening and releasing around his cock. He watched sweat break out along the potter's brow and body and leaned down to taste the droplets that gathered at Garrick's throat.

Slowly, Osric pulled nearly free from the potter's arse, then plunged back in again. He found his rhythm and began to plow Garrick's hole with abandon. Grabbing both of the man's ankles, Osric tossed his head back and closed his eyes, giving himself over to pure animal instinct. Sweat ran down his body and his hair, damp from the water and exertion, and slapped around his shoulders. He drove his hard, blunt member into Garrick faster and faster until he felt himself approach release.

"I am close," he gasped.

"Up inside me," Garrick replied. "Fill me up."

Osric let out a low, deep growl, and his hips bucked as he spent himself deep inside Garrick's body. He gulped ragged breaths and slumped forward over Garrick, supporting himself with his arms as he caught his breath. His cock remained tight inside Garrick as the potter furiously stroked his own leaking rod to orgasm.

"Oh...yes...aarghh!" Garrick's cock spat thick white seed up along their hairy, sweaty torsos. He raised his head and grunted until he was spent, then collapsed back onto the tabletop.

Osric slowly pulled himself from inside Garrick. He longed to remain here in the warmth of the potter's cottage all night, but he had learned his lesson. The shadows were lengthening along the wall; it was time for him to prepare to return to Sir Edward.

Osric bent down and licked the thinning seed from Garrick's sweat-drenched chest and stomach. Scooping up the fluid where it dampened his own furry torso, Osric stared down into Garrick's eyes as he raised his fingers to his lips and sucked them clean.

"Well," Garrick gasped as he caught his breath. "That was an unexpected surprise."

Osric grinned. "I like to keep you on your toes."

Garrick fixed him with a smile. "Or on my back."

"However it works," Osric replied with a shrug. "Come, let us clean up at the river."

They walked naked through the woods, carrying empty water jugs and pushing and touching each other playfully until they came to the cold, shallow river. They plunged into the icy waters, letting out howls of shock, then stood on the smooth, slippery rocks beneath the water and washed themselves.

Garrick watched as Osric waded to the riverbank and grabbed the jugs. The man stood with his back to Garrick as he dunked the jugs under the surface to fill. The muscles of Osric's hair-covered buttocks bunched and released and Garrick felt his desire flare up once again. Unfortunately, the afternoon was waning and Osric needed to return to the castle grounds.

"Come on, old man," Osric called out in good nature. He corked the last of the jugs and lifted it to the riverbank, then clambered out himself. "Get that saggy arse moving."

"The only reason it might be saggy is because you keep sticking that big trunk of yours into it," Garrick replied and accepted Osric's outstretched hand for assistance. The squire pulled him easily up the bank then grabbed him in a tight bear hug. They stood kissing for a time, their half-hard cocks rubbing casually together as their hands explored freshly washed and rinsed crevices.

Finally breaking the embrace, Garrick looked down at the slightly shorter man and caressed his face. "You bring me much joy, young squire."

"As you do me, old potter," Osric replied with a wicked grin. "Now let us return, and you can help me redress myself."

They carried the water jugs back to the cottage, and Garrick fell slightly behind to watch Osric's buttocks tighten and release as he moved. Once through the door, he helped Osric into his armor, fondling the long, heavy sword before passing it over. He kissed Osric one last time and smiled as the man stepped back, his armor quietly rattling. The man, almost a knight, reminded Garrick at times of a young, love-swept boy. And Garrick cherished this part of him.

Osric fixed him with a serious look and said quietly, "We are well-met, potter, but I must away."

A shiver traveled Garrick's spine, as always happened when Osric spoke his parting line. "I know. Come back when you can," he replied.

"I shall." Osric strode out the door and mounted his horse. He tipped a farewell to Garrick, then reined his horse around and headed off. Garrick stood, leaning nude in the doorway, and watched the young man make his way through the trees. The late-afternoon sun twinkled off Osric's broad armored shoulders, and Garrick watched until the squire was swallowed up by the trees of Farson's Wood.

Vinnie's Backyard Party

JIM MASON

The mailed, handwritten invitation is simple. "Party at Vinnie's. Bring yer butt and something else to eat." It gives the date for a Sunday afternoon in August, Vinnie's address in Boystown, Chicago, off Halsted Street, and his phone number.

Vinnie's a meat cutter for one of the big supermarket chains, so the food is always good. I know most of the guys 'cause we go to the same bars, but sometimes there's a new face, usually someone's trick from the night before. We have a great time together. OK, "great time" sometimes means sex, but these aren't always sex parties. There have been parties where all we did was eat and shoot the shit. Vinnie has a bowl of rubbers and bottles of lube available just in case they're needed.

His party last February, that's one to remember. We got trapped at his place for two days by an ice storm that fuckin' shut Chicago down. We were lucky the electricity stayed on so we were warm and could cook, but otherwise there were 12 guys with nothing to do but each other. Hell, even my butt got reamed out that weekend, and that doesn't happen often. We also all got crabs.

Like most of the crowd I hang with, I'm a regular guy who gets his rocks off with other regular guys. There's just a bit of gray in my beard and some in my chest hair, and the short hair on my head has receded some in front. Got more than enough fur on the rest of my body to make up for that loss, though. What's disappeared from my head seems to be reappearing on my back. The years' beer shows some in my gut, but I can still see my dick when I take a piss. Course I could say that's 'cause I got a 10-inch cock or something like that, but it'd be a lie. I'm average in that department, and it works fine.

August in Chicago can be hot and humid or rainy, hot, and humid. The day of the party is the former. With clear, sunny skies, the temperature is predicted to be in the 90s. I tug on a pair of ragged, cut-off 501 jeans, pull a sleeveless T-shirt over my head, and slip on a pair of sandals. With a one-pound container of store-bought macaroni salad in a bag, I get in my car and make the drive south to Vinnie's.

The house is in a tree-shaded residential area. It's a one-story place with a driveway that goes alongside to the back, leading to a detached garage. The backyard is enclosed from the house to the garage by a tall, wooden fence. "Don't want to spook the neighbors by our goings-on," Vinnie says.

I park in the driveway and note that Wes's Jeep is already there. I spot C.B.'s Harley parked on the walkway leading from the drive to the front door. *Well, we've got a party of four so far,* I think.

Vinnie's fence has a door between the drive and the yard, so I knock and wait to be let in. A feature of this door is a peephole at eye level, so Vinnie can see who's knocking before he opens it. First-timers always make some crack about Al Capone having lived there, but Vinnie says, "Naw, it's a glory hole for basketball players." Soon after I knock I see Vinnie's eye lookin' out the peephole, hear a couple latches being thrown, then the door opens and Vinnie's standing there wearing only a pair of worn, faded maroon gym shorts. His basket, hanging to the right, is clearly outlined under the old material. Vinnie's a hefty, very hairy man, and his face has more of a heavy stubble than a beard, but he has a thick black mustache. He looks like your local Italian grocer with hairy shoulders.

Vinnie smiles big, opens his arms, gives me a smooch and a sweaty hug. The sweat from his chest hair leaves a wet mark on my shirt.

"Hey, Russ," he says, "come on in. You already know Wes and C.B. If what you brought needs the fridge, just take it on into the kitchen."

I wave at the other two guys and bound up the back stairs into the kitchen. Outside again, I see Wes is sitting on an aluminum lawn chair, the kind that leaves stripes on your back from the plastic webbing, and C.B. is laid out on a matching lounge chair. Vinnie hands me a cold bottle of beer from a styrofoam cooler, and I sit my ass down in a director's chair. The yard is half in shade and half in sun, but it's so damn hot that we all choose the shady side.

I haven't known Wes long, but he's a good-looking, friendly guy, a bulky, hairy redhead with a full, bushy, reddish-brown beard and handlebar mustache that he sometimes waxes out along his cheeks. Today his 'stache is just drooping down either side of his mouth, getting lost in his face fur. He's probably the youngest of us here. The red "StL" ball cap on his head betrays the fact that he's not a Chicago native. Wes is wearing jeans and sneakers but is shirtless. I have a hard spot in my pants for redheads and want to lick the sweat from his nipples. I've never gotten it on with Wes, but sure as shit wouldn't turn down an invitation.

C.B., on the other hand, I've known most of my life. Hell, I even know his real name, and it doesn't start with C. You know how kids can be cruel. As early as junior high, C.B. got a lot of teasing from the other guys on account of the size of his dick. They started calling him "Coke Bottle" 'cause "Beer Can" wasn't long and fat enough. I guess now I'd say they were envious. He also has this big fuckin' dick head, covered by a long, meaty foreskin. Shit. What man wouldn't envy that? The nickname caused C.B. some deal of embarrassment, though, especially when it was used in front of the girls or teachers, but as he got older he realized that, hey, having the biggest dong in school wasn't such a bad thing. The name stuck but was shortened to "C.B.," and now that's how most folks know him.

C.B. was also my first sex buddy. Puberty hit both of us early and at about the same time, so we were getting chest hair when most other kids our age had just fuzz above their dicks. In Boy Scouts we learned from the older troop members how to jack off. Then once while sharing a tent we discovered it felt good to let another guy tug your meat. Later, during a backyard campout at his parents' place, I let C.B. put his dick in my mouth, and he let me rub his asshole with my prick. The next night we reversed positions. The following weekend C.B. sucked me off and even swallowed my load of ball juice. He then fucked the shit outta my ass. Damn. Guess that's why I don't get fucked much anymore. I've already been had by the biggest. Now C.B.'s a grown, well-built hump of a man, over six feet tall, with a shaved head, a tattoo of barbed wire around one bicep, a deep voice, longish brown beard, and body hair just as thick as that on his face. He's also a big ol' bottom, proving true the saying "The bigger the dick, the faster the legs go into the air." Today he's in his biker clothes of jeans, black boots, and a white T-shirt.

Just as my dick's starting to twitch from remembering some of the cocksucking fun C.B. and I have had, there's a knock at the fence door. It's Greg, a second-generation American, who lapses into Polish obscenities when he's about to come. Yeah, I know that from personal experience. Greg's a handsome fuck, built like a fireplug. He and I were once standing next to each other, pissing into the trough upstairs at one of the bars. His hairy forearms and fingers got my attention first. The long black hairs sticking out the top of his T-shirt also held my interest. Then when I saw his lengthening cock pissin' a stream at the urinal, I was in lust, went down on him right there, and used my tongue to scoop precome outta his big piss-slit. Soon his jizz was flowing out of my mouth and into my beard. He gave me a full-mouth kiss, smearing his black beard with his own come.

Greg has a tattoo of Poland over his right pec and gets asked if his nipple marks the location of Warsaw. He got the tat before his chest hair had grown in, so it's now a heavily forested Poland. Greg arrives at the party wearing only his jeans and a Cubs ball cap.

Right behind Greg is Ray. I've never met Ray before, but he knows Vinnie and Wes. Ray's a tall, bearded black guy, probably younger than me but not by much. He's got some strands of gray in his beard and hair and is wearing jeans, sneakers, and a bar T-shirt. There's a gold ring through his left earlobe, and I see the outline of another ring through his right nipple. Ray takes a seat next to Greg on a blanket in the grass and introduces himself around.

Greg asks how many more guys are coming. Vinnie goes through a list of half a dozen names who'd sent their regrets and ends with, "So this is probably it, unless Gene shows up." The beer is going down easily and quickly in the heat of the early afternoon. We're all sweatin' like sons-a-bitches. Vinnie and I are letting our balls hang out the bottoms of our shorts, "just to let them breathe," we say. The few shoes and shirts that were worn on arrival are now off. Occasionally, someone goes to take a leak against a tree. Wes produces a small pipe and a bag of dope, which he shares with all of us. After a few tokes, we're red-eyed and a little giggly. Talk wanders from the weather to the bars to politics to a brief debate between Wes and Greg about the Cards and Cubs. The rest of us put a fast end to that.

C.B. stands up from the lounge chair and asks, "Hey, Vinnie. Is it OK to get nekkid out here?" Without waiting for an answer, he pops open his jeans, pushes them down to his ankles, slips them off his feet, and sits back down with one leg on either side of the chair, his dick and balls resting heavily on the webbing. "Ah," he sighs, "that's better," and he places his hands behind his head.

My dopey attention is focused on C.B.'s sweat-matted armpits when Vinnie suddenly appears from behind C.B., takes a one-kneed stance in front of the chair, yells "Gotcha!" and, with a finger over the nozzle of a garden hose, sends a blast of cold water square into C.B.'s nuts.

"Motherfuck!" shouts C.B., and he makes a lunge for Vinnie. Still stoned off my ass, I'm seeing all this in slow motion, thinking how great it is to watch C.B.'s equipment swing and flop around as he jumps from the chair. Vinnie and C.B. are on the ground grappling for the hose, which is sending water all over the backyard. I think, *Wallet! In shorts! Can't get wet!* and make a dash for the garage side door, tugging open the buttons on my shorts as I go. I open the door, shove the shorts down, and kick them into the doorway. Just as I bend down to push them in farther, my butt gets sprayed with water. I turn around and see that Greg, wearing completely soaked jeans, now has the hose. I go for 'im.

Vinnie's lying on his back, laughin' his ass off with C.B sitting on his chest. Just before I reach Greg, he yells "Catch" and tosses the hose to Ray. Ray must have been thinking like me, 'cause he's stripped down to his white Jockey underwear, which looks great against the dark brown of his body. Ray catches the hose, but with the nozzle pointed up toward his face. After a few snorts, he gets the water out of his nose and spots a now-nude Wes, having also tossed his pants to safety, wearing only his ball cap. I've never seen Wes naked before, and I like what I see.

Wes stands there for a moment, looking like a deer caught in the headlights, then does a fast backward walk away from Ray, who's advancing with the hose. Wes trips over the beer cooler, smashing the Styrofoam and scattering beer bottles. He's on the ground moaning in pain as Ray approaches with the limp hose, concerned that Wes has hurt himself. But as Ray gets within reach, Wes grabs the hose and shoves it down the front of Ray's underwear. "Bigger than anything else you've got in there," grins Wes. Ray's underwear becomes transparent from the water, giving an impressive show of cock and balls. The water fight continues with all of us running and wrasslin' for control of the hose. Besides one another, we wash down the side of the garage, the back of the house, and probably Wes's Jeep and my car in the drive. Finally we're laughing so hard we can't stand up, and we collapse onto the ground.

After a few minutes' rest, we get up and retrieve our beers or replace spilled ones. Vinnie tries to put the bottles back into the shattered cooler and piles ice on top. His wet gym shorts are dragging down to his crotch hair in front and half down his ass in back. He's got this great triangular "welcome mat" of fur on his lower back, just above his butt. I mention to Ray that if Vinnie's yard didn't have grass, we'd be in a mudpit. "Maybe next time," he grins. Vinnie lets his shorts fall from their own weight, kicks them off, and hangs them on the clothesline to dry along with the blanket. Greg and Ray shrug, say "What the hell," take off the rest of their clothes, and hang them up on the line.

There are now six naked men in the backyard drying in the heat of the day. I'm back in the director's chair, letting my cock and balls hang over the edge of the seat. C.B. is in the lounge again, with his head back but his arms down. Greg stands behind C.B. Wes and Ray sit on the grass and start playing with each other's nipples. Vinnie remains standing, scratchin' his nuts and tuggin' slightly and slowly at his prick. I think I see which way this party's gonna go.

Without saying anything, Greg lifts his dick and rests it on C.B.'s shoulder. C.B. turns his head, looks, sticks out his tongue, and takes a lick at Greg's piss slit. Greg's dick twitches and starts to expand. C.B. takes a second lick. Greg's dick expands more and starts to hover over the surface of C.B.'s shoulder. After a third lick, Greg's cock is off the shoulder and waving freely in the air. All of us are watching as C.B. takes Greg's rod into his mouth, and Greg slides all the way in until his balls rest against C.B.'s chin. Greg moves from behind to straddle the chair, faces C.B., and gets into position for some serious face-fucking.

Vinnie's half hard-on leads him over to Greg and C.B., where he nuzzles Greg's balls from behind with his stubbled chin. C.B.'s dick has risen up from the chair, but his balls are still laid out on the webbing. You've heard of dicks so big they don't get hard? Well, C.B.'s ain't that way. His wanger not only increases in length and girth, it points straight up and gets hard as a fuckin' tree branch. My own tool's calling out for attention now, and I'm giving it some help with my right hand.

Ray and Wes are up off the grass, and Ray is headed for the party on the chair. I see Wes going toward the tree. Now's the time to make a move. I go up to Wes and kneel down behind him. His piss splatters on his furry toes and my knees. I reach out for his butt cheeks, spread 'em, find his hole, and wet down the reddish hairs with my tongue. "I'll give you just half an hour to stop that," he says slowly. He's finished pissing but seems to be taking a long time to shake the drops off.

Wes turns around so his balls rest near my nose. His crotch fur is red-orange in color—the color of his armpit hair and without the brown that's in his beard. Wes strokes the shaft of his dick, letting the head pop in and out of his foreskin. He's already drooling a lot of precome. I reach for his cock and take over the stroking. He's got a great-looking piece of meat, the blue veins clearly visible. The head's a fat one. The foreskin doesn't quite close all the way over, like C.B.'s does, but that might be 'cause he's getting harder. With my other hand, I play with Wes's hairy nuts, squeezin' and tuggin' gently. Then I go down on him. After a few minutes of giving Wes some of my best head, I pull off, leaving a string of spit and precome between my mouth and his dick. I admit to him that I want to spend more time with him, but that I also don't want to miss any group play. Wes agrees and adds, "Let's go join the others, but I want to reserve some more time with you too." We tongue-wrestle for a moment, then I tweak his nipples and give his dick another tug before we head over to the group by the chair.

C.B. is off the lounge, on his hands and knees, still working his lips on Greg's prick. Vinnie is jacking his dick while lying under C.B. trying to take that big cock down his throat. Mostly he's just tonguing under the foreskin. Ray is rimming C.B.'s ass from the side, leaving a lot of spit in and around the pink hole.

Sensing our arrival, Ray looks up and asks, "Is C.B. a good fuck?"

"Yeah," we all answer at once.

There are a few chuckles. C.B. speaks up, "All right, all right. So each of you has had my ass 'cept Ray, but I've had two of yours."

"Jesus Christ," interrupts Greg, "which two of us took on that monster schlong and survived?"

"I'm not tellin,' " C.B. answers, but I'm also wondering who

211

besides me C.B. has fucked. Then C.B. continues suggestively, "But I haven't had all of you on the same day…"

Vinnie pipes up, "Shit, C.B.! Are you offering us an afternoon gang bang?"

"Yeah," I say, "Sounds like C.B. wants to pull train. And being surrounded by five boners, it looks like he's gonna get what he's after."

"Plus," C.B. adds, "I want all of you to pull out in time to shoot your spunk on me." He then sets the stakes. "Whatcha say, 10 minutes each per round?"

We agree. One man gets to fuck C.B. for 10 minutes, then another man takes over for 10 minutes. After the fifth has screwed, we go around again and again till we've all shot our wads on C.B. Vinnie is the only one wearing a watch, so he's the timekeeper. The next question is, who's gonna go first?

"I don't mind sloppy seconds," says Greg.

"Or thirds," adds Wes.

Vinnie decides, "Ray, you've already got him loosened up with your tongue and wet with spit, so you can go first."

"OK, I'll volunteer to bust his cherry, if he's grown one today," Ray grins.

"Naw, my daily cherry already got busted 'bout 2 o'clock this morning," says C.B.

There are a few more chuckles, then Ray gets two fingers full of lube and starts to work at C.B.'s bunghole. The first of many rubbers used this afternoon is taken from the bowl.

Ray doesn't bother starting with just one finger and tries two, which slip into C.B. easily. Ray is massaging his prostate while C.B. moans softly. "Damn, he's loose," Ray notes, "I hope this isn't going to be like throwing hot dogs down a hallway."

C.B. challenges, "Just get your hard black fucker in there, and I'll show you who's loose."

Ray works the third finger in, satisfied that C.B. is ready. C.B. turns over onto his back and pushes his feet into Ray's shoulders. Greg, wearing his Cubs cap backward, sits on C.B.'s face and drops his balls into the open mouth. He faces Ray, pulls on his prick, and waits to watch Ray enter C.B. Ray's cock is long but not fat, and his shaft and balls are jet-black, darker than the rest of his body. Ray spits onto his hand, slicks up his cock, and presses forward. C.B. relaxes his ass to allow for easy entry, then flexes to tighten around Ray's piece. "Whoa," Ray exclaims as he feels C.B.'s muscles grab hold of his rod like a fist. He pumps slowly but fully in and out of C.B.'s chute. A couple times he pulls all the way out so he can enjoy the feeling of going back in.

"Fuck. That's great," he tells C.B.

"No shit," C.B. answers, muffled by Greg's balls, "and you're rubbin' me just the right way."

The rest of us are enjoying the show, but we're not just standing by, idly playing with ourselves. Vinnie's found a spot behind Ray where he can lap at Ray's balls while he fucks. I bury my face in Wes's moist armpits, loving the smell of a sweaty man, while he pinches my nipples. We're standing close enough to Greg that he reaches out and pulls Wes's dick into his mouth.

Much too soon, Vinnie suddenly calls out, "Switch!"

"Shit," Ray mutters, sweat pouring down his dark chest and back, as he withdraws from C.B.

Greg's next to go up C.B.'s fuck hole. His dick's already slick with precome. Greg's a rapid-fire pounder when it comes to fucking. He's not gentle. He grabs C.B. by the hips and in one push drives his prick all the way into C.B.'s guts. "Unh!" gasps C.B. Greg stays in for maybe five seconds, pulls all the way out, then drives all the way in again. C.B. is on his knees and forearms, trying to blow Vinnie, who's squatted down in front of him, but mostly C.B.'s hanging on to Vinnie's dick to keep from being pushed around the yard by Greg's hard thrusts. I'm acting as secondary anchor by standing next to Vinnie, easing my dick down his throat while he hangs on to my balls with one hand and runs another through my butt crack. Wes is going down on Ray and works a spit-wet finger up into Ray's asshole. After 10 minutes of jackhammer pounding and sweating, Greg's forested tat of Poland looks like a rain forest. He yields C.B.'s butt to me.

I lie on my back and hold my boner straight up in the air. C.B. slowly lowers himself onto my prick, facing me. He pushes back as I push up. We play with each other's nipples, thrusting and rocking, until Vinnie straddles my chest and feeds me his dick. Ray stands over me with his cock in Vinnie's face and wipes precome over his lips and 'stache. Vinnie rubs his stubble across Ray's dick head and nuts. I get a great view from underneath Ray's ass and balls. Greg stands beside Ray and gives Vinnie a choice of two dicks to slobber over. Wes comes up behind C.B. and pokes a finger into his hole, sliding it in and out alongside my cock. Greg, Ray, and Vinnie move off to the side to play and, with some adjustment, C.B. and I make room for Wes to position himself to enter C.B. for a double fuck. C.B. moans, "Unh, uh, oh, aah, ungh, fuck," as Wes pushes his prick forward. I feel every move Wes makes sliding in over the underside of my dick. I just shut my eyes and let them roll back into my head. C.B. rocks back and forth on both cocks, milking them with his clenching ass muscles. Wes and I pump slowly and at slightly different rates, making the sensation even more dramatic.

Then, "Switch! Sorry, guys," says Vinnie, grinning, "I really do hate to break that up, but I wanna fuck too."

"Aw, Christ," Wes sighs.

The three of us separate, but Vinnie tells Wes he still has five minutes left. Wes reenters C.B., but as a single, while I stand there strokin' my joint.

Vinnie mumbles, "This timer job really sucks shit," and he finally gets his turn after giving the watch over to Ray. C.B. is again on his back with his legs high in the air. Vinnie slaps each of C.B.'s ass cheeks, lifts his own arms and takes a long sniff of each pit, gives his balls a good tug, then drives his prick into the elevated butt. C.B.'s ass smacks hard against Vinnie's pelvis. C.B. again gasps, but it turns into a low moan. Ray and I latch on to one of C.B.'s bare feet, shrimping his toes and licking the grass-stained sole. Wes jerks off astride C.B.'s head, facing Vinnie, with his ass on top of C.B.'s nose, and gets his balls sucked. Greg alternates around, sucking any dick that's not being otherwise used. After 10 minutes, sweat is dripping off Vinnie's mustache, and Ray calls out, "Time. End of round one."

"Goddamn, you guys are good," says C.B., lying flat on his back. "I need a break. Just a quick one. My hole ain't satisfied yet." We get fresh beers, and Greg and Ray go to the tree to piss. Wes breaks out the pot again, and we have a couple hits to refresh the high.

After maybe five minutes, C.B. asks, "OK. Who's first for round two?"

"I am," Vinnie answers quickly.

During the second bout, no one wants to come yet, so we each quit before our 10 minutes is up. Vinnie jacks his dick back to full hardness and picks up where he left off, with C.B. on his back. I tug at Vinnie's balls and slap them around a little while he's fucking. Ray sits on C.B.'s face for some nut-munchin' and sucks on Wes's cock. Greg stands stroking himself and pinches hard at Wes's nipples.

Suddenly, Vinnie announces, "Oh, fuck. I gotta stop."

"But you've got four minutes left," says Ray.

"Naw, I gotta stop before I shoot," Vinnie sighs.

"My turn," says Wes. He stands C.B. up against the garage wall with his legs spread wide and his arms out to brace himself. Wes goes in with one hard and fast shove and pounds that ass. C.B. grunts "Unh…unh…unh" with the beat of each thrust. I'm sitting in front of C.B., taking his dick halfway down my throat each time he gets pushed forward. "Yeah, Wes," I hear above me, "Fuck my ass as hard as I fucked yours." C.B.'s words are punctuated by each jab from Wes's prick.

So, I think to myself, *Wes is the other one of us that's taken C.B.'s huge fucktool up his butt.*

Greg comes up to my right, holding his cock out toward me. I take it between my lips and suck him in, freeing C.B.'s prick to slide up and down my face. Vinnie and Ray are watching while stroking each other. Wes suddenly stops and lowers his bearded chin to his hairy chest. Sweat runs down his back into his ass crack, streams down his chest into his pubes, and drips from his nose. He slowly pulls out, panting, "Shit. Hafta stop, 'else gonna pop."

I crawl up off the ground and take Wes's place with C.B. in the same position. Vinnie replaces me on the ground and starts sucking on C.B. while also squeezin' C.B.'s balls in his fist. I decide to follow Greg and Wes's style and punch-fuck C.B. His moans are getting louder and sounding more desperate. Ray, Greg, and Wes are in a three-way suck, but I'm not seeing too clearly 'cause sweat keeps runnin' into my eyes. Also, my balls are really aching to unload. Too soon, I have to quit, saying, "Oh, God. Who's next? I gotta pull out."

Ray steps up and plugs in. Greg comes up behind Ray and commands, "Spread 'em." Greg uses a finger to push against Ray's hole as he humps into C.B., then Greg jams his dick into Ray. Although a little uncoordinated at first, they get into sync for a three-way standing fuck. Vinnie is under all those hairy legs, tuggin' on and tonguin' balls. With C.B.'s arms outstretched against the garage wall for support, I take advantage of his exposed pits by lapping up the sweat. The funk makes my 'stache and beard smell so fuckin' good. Then I feed C.B.'s sweat back to him by some mouth-to-mouth.

Ray calls the early end to round two, saying, "Shit, man, two more humps either into C.B. or from Greg behind me, and I'd have blasted."

C.B., looking wasted and limp everywhere but his dick, announces, "Round three. No break."

The final fuck session goes quickly. Although our nuts are still hanging low from the heat, we all feel the ache of blue balls. Ray is the first one in, with C.B. on the ground and his legs wrapped around Ray's back. At one point, Ray has C.B. bent over so far that his butt hole is straight up in the air, and his body weight is being supported by his shoulders. C.B. is looking his own dick in the face. He squeezes precome from the shaft out the piss-slit and catches it on his tongue. I know C.B. can suck himself off. I saw him do it once on a bet at a bar. He even came in his own mouth, then spit the splooge into the mouth of the man who'd lost the bet. It looks like he's gonna go down on himself again, but Ray lowers C.B. back to the ground, and Wes moves in to attach his face to

216

C.B.'s prick. I volunteer to give C.B. something else to suck. The pounding in his ass and the sliding against his prostate causes C.B.'s bladder to release, and he pisses into Wes's mouth.

Surprised, Wes pulls off, gets the rest in his face, and sputters, "Shit. Wasn't expectin' that."

C.B. grins and says, "Sorry, I didn't feel it coming."

Vinnie and Greg reappear, coming up behind Ray. "Look at those tight black balls," Greg says. He and Vinnie begin to tug and tickle Ray's nuts.

"He's about to blow!" Vinnie announces.

I get out of the path between Ray and C.B., so C.B. can catch the wad as he requested. Ray's body tenses, he stops humping, screws up his face, and pulls out of C.B. with a pop. "Aw, fuck!" Ray shouts as the first four bolts of jism fire up from his nuts and out his piss-hole, hitting C.B. as far as his shaved head and bearded face. More wads of spunk land atop his chest and belly hair. I rub the slick goo around on his head. "Damn. I thought I could stop in time," says an exhausted Ray. "I need a fuckin' beer," he adds, walking slowly off to the nearby sideline, his dick softening and dripping come into the grass.

Vinnie is next. C.B. turns over onto his hands and knees. I go behind Vinnie to knead, twist, and lick his balls, getting so close to C.B.'s butt that I get lube in my beard. C.B. is gobbling Greg's shaft, while Greg nuzzles Wes's balls and tugs his nipples. Vinnie starts humping and talks at C.B., "Yeah, that was so fuckin' hot watchin' you eat your own fuckin' precome. I'll bet you can fuck your own ass with that big fuckin' dick. Yeah, I wanna watch you fuck your own ass. I wanna watch you shoot a load of your own fuckin' come into your own fuckin' ass…Shit!" Vinnie pulls out and with half a dozen strokes, comes onto C.B.'s back, the jizz running down his butt. Vinnie mumbles incoherently and goes to join Ray in the cheering section.

Greg's huffing, "Too close. Gotta be next." He wasn't shittin' about being close—he's in C.B. for maybe a dozen of his pounding ruts, then starts to curse in Polish. He pulls out and adds several more globs of the white stuff to C.B.'s backside.

My turn. C.B. turns over onto his back and hoists his feet up onto my shoulders. "I hate to waste Vinnie's and Greg's ball juice on the grass," I tell him, "but I want you to watch me screw your hairy ass." Wes gives C.B.'s body a tongue wash, starting with his feet, moving to his pits, biting his nipples, and chewing on his foreskin. Finally, Wes moves behind me to play with my nut sac and lick my hole. I pound into C.B., dripping sweat down onto him. Ray, Greg, and Vinnie are chanting, "Come, Russ! Come, Russ!"

Through the afternoon, C.B. has never been less than half hard—he's been fully hard most of the time, but he hasn't tugged on his dick much. Maybe 'cause someone else was always on it. Now he's stroking in earnest, switching hands or using both hands at once. I last maybe five minutes. Like Ray, I try to hold back. I stop, tense up, and yell, "Oh, goddamn! Fuck!" I pull out and let go a load of pent-up spunk that's been wanting release for a long time. My wad lands on C.B.'s face and chest, drips down my shaft, over my fingers, and off my balls onto his crotch. I bend down and lick some spew off C.B.'s forehead.

Wes is last. C.B. is hugging the tree, with his butt out toward Wes, who sticks a finger up into C.B.'s chute and comments, "Yeah, that's a hot hole." The veins in Wes's cock are visibly throbbing as he strokes himself for the final plunge. He starts slowly but quickly gets up to pounding speed. C.B. lets go of the tree and straightens a bit so he can jerk off with both hands. As Wes drives his meat up C.B.'s butt, C.B. thrusts forward, not so much jacking his dick as fucking his fists. Sweat runs off both men onto the grass around the tree. Greg and I come up behind Wes, each needing to take a leak. Going for the "StL" on his backward sweat-stained red cap, we aim high and force our streams up against the back of Wes's head. "You shits," Wes gasps, "but that's hot as fuck." Our piss washes down his back, through his ass-crack to the ground, and triggers his nuts to let loose. Wes grunts and pounds once, twice more, pulls out, and erupts. The first blast gets C.B. on the neck, while the rest splatters and globs onto his back and butt cheeks.

I don't wanna miss catching C.B.'s load, so I sit on the grass, wet with piss and sweat, in front of him. C.B.'s strokin' hard and fast. His nuts are swingin' through the air and thwappin' against his fist and thighs. Wes comes around to where I sit, his feet squishin' on the wet ground, takes off his cap, looks at it, and says to me, "You asswipe." But he grins when he says it and smears off his come-covered cock through my beard. C.B. has started a low growl that increases in intensity. I stare at his dickhead, waiting for the first sign of a spurt. "Ah! God! Aw, fuck! Arhhh!" C.B.'s nuts are scrunched up hard against the base of his cock, and he fires off several hot wads of spunk, splattering me from face to crotch. A very tired C.B. turns and weakly looks around as applause breaks out from Vinnie, Greg, Ray, Wes, and me.

The bowl of rubbers and two big bottles of lube are empty. C.B. looks like a glazed doughnut that's been dropped on the barber-shop floor.

"How's your butt, C.B.?" Ray asks.

"Satisfied," C.B. answers.

Everyone is gathered around the remains of the cooler, sitting naked on the grass and drinking beer cooled by fresh ice dumped on top of the bottles. I like the way the grass tickles the hairs up my ass and those on my nuts. It's still sunny, but the temperature is down to the upper 80s now. Although we're tired and look like shit, we feel good. We're sweaty and dirty with spilled beer, piss, come, grass stains, and lube. Some folks might even complain that we stink, but we'd just sneer and answer that we smell of hot, raw, naked sex.

We sit quietly for a while, except for the occasional fart from C.B.'s ass. "Hey, you guys pumped a lot of air up into me," he defends himself. Vinnie leaves briefly, goes into the house, and returns with a camera. "Gotta fuckin' immortalize this day," he says. He props the camera up on a chair and sets the timer while we stand up against the garage wall, grinning with our arms around one another. For the second shot, C.B. bends over and winks his hole at the camera, while the rest of us point at his ass with our dicks.

"Anyone else got the munchies?" I ask.

"Let's wash off first," Greg says as he gets the hose.

We spend a good 15 minutes hosing off feet, faces, balls, heads, armpits, mustaches, beards, bellies, chests, backs, navels, dicks, hairy assholes, and under foreskins. Ray and Greg are getting hard again and start to tug on each other.

"Shit! Aren't we ever gonna fuckin' eat?" I wonder aloud and plop down onto the grass. My view is suddenly blocked by a butt at my nose.

"Here, Russ," says Wes, "eat this."

I spread his furry buns and begin butt-munchin'.

"Round four?" C.B. asks.

The rest of us stop what we're doing, pause to think, then get up off the grass and say, "Naw, let's get some food."

The Bear Who Knew Too Much

BRUTUS

Another sunny Tuesday as I squinted through the glare
While driving through the humid haze of downtown city air,
My lunch break almost over as I headed into town,
My drive-thru garbage at my side, I rolled my window down.
I turned my head to check both ways as I let off the brake,
But as I looked, I saw a man who made me double-take.

He stood by Bucky's Hardware by the open corner door.
He had a rather solid bulk and stood at six-foot-four.
He had a short-cropped haircut with some silver on each side,
His beard was full and neatly trimmed, his mustache thick
     and wide.
His sleeveless tank displayed his arms and shoulders round
     and strong:
He's just the kind of guy that I could stare at all day long.

The way his jeans showed off his goods was perfect as can be—
His eyes were dark and hungry—he was looking back at me!
My stomach leapt into my throat as I drove slowly by;
He bent his head and met my stare as we matched eye to eye.

And though my pulse was racing, I could feel my spirits drop—
My car kept right on moving, though my brain was screaming
    Stop!
And as my car moved down the street, I bubbled with regret,
And then a thought occurred to me: *This wasn't over yet.*
I knew that I should not play games—I was still on the clock.
I knew I should return to work, but I drove around the block.
I hoped he would be standing there when I came back around,
But the storefront was deserted—he was nowhere to be found.

When I got back, my office desk was piled high with work.
I plopped into my office chair, still feeling like a jerk.
The office snitch came by to glare and pointed at his watch;
I smiled just to piss him off and pointed at my crotch.
The moment was corrupted by that old familiar tone
Of the loud, incessant chirping of my busy office phone.

I lifted the receiver and I barked my standard line:
"You've reached the downtown office; can I help you at this time?"
A deep and husky voice replied in a rather playful tone:
"Why did you go and leave me on the corner all alone?"
Was this the guy I just drove by while heading into town?
Where did he get my number? How did he track me down?

Before I could reply to him, he spoke to me once more:
"Perhaps you might drive by again, around a half past four."
I heard a click as he hung up; I sat there like a stone.
I felt my pecker twitching as I slowly dropped the phone.
I felt my stomach tingle as the blood raced for my cock—
My hard-on tented visibly as I glanced at the clock.

Maybe this was all a prank and maybe it was real—
But either way, I really loved the way this made me feel!
And though he was a stranger and there was some cause to fear,
My dick told me to ride the wave, and soon all would be clear.

So when the time had come to leave, I locked my top desk drawer
And tried to hide my woody as I took off out the door.

I drove back to the hardware store and rolled my window down;
Apart from random passers-by, I saw no one around.
I heaved a sigh and just as I was ready to head home,
I heard the nearby ringing of the corner public phone.
The church bells rang four-thirty, so it sure seemed plain to see—
I didn't have to wonder if that phone call was for me.

I threw on my emergency and got out of the car;
To park there was illegal, so I'm glad it wasn't far.
I picked up the receiver and I whispered a "Hello,"
The voice said, "Hello, buddy. I'm so glad that you could show."
I finally asked, "Who is this?" But he gave me no reaction.
Instead he asked me playfully, "You ready for some action?"

Dear readers, there are times in life when I should use my head
So I don't end up victimized, ripped off, or even dead.
I didn't know who this guy was; I didn't know his plan—
I threw it all into the wind and answered, "Yes, I am."
"I'm closer than you think I am. I'm somewhere right nearby!
Just look around to spot me: You can see me if you try."

I looked around the phone booth, and I glanced around the store,
And there across the street, I saw him leaning by a door.
He put away his cell phone, and he nodded with a grin;
He opened up the unmarked door and, smiling, he went in.
My hard-on was returning as I ran across the street
I felt my body tingling from my head down to my feet.

The door was not a storefront. When I pulled it open wide,
I took a breath and let it out, and then I went inside.
Straight down a darkened hallway, I moved without a sound—
I couldn't see or hear too much as I looked all around.

My senses ached for input, and I felt so deaf and blind,
Then I felt two meaty arms slide round me from behind.

His body pushed against my back, his hands slid cross my chest;
His hips on mine, I felt his stony pecker as he pressed.
I turned around to face him, but I had no chance to quip;
He held his meaty finger out and pressed it on my lip,
"I know your home phone number. I also know your name.
I know you want the Red Sox in tomorrow evening's game.

"I know your favorite color; I know your brand of beer.
I know your boss would fire your ass if he found out you're
        queer.
I know so much about you, bud—don't even ask me how—
And I know that you would love it if I fucked you here and now."
His eyes stayed locked upon my eyes as he undid my shirt,
His bearded face attacked my chest and gnawed until it hurt.

His arms were damp and solid as they slid down to my waist,
His kiss was strong and urgent and was salty to the taste,
My hand grabbed on his denim bulge and traced its ample size,
And when I had unleashed it, I could not believe my eyes!
Sinking down to take it in, I kissed the very tip,
And just to tease I started with my tongue upon his hip.

As my tongue circled closer, I could feel his muscles shudder,
Then I engulfed his hard-on like a calf attacks an udder.
Soon I felt him tensing, so my rhythm action slowed;
I pulled away before he had the chance to fire his load.
He stood before me, heaving, as the sweat rolled off his nose—
And staring in my eyes again, he took off all his clothes.

He opened up my trousers, and he pulled them past my knees;
His hand slid round my nut sac as he tugged it with a squeeze;
He paused for just a moment, then I felt him touch my prick;

A slippery hand of KY made my hard-on smooth and slick.
He grabbed my legs and hoisted them so gracefully and fast;
Slathering his cock with lube, he pushed it in my ass.
Each stabbing thrust convinced me that his strength was so
    profound,
My hands were on his shoulders and my feet were off the ground!
Completely at his mercy, I leaned back and took the ride;
I felt him getting ready to unleash his spunk inside.
I also felt my climax start to build from underneath;
I shouted out, "I'm coming!" through my grinding, clenching teeth.

He erupted with a final thrust, his muscles hard as stone;
As I fired off my jism, I let out a heavy moan.
Then we stood there heaving air, our sweat mixed with our come.
He slowly placed me on my feet and kissed me with his tongue.
He started to get dressed again without a single word;
I almost spoke, but then I thought that silence was preferred.

And when he finished dressing, he touched me on the chin,
He bent to kiss me one more time and stood there with a grin.
And as I tried to speak to him, he walked back down the hall;
He gave me no reaction—just like talking to a wall.
I got myself adjusted, then I walked out to the door,
The sunlight brightly blinding as I stepped outside once more.

I looked to see which way he went, but when I turned around,
He wasn't anywhere in sight; he was nowhere to be found!
And then the thought occurred to me something else was wrong:
I'd left my car across the street, but now my car was gone.
And as my eyes adjusted to the burning light of day,
I realized that, while inside, my car'd been towed away.

A couple phone calls later and a nasty cab ride home,
I stood out in my driveway in the darkness all alone.
A part of me was deeply sad this was a one-time deal,

The rest of me was basking in the glow of the surreal.
Although my legs were sore as hell, my ass still moist with come,
I still felt oddly peaceful—quite relaxed and somewhat numb.

The moon smiled down upon me as I looked up in the sky
And all at once, it dawned on me that I'm a lucky guy.
I quietly resigned myself and headed in once more.
I saw a little envelope attached to my front door.
There was no card inside, just a little note instead,
Written by my very best friend, and this is what it said:

You really mean the world to me; it's corny but it's true.
If I could grant you any wish, what could I do for you?
Can't get no silly token gifts. You know that's not my style,
So what could I arrange that you'd remember for a while?
I figured that you'd like a trick with someone big and burly,
So hope you had a good one—happy birthday one week early.

ABOUT THE CONTRIBUTORS

Louis Anthes is a writer living in Paris, France, and Cleveland, Ohio. He earned his doctorate and law degrees from New York University in 2000. He has previously published a history of lawyers and immigrants in New York City. This is his first work of fiction.

Adam Ben-Hur works at home in Cupertino, Calif., in computer graphics, animation, and illustration. Several stories from his erotic memoirs have been published online by Men's Web and in print in West Beach Books's *Buttmen* series. He has also written, illustrated, and self-published a chapbook, *Summer Island & Other Memories*. His drawings appear in the art gallery of the Italian bear Web site www.sbqr.com. Readers may contact the author at adambenhur@yahoo.com.

Tulsa Brown has been feeding the same bear for the last 22 years up in the cold Canadian North, where the bears grow longer and thicker…coats. Tulsa's work has appeared in *The International Journal of Erotica* and *Moist* Magazine.

Brutus, also known as Bob Cunningham, created the cartoon "Grizzly Tales" for *Bear* magazine and currently produces "Beercan and Saurus" for *100% Beef* Magazine. He resides in Buffalo, New York, and is a staff trainer for an agency that serves people with special needs. He is president of the Buffalo Bears.

Dale Chase has been writing erotica for six years and has had more than 100 stories published in *Freshmen, In Touch,* and *Indulge.* His work has appeared in a dozen anthologies and has been translated into German. Cinema Bravo has acquired one story, and hope remains that it will some day reach the big screen. Chase lives near San Francisco.

Hank Edwards's humorous erotic novel, *Fluffers, Inc.,* is currently available from Alyson Publications. His stories have appeared in *Honcho, Mandate,* and *American Bear* as well as the anthologies *Full Body Contact* and *Just the Sex.* Hank lives in a northern suburb of Detroit with his very patient partner of many years and their orange tabby cat, who believes he is a dog. To feed himself, Hank organizes software testing. Visit his Web site at www.hankedwardsbooks.com.

Furr's work, published seven times in *Bear,* has also appeared in *Drummer, PowerPlay, Hippie Dick!* and *The Bear Fax.* This story marks his return after several years to published bearotica. He likes motorcycles, cigars, and good whiskey, and feels there's no such thing as a beard "too long" or a man "too hairy."

Daniel M. Jaffe's novel, *The Limits of Pleasure,* was excerpted in *Best Gay Erotica 2003* and was a Finalist for *ForeWord* magazine's Book of the Year Award. Dan is a frequent contributor to anthologies, literary journals, and newspapers. Read more at danieljaffe.tripod.com.

Shaun Levin's 2003 novella, *Seven Sweet Things,* is available from his Web site, www.shaunlevin.com, and U.K. bookstores. His short stories appear in anthologies as diverse as *Modern South African Short Stories, Boyfriends from Hell, Tales from the Bear Cult, Best Gay Erotica 2000, 2002,* and *2003,* and *The Slow Mirror: New Fiction by Jewish Writers.* He teaches creative writing and runs Gay Men Writing, an organization to encourage and promote writing by gay men—www.gaymenwriting.co.uk.

Jeff Mann has published three award-winning poetry chapbooks—*Bliss, Mountain Fireflies,* and *Flint Shards from Sussex.* Also appearing in 2003 were a full-length collection of poetry, *Bones Washed With Wine;* a collection of essays, *Edge;* and a novella, *Devoured,* included in the anthology *Masters of Midnight.* He lives in Charleston, W.Va., and Blacksburg, Va., where he teaches Appalachian Studies, Creative Writing, and Literature at Virginia Tech.

A native of Illinois and former resident of Kansas, **Jim Mason** lives with his partner of more than 25 years in San Francisco and is a regular patron of Saturday afternoon beer busts at the Lone Star Saloon. His fiction has been published in *Bearotica* and *100% Beef* magazine.

Attracted to husky, hairy men since birth, **Jay Neal** has written about them since late last century. His stories have appeared in *American Bear, American Grizzly,* and *100% Beef* magazines, and the anthologies *Bearotica; Best Gay Erotica 2002, 2003,* and *2004; Kink;* and others. He lives in suburban Washington, D.C.

R.E. Neu has written humor for publications such as *The New York Times Book Review, Los Angeles Times,* and for the anthology *Bearotica.* For many years, he was a contributing writer for *Spy* magazine. His column "Sucks in the City" appears irregularly in *Frontiers* newsmagazine.

R.G. Powers has published *A Wind Across the Century,* a Gothic-Romantic coming-out bear novel, now available in bookstores. He also contributed an essay for *The Bear Book.* His *Beartime Stories for Bed,* a collection of erotic coming-out and well-being stories for bears, is currently in production. R.G. is presently working on *Highland Son,* an erotic period piece set in the northwest highlands of Scotland. He lives in Long Beach, Calif. Visit him online at www.rgpowers.net.

ABOUT THE CONTRIBUTORS

Simon Sheppard is the author of *Kinkorama: Dispatches From the Front Lines of Desire* and *Hotter Than Hell and Other Stories*, with another collection, *In Deep*, forthcoming from Alyson Books. His work has been published in nearly 100 anthologies, including *Best American Erotica 2004*, *Best Gay Erotica 2004*, *Friction 7*, and *Bearotica*. He's also the coeditor, with M. Christian, of *Rough Stuff* and *Roughed Up*. He lives in San Francisco and loiters shamelessly at www.simonsheppard.com.

Jay Starre stays busy creating hot stories for gay men's magazines, including *Bear, American Bear, American Grizzly, Honcho, Torso,* and *Men*. His fiction has also appeared in gay-themed anthologies, including the *Friction* series for Alyson, *Sex Buddies, Straight?, Full Body Contact, Three the Hard Way,* and the *Buttmen* series from West Beach Books. From Vancouver, B.C., Canada, Jay was first runner-up in the Mr. BC Leather contest of 2002. His Web site is members.shaw.ca/jaystarre.

Thom Wolf is the author of two erotic novels, *Words Made Flesh* and *The Chain*. His short fiction has appeared in *Bearotica*, Alyson's *Friction* series, *Twink, Three the Hard Way, Just The Sex, Manhandled,* and *Buttmen 3*. He likes vodka, Kylie Minogue, and vintage horror films. Thom lives in northeast England with his boyfriend, Liam.

ABOUT THE EDITOR

Ron Suresha, whom *Lambda Book Report* has called the "all-things-bear expert," is a journalist and editor chronicling the evolution of the gay and bisexual men's bear subculture. In 2002, he authored *Bears on Bears: Interviews and Discussions,* which Salon.com declared "invaluable" and the *Village Voice* acclaimed as "required reading for anyone interested in gender studies." Also that year, he edited the fiction anthology *Bearotica: Hot, Hairy, Heavy Fiction.*

Ron is also author of a self-published recipe book, *Mugs o' Joy: Delightful Hot Drinkables.* In 2004, he coedited with P.J. Willis a gay men's fiction anthology, *Kink: Stories of the Sexual Adventurer* (2004, STARBooks Press). Current projects include *Bi Men: Every Which Way Out,* a nonfiction anthology about bisexual men (coedited with Pete Chvany), and *Bi Guys: Firsthand Fiction on Bisexual Men,* a fiction anthology, both forthcoming from Haworth Press.

Ron's nonfiction writing has appeared in Advocate.com, *The Gay & Lesbian Review Worldwide, GCN, Transgender Tapestry, White Crane Journal, RFD,* and many other periodicals and Web sites. His erotica has been featured in the magazines *American Bear, 100% Beef,* and *Holy Titclamps* as well as the anthologies *Quickies 2* and *3, Bar Stories, Tales From the Bear Cult, Sex Buddies,* and *Men, Amplified.*

Ron's good fortune has taken him to regions where some of the world's most exotic bears and working-class men reside: India, Israel, Turkey, Spain, and Detroit. His pastimes include calligraphy, guitar, and running Rhode Island's bear club, Bears Ocean State. Ron lives in Providence, and his online presence resides at www.suresha.com, where he makes his writings and other resources available to all.

ACKNOWLEDGMENTS

Intense gratitude and consideration go to dearest daddybear, Rocco, whose presence at the 2003 Lambda Literary Festival in Provincetown magically transformed not only that weekend but also a difficult autumn and winter of cancer treatment and recovery (doing fine now, thanks!) and, if his nefarious plan succeeds, the rest of my days.

Multithanks to my dear Webdaddy, Jeff Shaumeyer, whose support and collaborations have greatly enhanced my work and life; to faithful Webwolf Nickolas Vannello; and to Steve Rohde for further cybersupport.

Deep personal thanks for everything to Chris Nelson and Michael Paul Smith. Salutations to bearbuds Jim a.k.a. Punkin, Michael a.k.a. MadCubb, Jerry, and Russell. I offer throbs to "Big Easy" daddybears Sergeant Boudreaux, Dale, Dave, and Ray.

For their photographic contributions, my appreciation goes to Chris Komater and Edward Scott Valentine as well as to Lynn Ludwig and Ray Beausejour.

Many thanks also are due to Michael Bronski for his words of priase and encouragement. For bearotic and editorial considerations, thanks to Tim Martin at *American Bear*, Scott McGillivray at *100% Beef*, D & D at *Handjobs*, Jack Fritscher and Mark Hemry at Palm Drive, Michael Huxley at STARbooks, Ian Philips and Greg Wharton at Suspect Thoughts, Richard Labonté, Michael Bronski, David Bergman, Paul Willis, Greg Herren, Felice Picano, Danny

Jaffe, Pete Chvany, Larry-Bob, Andy Mangels, Mark Wylder, Mike Frisch, Meir Amiel, and Andrew Sullivan. My gratitude extends to bear lovers Martha Stone, Tristan Taormino, Susie Bright, and Rachel Kramer Bussel; the folks associated with Bears Mailing List, Bears Ocean State, and the Erotica Readers & Writers Association; and once again to all the *Bearotica* contributors.

Indeed, I am deeply indebted to bearfolk every which way for their kind and enthusiastic support for my work. Heartfelt hairy hugs to bear clubs and grrr-pals everywhere, and to the wonderful readers and reviewers of *Bearotica* who sent feedback. I welcome spam-free correspondence through my Web site, www.suresha.com.

Finally, my thanks to the good folks at Alyson.

RESOURCES

American Bear and _American Grizzly_
American Bear, a bimonthly men's magazine, has been published since 1994. _American Grizzly,_ his big-boned brother, is published quarterly. Both feature photo spreads and erotic fiction; _American Bear_ includes cultural news, health reports, and feature articles as well as reports on bear clubs, events, contacts, and much more.
Amabear Publishing, P.O. Box 7083, Louisville, KY 40257-7083; amabearinc@earthlink.net; www.amabear.com.

Brown Bear Resources
Ron Suresha donates a portion of his proceeds from sales of _Bear Lust, Bearotica,_ and _Bears on Bears_ to Brown Bear Resources (BBR). Since 1989, BBR has worked proactively to give humans understanding and respect for grizzly bears. This nonprofit research corporation is endorsed by federal, state, and tribal agencies. Readers are encouraged to inquire and contribute.
Brown Bear Resources, 222 North Higgins, Missoula, MT 59802; (406) 549-4896; ursus@montana.org; www.brownbear.org.

The Erotica Readers & Writers Association
Dedicated to readers and writers of erotica since 1996, this has become a popular online oasis for the finest in original erotic fiction and poetry, with articles, author resources, and news about erotic books, adult videos, and sex toys.
www.erotica-readers.com.

Nashoba Institute/Bear History Project
This longstanding nonprofit organization can always use volunteers and donations. It advocates for the preservation and promotion of bear history, and it sponsors a variety of cultural and health-related activities. Its Web site contains a vast reservoir of information and links; an art and gift shop; and an online masculinities magazine, *Verisimilitude.*
Nashoba Institute/Bear History Project
P.O. Box 926, Fitchburg, MA 01420; www.bearhistory.com

100% Beef Magazine
This bimonthly adult men's magazine founded in 2002 features photo spreads, erotic fiction, cultural news, feature articles, reports on bear clubs and events, contacts, and more.
J & L Productions, P.O. Box 1344, Palm Springs, CA 92263; (800) 672-3287; info@beefmag.com; www.beefmag.com.

Resources for Bears (RFB)
Your first online stop for all things bear: club and event listings, profiles of men, bear-related businesses and services, an explanation of the Bear Codes, and plenty of other cultural information. Here's another fine nonprofit organization that can always use volunteers.
www.resourcesforbears.com.